Dark Hunt

Olive King

Published by Olive King, 2024.

This is a work of fiction. Similarities to real people, places, or events are entirely coincidental.

DARK HUNT

First edition. November 9, 2024.

Copyright © 2024 Olive King.

ISBN: 979-8224205301

Written by Olive King.

Chapter 1: The Web of Fate

The wind whipped through my hair, tangling it into a wild, dark knot that matched the chaos in my chest. I peered over the edge of the crumbling rooftop, the street below an endless stretch of broken glass and forgotten dreams. Crescent City always felt like this—drenched in the scent of rain-soaked pavement and the faint, metallic bite of old blood. It thrummed with a pulse all its own, an undercurrent of danger that ran through every cobblestone, every alleyway, and every crooked building.

I had been chasing a ghost for the past two months. But tonight, the trail had gone cold. The only thing left to catch was him. Vance Callahan. The name alone was enough to make anyone's skin prickle with a mix of dread and... something else. Something far more dangerous. He had a reputation, sure, but that wasn't what kept me awake at night. No, it was the way he watched me. The way he seemed to know exactly what I was thinking, even before I did. And tonight, I was going to make sure I was the one who came out on top.

The flickering streetlights below cast sharp shadows, bending and stretching as though they were alive. I couldn't help but smile. In this city, everyone had a secret, and mine was that I was willing to do anything to expose them. Even if it meant dangling over the edge of a roof, half a second away from tumbling into the abyss. I wasn't afraid of heights. What I feared was what awaited me down there—Vance. Because if I wasn't careful, the next time I faced him, I might not make it out.

The scrape of boots against gravel echoed behind me, and I spun around instinctively, my fingers tightening on the jagged ledge. He was there, of course. Standing just beyond the reach of the faint light, his silhouette tall and impossibly still. Vance didn't need to move much to make an impression. His presence filled the space, oppressive, magnetic. He stood like a shadow himself, blending with the night.

"You really ought to be more careful, little bird," he said, his voice low and smooth, like velvet slipping over glass. Every word seemed to linger in the air, pulling at the edges of my resolve.

I forced myself not to flinch. "You've been watching me. How charming."

"Not watching," he corrected, taking a step closer. "Waiting."

There it was again—the confidence. The certainty that he was in control. And that, for whatever reason, unsettled me more than anything else. He was like a riddle wrapped in a riddle, and every time I thought I had him figured out, he shifted, just out of reach. He didn't speak much, but when he did, every syllable seemed to slice through the silence, carving out a space for him that was impossible to ignore.

I narrowed my eyes, the wind pulling at my coat, urging me to either jump or retreat. Neither option appealed to me. "If you've been waiting for me, Callahan, I hope you brought something interesting. I'm not the type to waste time."

A smirk tugged at the corner of his mouth, though his eyes—those damned eyes—never left mine. "You always were impatient. Reckless, even. I admire that. It's what makes you dangerous."

I swallowed hard, the usual thrill of our encounters now tinged with something deeper. Something that felt like a challenge wrapped in a dare. He was playing a game, and I was too caught up in it to remember the rules.

I took a step back, eyeing the distance between us. The roof groaned beneath me, and I fought the urge to look down. "I'm not here to flirt with danger, Callahan. I'm here to finish what we started."

His gaze flickered briefly toward the far end of the rooftop, as though contemplating something, before returning to me with a sharp, focused intensity. "We finished nothing, sweetheart. You've been running from me for months. I'd say that makes us even."

A flash of anger sparked inside me, and I straightened, pushing past the instinct to back down. "I don't run. You're just too damn slow."

He laughed then, a soft, dangerous sound that had a way of making the air feel thick with tension. "Don't be so sure, darling. I'm always right behind you."

My fingers tightened on the ledge, my heart beating faster, a mix of frustration and something else—something I didn't want to acknowledge. I hated that he had this hold over me, hated that he could reduce me to this strange, off-kilter state with nothing more than a few words. I was supposed to be the one in control, the one pulling the strings. But here I was, standing on the edge, the taste of failure bitter on my tongue.

The night air shifted, and I caught a glimpse of movement in the corner of my eye. A shadow, slinking toward the alley below, a figure too quiet to be ignored. Before I could process it, Vance was already beside me, his hand on my wrist, pulling me back from the edge with the gentleness of someone who had done this too many times.

"Get a grip," he muttered, his voice hard now, a hint of something darker threading through it. "You don't want to end up like them."

I wasn't sure who "them" were, but I didn't need to ask. The city had its share of bodies—lost, forgotten, left to rot in the dark corners where even the light wouldn't dare to venture. This city had a way of swallowing people whole, and I wasn't sure whether I'd ever make it out.

I jerked my arm away from him, glaring as the cool night air pressed against my skin like a reprimand. "Don't touch me."

Vance didn't flinch, didn't back away. He simply looked at me, his gaze unreadable, as though he were seeing straight through me. "I'm not the one you need to worry about."

I glared at Vance, my teeth clenched and my hands curling into fists at my sides. If there was one thing I hated more than his presence in the dark corners of this city, it was the way he made me question myself. He was always in control, always five steps ahead, and always so goddamn sure of everything.

He took a step forward, his dark coat swirling around him like a shadow, his expression unreadable. "You can fight it all you want, but we both know it's not the danger you're worried about."

I swallowed, trying to tamp down the surge of emotion that threatened to rise up and spill over. It wasn't fear that made my heart race. It wasn't the rush of adrenaline from the rooftop, or the knowledge that every move I made could be my last. It was him. Vance Callahan had a way of getting under my skin, of making me feel like I was teetering on the edge of something I couldn't quite grasp—something that I didn't even want to understand.

"I'm not interested in your mind games," I said, the words sharper than I intended.

Vance's lips curled into that infuriating smirk, the one that always made me want to punch him in the face. "Funny, because you're still standing here, aren't you?"

I didn't respond right away, letting the weight of the silence settle between us like an old, unwanted acquaintance. He was right. The tension between us had always been more than just the hunt. It was something more, something I couldn't pin down. It was this ridiculous, undeniable pull that kept me here, and that was more dangerous than any of the other risks I was willing to take tonight.

I glanced down again, more out of habit than curiosity, at the alley below. There was no sign of the shadow that had slipped into the darkness earlier. Whoever it was had vanished, and I was left with nothing but the pressing sense that I was missing something.

Vance's eyes flickered toward the same alley, and I could almost hear the calculation running through his mind. His hand twitched at his side, like he was reaching for something—his weapon, no doubt. But that wasn't what made my stomach tighten. It was the way his body language shifted, the subtle tension that was always there, but that I'd learned to ignore.

He wasn't worried about the shadow. He was worried about me.

That realization sent a rush of heat to my face, and I turned my back on him, facing the open air and the cool breeze that brushed against my skin. "You don't know anything about me, Callahan."

His footsteps echoed behind me, and I clenched my jaw as his voice cut through the night. "I know more than you think." There was a pause. "More than you want me to."

I bit back the sharp retort that wanted to come. I wasn't about to admit to him, to anyone, that he might be right. That he did know me in ways that made me uncomfortable—ways I wasn't prepared to confront just yet.

"You're not the only one who knows how to play the game," I said, my voice steadier now, more controlled. I turned back to face him, locking eyes as I said it, the words like a challenge hanging between us. "If you think you've got the upper hand, you're wrong."

Vance tilted his head slightly, studying me as if I were some intricate puzzle he was just about to solve. His lips twitched, but he didn't say anything. Instead, he moved in closer, his presence so overwhelming that I could feel the space around me contracting, tightening until it was hard to breathe. His gaze never wavered, and it was enough to make my pulse quicken in response, whether I wanted it to or not.

"I'm not trying to get the upper hand," he said, his voice like a low murmur in the night. "I'm just trying to get you to stop lying to yourself."

My stomach twisted, the words striking too close to something I hadn't even realized I was hiding. It was always like this with him—everything felt too raw, too exposed. "I'm not lying to anyone," I snapped, my voice a little too sharp for comfort. "Least of all to you."

He didn't flinch at my outburst. Instead, his eyes softened—just slightly, but enough to make my heart trip in my chest. "You say that, but you're still standing here. Waiting for something to happen. Waiting for me to do something."

I shook my head, frustrated. He wasn't wrong, but it didn't matter. I was here to find the answers I needed, to uncover whatever dark secret Crescent City was hiding, and if I had to fight my way through every twist and turn of this city to do it, then so be it.

The wind kicked up again, tugging at my coat, and I stepped back from the ledge. The temptation to stay in the dangerous quiet of this rooftop, this moment, was almost overwhelming. But I wasn't a fool. I knew better than to let my guard down.

"Whatever it is you think you know, Callahan," I said, forcing my voice to remain steady, "you don't. I'm not some damsel in distress, and I'm not going to sit here and wait for you to save me."

He looked at me like I had just said something profoundly absurd, his lips curling into the faintest smile. "I never said you were," he replied softly. "But I think you might be starting to realize you can't do it alone."

There it was again—the weight of his words, the pull of them that was impossible to ignore. It wasn't just a statement. It was a question. And for the first time, I wasn't sure how to answer.

"Don't pretend like you care," I muttered, though the words came out more defensive than I had intended.

Vance didn't react to the challenge in my tone. He merely stepped forward again, closing the distance between us until I could feel the heat of his body against mine. He looked down at me, his eyes dark with something I couldn't quite read, and for a moment, the city seemed to hold its breath.

"I don't have to pretend anything," he said, his voice soft, almost tender, and yet the words still made my heart stutter. "The truth is, I've always known exactly who you are."

The chill of the night pressed closer, like the city itself was holding its breath. Vance's words hung in the air, heavy and still. There was something in the way he said it—I've always known exactly who you are—that twisted in my gut. It wasn't arrogance that cut through the space between us, though he had more than enough of that. It was something deeper, something that made me feel exposed in ways I couldn't shake off.

I wasn't afraid of him, or at least, I told myself I wasn't. I had learned long ago to face my fears head-on—whether it was leaping into the unknown or crossing into territory that should've been left alone. I had my own secrets to protect, and those had always been enough to keep me going. But now, standing on the edge of this rooftop with Vance so close, so present, it felt like he had unlocked a door I hadn't known existed. And I didn't know if I was ready to step through it.

"You don't know anything about me," I said, my voice shaky despite my best efforts to steady it. My fingers twitched at my sides, desperate to do something—anything—to regain control over this situation.

Vance stepped closer, his gaze never leaving mine. He didn't need to speak. His silence said it all. He wasn't the type to repeat himself. He was the type to let you squirm until the weight of his presence forced you to confront whatever truth you were hiding from.

"I'm not some open book for you to read, Callahan," I added, a little more forcefully this time. "So why don't you just drop the act and tell me what you really want?"

His eyes glittered with amusement, the smallest of smirks dancing at the corner of his lips. He knew exactly what I meant, even if I wasn't ready to admit it aloud. But instead of responding, he simply stepped back, his hand gesturing toward the alley below, the shadows there growing darker and deeper by the second.

"I want what you came for," he said softly. "The truth. You've been chasing it for so long now, but you're still just a step behind."

The insult stung, but I swallowed it down. If there was one thing I could hold onto in this city, it was my pride. And I wasn't about to let him strip that away too.

I glanced down at the alley again, my pulse quickening. I could feel something moving in the air—something wrong. The shadows weren't just shadows anymore. They had taken on a shape, a presence. I wasn't imagining it. Someone—or something—was waiting.

Without another word, I moved toward the edge, my hand gripping the rough brick of the building. My heart raced, but not from fear. From anticipation. There was no turning back now. The truth had always been a dangerous game, and I had played it so many times before, but tonight... tonight it felt different.

Vance followed my every move, his footsteps so quiet that I could hardly hear them over the pounding of my own heartbeat. "I wouldn't go down there if I were you," he warned, his voice low, almost a growl.

I didn't stop. "I didn't ask for your advice."

A shadow moved again, closer now. It was unmistakable. There was someone—or something—lurking just out of sight, watching, waiting for me to make the first move. My hand tightened on the ledge, my fingers digging into the stone, the coldness biting into my skin.

I wasn't about to let whatever was down there make a fool of me. I could handle this.

But as I started to lower myself down, a firm hand shot out from behind me, wrapping around my wrist. Vance's grip was strong, unyielding. It didn't feel like he was trying to stop me, though. No, it felt like he was trying to keep me from making a mistake, something I hadn't quite figured out yet.

"You don't know what you're about to walk into," he said, his voice just above a whisper, but the urgency in it was unmistakable. There was something there, something deeper than his usual mocking tone. Something real.

I didn't look at him. I couldn't. If I did, I might lose my nerve, and that was the last thing I needed.

"Let go of me," I snapped, pulling my wrist out of his grip.

For a moment, he hesitated, but then he let go, stepping back as if he'd known I wouldn't take his advice. "You're right about one thing," he said softly, almost to himself. "You're not afraid to jump into the unknown."

I didn't respond. The air felt thick with tension, and I knew, deep down, that something was about to shift. Whatever had been chasing me for months was finally cornering me, and I didn't know if I was ready for what that would mean.

I slipped over the side of the building, my feet finding purchase on the edge of a lower rooftop. I had done this before, climbing and scaling buildings in the dead of night. But this time, something felt different. The streets below, dark and empty as they were, seemed alive with danger. Every step I took sent a ripple through the air, and I could feel the eyes of whatever waited in the alley following my every move.

The shadows seemed to grow taller, more menacing, and I realized with a sudden shock that I wasn't alone.

There was a figure at the far end of the alley, just out of the reach of the dim streetlights, standing perfectly still. It wasn't just the darkness that concealed them—it was the silence. The figure was too quiet, too still, like it was waiting for something, or perhaps, someone.

I froze mid-step, my breath catching in my throat.

And then, in the next heartbeat, I saw it: the glint of something sharp, something cold and deadly, catching the last of the moonlight.

I wasn't alone.

Vance's voice came through the darkness, a low warning. "Get out of there now."

Chapter 2: Threads of Deceit

The streetlights flickered, casting long, jagged shadows that seemed to stretch and claw across the cracked pavement, trying to escape their own light. The night felt too alive, as if the city itself was holding its breath, watching, waiting. I pressed my palms against the cold brick of the alleyway, trying to steady my racing pulse. The air was thick, heavy with the scent of rain that had yet to fall, mixing with the faint traces of diesel and something sharp—perhaps the distant promise of a storm.

I didn't need to look up to know that Vance was still standing there, perched on the edge of that fire escape like some kind of elusive phantom. His form was just a dark blur against the silvered sky, his presence taunting in the way it always did. He was a man who knew how to keep you off balance, how to wrap his words around you until you didn't know if you were being pulled closer or shoved away.

"You know," his voice drifted down to me, low and dangerous, "it's funny. You still think you have control of this game."

I clenched my fists, biting back the instinct to shout at him, to demand that he tell me what I needed to know. But I couldn't. Not yet. Not when I was so close. I could feel the weight of the dossier burning a hole in my jacket pocket, each page a piece of a puzzle that had taken months to put together. A puzzle with one missing piece—the very piece Vance was holding in his hands, even if he didn't know it yet.

"You know nothing about control," I replied, forcing my voice to stay steady. The last thing I needed was to show weakness, especially now. "I didn't come here to play your games, Vance."

He chuckled, a dark, rich sound that curled around me like smoke. "Oh, but that's exactly what you're doing. You think you're playing the game, but I've already written the rules."

I could almost feel the smirk on his lips, even though I couldn't see it. It was that smug, superior kind of grin that made you want to punch him—and then kiss him, just to mess with his head. He had that effect on me, and I hated it.

The tension between us crackled like static, an invisible current that pulled me in every direction. His presence was like a magnet, forcing me to be aware of every movement, every breath, even when I tried to ignore him. He was everywhere—his influence, his games, his lies. But tonight, I wasn't here to be another one of his pawns.

"I came here for information, not a lecture," I said, my tone colder now, sharper. I stepped away from the wall, forcing myself to move despite the way my legs felt weak, as if they were betraying me.

"Information," he repeated, drawing out the word like it was a secret, a treasure he was reluctant to give away. "You always think you're so close to the truth, don't you?"

"I don't need to think, Vance," I replied, my voice hardening. "I know I'm close. You can't hide it forever."

For a moment, I thought he might laugh again, that cold, knowing laugh that always seemed to hint at something darker underneath. But instead, there was silence. The kind of silence that swallowed everything, even the street sounds around us. The kind of silence that made the air feel tight, as if the world was waiting for something to break.

When he spoke again, his voice was softer, more dangerous. "You're playing a dangerous game, you know. What if you're wrong? What if you've been chasing shadows all along?"

I swallowed hard, fighting the wave of doubt that threatened to crash over me. He had a way of getting under my skin, making me question everything I thought I knew. But I couldn't let him win—not now. Not when I was so close to the truth.

"I'm not wrong," I said firmly, my eyes narrowing. "And I'm not walking away until I have what I came for."

For a long moment, we stood there, locked in a battle of wills, neither of us willing to break first. Then, finally, Vance moved, stepping off the ledge with a grace that was unnerving, as if the fall had never been a risk at all. He landed on the ground in front of me with barely a sound, his boots scuffing against the concrete.

His eyes were dark, inscrutable, but there was a flicker of something in them—something almost like curiosity. "You really think you're ready for this? Ready to know what's at the end of the line?"

I didn't hesitate. "I'm ready for anything."

He studied me for a moment, as though weighing my words, and then a small, wry smile tugged at the corner of his mouth. "You don't even know what you're up against."

Before I could respond, he turned and started walking toward the shadows, his movements fluid, almost feline in their grace. My heart raced in my chest, the anticipation building, but I kept my focus on him, forcing myself not to react to the surge of emotion inside me. Vance had a way of making you feel like you were losing control without even trying, but I couldn't let him win.

"You're not going to get away with this," I called after him, the words sharp and clear.

He paused just long enough to glance over his shoulder, his expression unreadable. "Who says I'm trying to get away with anything?"

I didn't know how to answer that. Maybe he wasn't trying to escape. Maybe he was already one step ahead, watching me like a chessboard, waiting for me to make my next move.

"I'll find you," I said, my voice low, almost a whisper.

And for a fleeting moment, just as he disappeared into the darkness, I thought I saw something in his eyes—something that flickered between amusement and something far darker. A promise, perhaps. Or a warning.

Either way, I wasn't backing down.

I followed Vance deeper into the labyrinth of alleys, my boots scraping against the damp asphalt, every step reverberating in the thick, suffocating air. The city was alive with its usual noise—distant car engines, the occasional shout from a nearby street vendor, and the soft rustle of wind through a tangle of stray newspaper pages. But there was something different tonight. Something heavier. I couldn't put my finger on it, but the weight of it settled in my chest, a slow pressure that wouldn't let up.

Vance's footsteps were silent, almost unnatural in their quiet precision. It was one of the many things that unsettled me about him—the way he seemed to glide through the world, untouchable, unaware of the messes he left behind. He didn't need to make a sound to know someone was following him, didn't need to look back to see who was on his trail. It wasn't a gift; it was a habit—one born from years of being far too aware of the power he wielded. The power he thought he still held over me.

I should've been angry. Should've called him out for his arrogance, his games, his smug insistence that I was just another piece on his chessboard. But the truth was, I was playing this game, too, and he had no idea how much I was willing to sacrifice to win it.

"Not planning on giving up anytime soon, are you?" His voice sliced through the tension, a whisper that seemed to wrap itself around my thoughts, tugging at the edges of my concentration.

I didn't answer right away. Part of me wanted to remind him that I'd been chasing this for far longer than he realized, that I'd learned how to stay focused through worse than his ridiculous taunts. But there was no time for that. Not anymore. Whatever he had planned, I needed to stay ahead of him.

The alley opened into a small courtyard, the kind of place where the light never quite reached. A patchwork of rusted metal sculptures lined the walls, twisted pieces of forgotten art that seemed to shimmer in the pale glow of the streetlights. It was one of the many hidden corners of the city, the places where you weren't supposed to ask questions and the people you met never expected answers.

Vance turned to face me, his hands shoved deep into the pockets of his coat. There was something almost tender in the way he looked at me, as if I were a puzzle he had yet to solve, and I was getting dangerously close to a breakthrough.

"You've got a lot of questions, I can tell," he said, his tone light, almost teasing. "You think this is all a game, don't you?"

"I think you're the one who's playing games," I shot back, stepping closer, narrowing the distance between us. I refused to let him control the space. "But I'm not here to entertain you, Vance. I'm here to finish what I started."

His eyes flickered, a shadow passing over them, before he smirked again, that same, maddeningly charming smirk that I could feel deep in my bones. It was as if he was daring me to take a step too far, daring me to push him until he showed me just how far he was willing to go to win.

"I don't think you understand the game you're playing," he said softly, the words almost a caress. "This isn't about finding the truth. It's about surviving long enough to find the people who will tear you apart for even looking in the wrong direction."

I swallowed hard. It was a warning. A threat. And yet, there was something in the way he spoke, something in the tension that laced his words, that made me wonder whether he was trying to protect me or lead me deeper into the trap.

"I'm not afraid of the truth," I said, my voice steadier than I felt. "And I'm not afraid of you."

Vance's lips twitched upward, but his eyes darkened. "Oh, but you should be. The truth isn't something you can fight, not when it's bigger than you. You'll just end up lost in the details, like everyone else."

I tilted my head, studying him carefully. "You talk like you know the truth. Like you're the only one who has it."

His gaze flicked to the side for a brief moment, his expression momentarily unreadable. I knew I'd struck a nerve. There was something about the way he always danced around the truth, like it was a secret he was desperate to keep buried.

"You're right about one thing," he said, his voice low, almost reluctant. "There's more going on here than you understand. But if you really think you can just waltz in and claim victory, you're in for a rude awakening."

I felt the words in my chest like a punch, sharp and unrelenting. Was he trying to warn me, or was he simply toying with me, like he always did? It was hard to tell, but I couldn't afford to second-guess myself now.

"I'm done being your pawn, Vance," I said, my voice firm. "Either you help me, or you get out of my way."

For a moment, he simply looked at me, that unreadable expression settling back into place. Then, as if deciding that the conversation had reached its end, he straightened and turned, his coat flaring out behind him in the cool night breeze.

"You're making a mistake," he called over his shoulder, his voice drifting back to me. "But it's your mistake to make."

I watched him disappear into the shadows, my heart pounding in my chest. Every instinct told me that he was dangerous, that he was right—that this was all too much, too far, too risky. But I wasn't about to turn back. Not now. Not when the truth was within reach.

I took a deep breath, steeling myself for what was to come. The road ahead was darker than I had imagined, but I was done running. Whatever Vance's game was, I was ready to play.

The sound of Vance's footsteps faded as he disappeared into the maze of alleyways. I stood there for a beat longer than necessary, unwilling to let the weight of his words take root in my mind. He thought I was playing a game, but I knew something he didn't: the truth wasn't a game. It was a weapon, one I'd wield with precision if it meant uncovering the lies that had kept me on this path for so long.

With a deep breath, I pushed away from the brick wall, the damp air biting at my skin as I squared my shoulders. If Vance wanted to disappear into the shadows, that was fine. I would find my own way to the answers—answers that didn't hinge on his smirking face or cryptic warnings. There was something else at play here, something bigger than either of us, and it was about time I saw it for what it really was.

I made my way through the twisting alleys, the narrow streets growing darker the further I went. The low hum of distant traffic felt miles away, muffled by the oppressive silence of this part of the city. The further I ventured, the more it felt like the walls were closing in on me. The lights flickered above, casting fractured shadows across the broken pavement. This wasn't a part of the city people usually talked about, let alone walked through.

I had no idea where I was going, but I knew I wasn't going to stop. Not until I found what I needed. The clock was ticking, and the answers were slipping farther out of reach with each minute I wasted.

I reached a corner, paused to check my bearings, and immediately froze. The distinct sound of a door creaking open behind me sent a shiver up my spine. It was subtle, but unmistakable. My hand slid instinctively to the gun at my waist—just in case. A moment later, I heard the soft shuffle of footsteps. Too light, too deliberate to be an accident. Someone was following me.

I spun around, scanning the darkness. At first, nothing. Then, a figure emerged from the shadows.

"Not as good at hiding as you think," Vance's voice sliced through the air, smooth and unbothered, like he hadn't just disappeared on me moments ago.

I swallowed my irritation. "You've been following me."

"I'm not following you," he corrected, stepping closer. "I'm just... making sure you don't make any mistakes."

I studied him for a beat, trying to gauge whether he was lying. It wasn't as if I could trust him. Trust wasn't even on the table at this point. But there was something in his expression now, something more than the usual cocky grin. His eyes were darker, harder, and there was no mistaking the way he was watching me—like he was assessing whether I'd break under the pressure.

"You seem awfully concerned for someone who claims to have nothing to do with this," I replied, my tone sharp, keeping my distance as I took a slow step back.

"I'm not concerned," Vance said, his lips curling slightly. "I'm just curious. You've been chasing something, haven't you? Something you don't fully understand."

I didn't answer. I wasn't here to get pulled into one of his mind games. The truth, my truth, was waiting somewhere, and I would find it—whether he helped me or not.

"Tell me what you know," I said, my voice low, controlled. "And then I'll leave you alone. No more games."

His smile turned rueful, but there was no humor in it. He took a step closer, the air between us growing thick with something I couldn't name. "You really think I'm the one playing games here?"

I shook my head, more out of frustration than anything else. "You're the one who's been running the show from the start. All I'm doing is trying to catch up."

He tilted his head, studying me with an intensity that felt almost suffocating. The world felt like it had narrowed to just the two of us—no alleyways, no shadows, no city around us. Just him, with his sharp eyes and that maddening smile.

"You're not playing catch-up, sweetheart," he said, his voice almost too smooth. "You've been in the game all along. You just didn't realize it."

The hairs on the back of my neck stood up, a chill creeping through me. For a moment, I almost believed him. Almost.

"Enough with the riddles," I snapped, my patience wearing thin. "I'm not here for your cryptic little games. Tell me what you know."

Vance didn't move, but his eyes flicked toward something behind me. My instincts kicked in, the hair on the back of my neck rising again. It was too quiet. Too still.

"Why don't you take a look for yourself?" he said, his tone suddenly different, almost... amused.

I spun around just in time to see the shadow shift.

A man—dressed in all black, his face obscured by the hood of his jacket—emerged from the darkened doorway. His movements were slow, deliberate, like a predator circling its prey. I felt a rush of adrenaline flood my system, a wave of tension so strong that it nearly buckled my knees.

Vance took a half-step back, his expression unreadable. "I didn't think they'd show up so soon."

The man stepped forward, the soft clink of metal against leather ringing in my ears. He didn't speak, just moved with an eerie, silent precision, his eyes locked on me like I was the only thing in the world that mattered.

I reached for my gun, but before I could fully draw it, I heard a sound—a distinct click. Not the sound of a gun cocking, but something worse. A tranquilizer dart.

I turned just in time to see the dart sinking into my shoulder, the world around me spinning as the darkness crept in, pulling me under.

Vance's voice was the last thing I heard before everything went black.

"Game over."

Chapter 3: The Hunter and the Hunted

The streets of Crescent City had a pulse all their own, thrumming beneath the weight of the storm that hung heavy in the air. Neon lights flickered above me, casting their sickly, colorful glow over the asphalt, the glow of a thousand different stories waiting to be told. The steady hum of traffic was accompanied by the occasional screech of tires or the clinking of glass bottles in dark alleyways. It was a city built on secrets, where the sky was always a bit too gray, and the shadows always seemed to stretch just a little longer than they should.

I tried not to look at Vance, but it was impossible. Even now, after everything, his presence wrapped itself around me like smoke—unwanted but impossible to ignore. His stride was effortless, predatory in the way he moved through the crowded streets, scanning every face, every corner, with a precision that unnerved me. He looked like someone who had spent too many nights hunting in places like this. His dark jacket blended with the night, his eyes sharp, calculating, but his jaw—there was something unmistakable about the tension there. Something almost... vulnerable.

"Don't get too comfortable," he said, his voice low but sharp, like the edge of a blade being drawn across skin. "This isn't the kind of place where trust comes easy."

I shot him a sideways glance, trying to keep my expression neutral, despite the heat building in my chest. "I didn't come here to make friends," I muttered, my fingers tightening around the strap of my bag.

His lips curled slightly at the corners, an expression that might have been a smile if I didn't know better. "That's good," he replied, voice dripping with a mix of amusement and warning. "Because trust won't save you when it all falls apart."

I was tempted to snap back, tell him that I was fully aware of the stakes, but something about the way he said it—like he was speaking from experience—stopped me. Instead, I pressed my lips together, my gaze hardening.

We turned down an alley, the neon lights fading as we moved deeper into the shadows. The air smelled of wet concrete, old cigarette smoke, and something metallic, like the taste of blood lingering on the tip of your tongue. My skin prickled with the sensation of being watched, but I kept my steps steady, refusing to show fear. I didn't trust Vance, not even a little, but there was something undeniably magnetic about him. Maybe it was the way he seemed to know this city like the back of his hand, or how he never seemed to blink when danger loomed. Whatever it was, I couldn't shake the feeling that we were tangled up in something far bigger than either of us.

"You're quiet," he observed, his voice almost too casual, like he didn't care whether or not I answered. But I could feel the weight of his gaze on me, steady and unyielding.

"I'm trying to ignore you," I said flatly, though I knew he wasn't the kind to be ignored. And honestly, I wasn't sure if I even wanted to.

"Good luck with that," he chuckled darkly, the sound low and dry. "You've got a long way to go before you can pretend I'm not here."

The streetlights above flickered once more, casting long shadows that twisted and shifted like something alive. It made me uneasy, the feeling that we weren't alone. But as always, Vance remained unbothered. He moved with the grace of a predator, taking everything in—every slight shift in the air, every muffled sound.

I glanced over my shoulder, half expecting someone to be following us, but the alley remained empty. Still, I couldn't shake the sense that we were being hunted.

"We should be careful," I said, my voice a little more cautious than I intended. "If we keep going like this, we're going to walk straight into the storm."

"Good," he replied, his eyes narrowing as he glanced back at me. "I don't do anything unless there's a storm."

It wasn't the answer I'd expected, but it didn't surprise me either. Vance was a man who thrived on chaos, a man who would push forward even if it meant standing in the middle of a wildfire. It was what made him dangerous. And it was also what made him so hard to resist.

As we rounded another corner, the faint sound of music drifted from a nearby club. It wasn't the kind of music you heard on the radio. No, this was raw—dirty, gritty jazz that seemed to swirl around you, pulling you in, like it had a life of its own. I caught a glimpse of a neon sign hanging above the club's entrance: The Broken String.

Vance stopped in front of the door, his posture stiffening just slightly. I could tell he didn't want to be here, but there was no avoiding it.

"You know what you're walking into?" I asked, my voice softer now, more tentative.

"Not really," he said with a shrug, "but I figure I'll know when we get there."

I raised an eyebrow, my skepticism barely contained. "You're a real piece of work, you know that?"

Vance didn't respond at first, but I saw the faintest glimmer of something in his eyes. Maybe it was amusement, maybe something else. But he didn't let it linger. Instead, he grabbed the door handle, twisting it and pulling it open without hesitation.

Inside, the air was thick with smoke and the low hum of a saxophone. A bartender with a weathered face wiped down the counter, his eyes flicking over us briefly before going back to the endless glasses in front of him. A few scattered patrons lingered in the dim light, none of them looking particularly friendly. This wasn't the kind of place for casual conversation, and everyone here seemed to know it.

Vance didn't waste time with pleasantries. He headed straight for the back, where a set of stairs led to a shadowy room above. I followed, my footsteps echoing in the hollow silence between us. My heart was pounding, and I knew the storm was about to break. What I didn't know was whether we were the ones caught in the downpour—or whether we were about to bring it with us.

The stairs creaked underfoot as we ascended into the darkness above The Broken String. The low hum of the jazz band below faded with every step, swallowed by the oppressive silence that had settled over us. The light was dim up here, just enough to outline the edges of the room—a smattering of mismatched chairs, a couple of men hunched over a table, whispering in low, urgent tones. The air felt thick, almost stifling, and the distinct scent of sweat and whiskey lingered, mingling with the faint traces of tobacco smoke that seemed permanently embedded in the walls.

I couldn't tell if I was walking toward danger or toward the very thing I was trying to avoid. All I knew was that I was tethered to this place, to Vance, and to the tangled mess of choices that had led me here. My fingers brushed against the cool metal of the banister, and I glanced at Vance, whose back was straight, his eyes scanning every inch of the room as if he were already calculating his next move.

"Do you ever get the feeling that we're the only ones who didn't get the memo on how this game is supposed to be played?" I asked, unable to keep the edge of sarcasm out of my voice.

Vance's lips twitched, the smallest of smiles tugging at the corners. "I don't play games," he replied, his tone smooth and dismissive. "I just win them."

"Well, that's convenient," I muttered, rolling my eyes. "Because the last thing I need right now is someone who thinks the rules don't apply."

"You're still in that 'trying to save the world' phase, huh?" He shot a glance over his shoulder, his expression unreadable. "It's cute. Almost makes me think you're still naïve enough to think you can change anything."

I bristled at the implication, but he was right, wasn't he? I was still holding on to that desperate hope that, somehow, I could stop the wheels of chaos from turning. Maybe I wasn't the best person for the job, but I couldn't let go of the idea that something—anything—could make a difference.

"Maybe I'm just tired of standing by while the rest of the world burns," I said, my voice quieter now, though it still held a sharpness that matched my growing frustration. "Not everyone is looking for a quick way out."

Vance didn't answer. Instead, he pushed open the door to the back room, and the air in front of us shifted again. The temperature dropped, and the sharp scent of something metallic—something foul—filled my nose. A man stood in the center of the room, his back to us, one hand resting on a table cluttered with papers and half-empty glasses. The tension in the room thickened immediately, and I could feel the hairs on the back of my neck rise.

This was it. The person we'd been tracking, the one pulling all the strings behind the chaos that had swept through the city.

He turned, his movements slow and deliberate, as if he had all the time in the world to make us wait. His eyes flicked to Vance first, then to me, assessing, calculating. And for the briefest of moments, I thought I saw a flicker of recognition in his gaze.

"Ah," he said, his voice smooth, with the hint of an accent I couldn't place. "The hunter and the hunted, finally together in the same room."

I crossed my arms, unwilling to give him the satisfaction of seeing me flinch. "I'm not here for games. You've been running things from the shadows, and now it's time for you to step into the light."

His smile didn't reach his eyes. "Oh, sweetheart, the light's overrated," he said, his gaze drifting lazily from me to Vance. "It's the shadows where the real power lies. You should know that by now."

Vance stepped forward, his presence commanding, though there was something different about the way he carried himself now. No longer the cool, detached figure from the alley, he was suddenly on edge. The air between us thickened again, charged with a tension I couldn't quite place. It was as if the walls were closing in around us, every word now a weapon in a battle that was far from over.

"Let's skip the small talk," Vance said, his voice low, but sharp. "You know why we're here."

The man's smile deepened, and he finally took a step closer to us, his hands sliding casually into the pockets of his coat. "Oh, I'm well aware." He looked me over again, his eyes lingering just a second too long. "But the question is, why are you still here?"

I narrowed my eyes, not understanding his meaning. "What are you talking about?"

He let out a slow, almost pitying laugh. "Didn't you get the memo, darling? This city isn't yours to save. It never was." His gaze shifted to Vance, as though expecting a reaction, but Vance remained silent, his jaw clenched. "And you? You're already too far in. You can't back out now. Not without losing everything."

The weight of his words landed heavy in the room, pressing down like the weight of the storm outside. I swallowed hard, unsure whether to feel angry or fearful—or both.

"I didn't ask for this," I said, my voice tight, but it came out stronger than I expected. "But I'm not backing down now."

The man chuckled softly, the sound dripping with contempt. "No, you won't," he said, as if it were a foregone conclusion. "None of you ever do."

There was a moment of silence, thick with unspoken threats. I knew, without a doubt, that whatever we were about to face next was going to change everything. And as much as I hated to admit it, I was starting to wonder if maybe, just maybe, Vance was right about one thing: this wasn't a game anymore. This was a war.

And we were already caught in the middle of it.

The room had gone still, the air thick with the kind of tension that made your skin prickle, your pulse quicken. The man—whose name I still hadn't learned but whose eyes told me enough—took a slow, deliberate step toward us. His boots clicked against the worn wood, echoing like the steady beat of a drum. I could feel the weight of his presence, the heaviness of something dark and ancient creeping along the edges of my thoughts.

He didn't look like the kind of person who needed to speak in riddles. His every move screamed that he had no intention of letting us walk away from this conversation in one piece.

"You're both so eager to play hero," he mused, his voice dripping with amusement. "But the game you think you're playing is already over. You just don't know it yet."

I resisted the urge to step back, to put more distance between myself and the man whose every word felt like a countdown. Instead, I narrowed my eyes, clenching my fists at my sides. I didn't come here to play games. "If the game's over," I shot back, my tone as sharp as I could muster, "then why am I still standing here?"

The man paused, his lips curling into a smile that didn't reach his eyes. "Because, darling, you're already in it. Whether you like it or not."

Behind me, Vance shifted, the tension in his posture a clear sign that he was calculating something in his head—looking for the next move, the next opening. He wasn't the type to let anything slip. But there was something about the man before us that made even Vance falter for just a second.

For a brief, unsettling moment, I thought I saw Vance's jaw tighten ever so slightly, his eyes narrowing in a way I hadn't seen before. Something about the man, something I hadn't yet pieced together, was rattling him. But I couldn't afford to be distracted. Not now.

"Enough with the riddles," I said, my voice firm. "Who are you? What do you want with Crescent City?"

The man's smile faded, and he took another deliberate step toward us. There was a coldness in his eyes now, something that made the hair on the back of my neck stand on end. "I've already got what I need," he said simply. "I've been working toward this for a long time. And now, the city is just... a distraction. It's you two who have made things interesting. A lot more interesting than I anticipated."

I glanced at Vance, whose expression remained unreadable, but his hand twitched, like he was resisting the urge to reach for the gun he kept tucked beneath his jacket. I could feel his focus sharpening, his attention zeroing in on the man like a predator about to strike. But I knew Vance well enough to understand that he didn't make moves without a reason, without a plan. So why the hesitation?

"Interesting how?" I asked, trying to keep my voice steady.

The man's eyes flicked over to Vance, and for the briefest of moments, a glimmer of recognition passed between them. It wasn't much, just a flicker of understanding—something old and dangerous—but it was enough to make me pause.

"Because," the man began, his voice low and smooth, "you two don't even realize what you're standing on. You're sitting in the center of a storm you can't control, and the more you struggle against it, the more it'll tear you apart. You should've stayed out of it, but now... now you're part of the equation. Whether you like it or not."

I was no stranger to cryptic threats, but something about his words chilled me more than I cared to admit. His presence felt like a weight pressing down on my chest, making it hard to breathe. I glanced at Vance again, but his eyes were fixed on the man now, his muscles taut with barely contained frustration. It was like he was fighting to keep a lid on whatever storm was brewing inside him.

"You've made a mistake," Vance said, his voice steady, but I could sense the undercurrent of something darker there. "You think we're the ones who don't know what we're up against? We've been in this game long enough to know that nothing is as simple as it seems."

The man's smile returned, but this time, it was colder. "That's where you're wrong, my friend. You think you have the upper hand, but the reality is, you've been playing catch-up from the start. You're not the ones holding the strings. You never were."

The words hit me like a slap, leaving me momentarily disoriented. My mind raced to process them, but there was no time. Without warning, the man's eyes flicked to the door, and before I could even react, the sound of footsteps—too many, too fast—brought the air to a screeching halt.

Someone else was coming.

The man's smile never wavered. "I'll leave you with that thought," he said with an eerie calmness. "But be careful. You're not as invisible as you think."

With that, he turned, moving toward the back of the room with a deliberate, almost leisurely pace. The door creaked as he pushed it open, vanishing into the shadows beyond.

Vance was already moving, his steps quick and measured, but I wasn't far behind. The adrenaline surged, a jolt of energy shooting through me as I followed him down the narrow hall. The sudden rush of motion was both exhilarating and terrifying, and I couldn't tell which feeling was winning out.

I could hear voices now—low, urgent murmurs coming from the far side of the building. The footsteps were getting louder, closing in. Whoever was coming, they weren't alone.

"Vance, what the hell just happened?" I hissed, my breath shallow as we rounded another corner, the sound of our footsteps pounding against the old wood floor.

Vance didn't answer at first, but I could feel the tension rolling off him, the uncertainty that had crept into his movements. The calm façade was cracking, and I wasn't sure whether I was relieved or terrified by that fact.

"Get ready," he muttered. "This is far from over."

Just as the door at the end of the hall burst open, the room beyond flooded with light, and I was barely a step away from understanding what he meant when a voice I recognized too well echoed through the space.

"Glad you could make it."

And standing there, grinning like the devil himself, was someone I had never expected to see again.

Chapter 4: Unraveling Secrets

The air inside the factory was thick with dust and the weight of forgotten memories. Each step I took echoed off the hollow walls, reverberating with the sounds of a past that was better left behind. Rusted machinery loomed in the corners, their jagged metal arms outstretched like the fingers of long-dead giants, their intentions unclear. The flickering lights overhead cast eerie shadows, as if the factory itself were alive, watching, waiting for the right moment to swallow us whole.

Vance moved ahead of me, his broad back cutting through the gloom with the kind of silent confidence that made me wonder if he had any real fear. I'd seen him play the part of the fearless leader before, but this was different—there was something in his movements now that hinted at doubt, or maybe it was just the weight of all the things left unsaid between us. His leather jacket creaked as he shifted, and the faint scent of his cologne, something woodsy with a hint of spice, clung to the air. The smell, oddly comforting in such a desolate place, did nothing to ease the tension coiling in my stomach.

I forced myself to keep my focus. One wrong move here, and everything could fall apart. The mission was simple: infiltrate, gather what we needed, and leave. But as we stepped deeper into the belly of the beast, I couldn't shake the feeling that the lines between mission and something personal were starting to blur. I'd spent enough time with Vance to know he wasn't the type to let his guard down, especially not around someone like me. So why was it that, every time our paths crossed in this crumbling factory, I felt like he was trying to tell me something without speaking a word?

The floor creaked beneath us, a sound far too loud for comfort. I stopped, holding up a hand, signaling for him to wait. Vance shot me a quick glance, his sharp eyes narrowing with the kind of curiosity I'd seen him reserve for things he wasn't sure he could control.

"Something wrong?" he asked, his voice low, almost hesitant. For a split second, I thought I caught a flicker of something vulnerable in his expression, but it disappeared too quickly for me to be sure.

"I don't know. Just...feels off," I replied, trying to ignore the strange flutter in my chest. My senses were on high alert, and my instincts were screaming at me to turn back, to abandon the mission before it all unraveled. But I couldn't. Not now. Not when we were so close to uncovering what lay hidden in these decaying walls.

He didn't push, just gave me a curt nod and moved forward, his boots crunching over the debris that littered the factory floor. I followed him, keeping my distance just enough to be unnoticed, but close enough to feel the heat radiating off his body, the faint pulse of his heartbeat that I could almost sense through the air. Every time I tried to distance myself, to remind myself that this was a mission, not a game, that strange connection pulled me back.

The hallway ahead opened up into a cavernous room, its walls lined with shelves of outdated equipment and broken tools, abandoned decades ago. The smell of oil and metal mixed with the musty scent of decay, and I gagged, momentarily distracted by the overpowering stench. Vance led the way again, his steps confident, his hand brushing the edge of a table that had long since lost its purpose. He paused, scanning the room, his eyes darting from corner to corner, searching for something only he seemed to see.

"You think this is the place?" I asked, breaking the silence that had settled between us. My voice felt too loud in the stillness, but Vance didn't flinch. He never did. It was one of the things I both envied and hated about him.

"Doesn't matter if I think it's the place," he muttered, his voice steady and cool. "We're here. We're committed. We find what we came for, and then we get the hell out."

It was his usual rhetoric—pragmatic, unemotional—but there was a slight tremor in his words that betrayed him. I knew it wasn't just the factory's oppressive atmosphere that had him on edge. It was something else. Something I didn't know, but I was starting to realize I wanted to.

I moved closer, narrowing my eyes as I scanned the room. Something glinted in the corner, barely visible beneath a stack of broken crates. My pulse quickened. That was it. Whatever had brought us here, whatever had been hidden so carefully, was right in front of us now.

"Vance," I whispered, my voice sharp with urgency. "Over there."

He didn't hesitate. In one fluid motion, he crossed the room, his gaze fixed on the pile. My feet followed, almost of their own accord. When we reached the crates, I half expected him to make some sort of dramatic declaration, but he simply lifted the top one, his hands moving with a practiced precision that spoke volumes of his experience.

The moment the crate gave way, my breath hitched. Beneath it was a small, rusted chest, its edges marked by years of neglect. My fingers itched to touch it, to unlock the secrets it held, but there was a hesitation, a gut instinct warning me that what we were about to find would change everything.

"Are you ready for this?" I asked, my voice barely more than a whisper. It felt ridiculous to ask. Vance had been ready for far worse, but something in me needed to know that he, too, felt the weight of what we were about to uncover.

He glanced at me, and for the first time since we'd entered this mess, his usual mask slipped. The hardness in his eyes softened, just a fraction, and something flickered there—a recognition, maybe, or perhaps it was just exhaustion.

"Ready as I'll ever be," he muttered, and for the first time, his voice wasn't just cold—it was strained, as though the weight of whatever lay ahead was beginning to wear on him too.

He opened the chest, and the room seemed to hold its breath.

The chest creaked open with a sound that was almost mournful, as if it, too, knew the weight of what was about to unfold. Inside, nestled among yellowed papers and brittle leather-bound books, was a small, unassuming envelope—its edges frayed with age, the wax seal still intact. It was the kind of object that should have been lost to time, but somehow, it had survived, preserved like a secret too dangerous to let go.

Vance's hand hovered over it for a moment, his fingers twitching as if reluctant to disturb the fragile peace the chest had held for so long. I could feel my pulse quicken, the tension crackling between us, thick enough to touch. There was something profoundly personal about this moment, as though we were standing on the precipice of something neither of us was ready to face, but both of us were too far gone to turn back now.

"What is it?" I asked, my voice low, unable to hide the curiosity that gnawed at me. I tried to keep my tone neutral, but I knew the words came out sharper than I intended. The silence between us was loaded, thick with the promise of whatever truth this envelope carried.

Vance didn't answer immediately. His eyes scanned the seal, his brow furrowing as he weighed his options. I couldn't read him—not now, not in this place where the lines between truth and lies had started to blur. But then he seemed to make a decision. Slowly, deliberately, he broke the seal.

The crack of wax sounded like the final toll of a bell, and I swore I could almost hear the echoes reverberating through the hollow factory. He pulled out the contents—a single sheet of paper, worn at the edges, the ink faint but legible. He glanced at it, his face going still, almost too still. The kind of stillness that made the air around us feel heavier, thicker, like it was holding its breath, waiting for something to snap.

"What's on it?" I pressed again, though I already knew. I could see the way his jaw tightened, the faint flicker of something passing over his face. This wasn't just information. This was history. His history.

"I didn't expect this," he muttered under his breath, more to himself than to me. But I heard it all the same. The words were heavy, laced with a history I wasn't sure I was ready to uncover.

Without asking, I moved closer, trying to catch a glimpse of the paper. He turned the sheet, so it was facing me, and I saw the familiar scrawl of a name—a name I'd heard only in hushed whispers, a name that had become a ghost story among those who knew the city's darker corners.

"Victor Hale," I read aloud, the name slipping from my tongue like something foreign. "What the hell does he have to do with any of this?"

Vance didn't immediately respond, his hand clutching the paper with an almost frantic intensity, as though he feared it would slip away and vanish into the air. There was a shift in him, something I couldn't quite place. His usual bravado was gone, replaced by a raw vulnerability I wasn't sure how to handle.

"You don't get it, do you?" His voice was low, almost gravelly, and when he finally looked at me, the mask had slipped entirely. His eyes were wide, and for the first time, I saw the storm brewing behind them. "This isn't just about us. This... this has been planned for a long time, and Victor Hale has been at the center of it all."

The name hit me like a punch to the gut. Victor Hale. A name that had been whispered in dark corners, a shadowy figure in the underworld that had always felt just out of reach. A man whose dealings had ruined lives, who had managed to stay untouchable for years, despite the countless attempts to bring him down.

"Wait," I said, taking a step back, my mind racing. "You mean to tell me... he's the one pulling the strings? The one who's been orchestrating everything?"

Vance didn't answer right away, his gaze fixed on the paper as if it held all the answers. But I saw the shift in him. The way his shoulders seemed to sag, the way his fingers trembled just slightly as he crumpled the paper in his hands. He looked like he had just uncovered something he hadn't been ready to face either.

"Not exactly," he said, his voice tight. "He's been the one keeping the strings in place. But..." His voice faltered, and for a brief, terrifying moment, he seemed almost unsure. "But I'm not sure what he wants anymore."

There it was—the crack in the armor. The vulnerability I hadn't expected to see. The man who always had a plan, who always knew how to stay one step ahead, had lost his footing. I wasn't sure if it was the weight of Hale's name or something else that had thrown him off balance, but whatever it was, I could feel the shift between us. The fragile alliance we'd built seemed to teeter on the edge of something far darker than either of us had bargained for.

"I thought we were here for answers," I said, trying to push through the growing tension, my words coming out sharper than I'd intended. I wasn't sure if I was angry or scared—or both—but I needed something. Anything that would make sense of the mess we were standing in.

Vance's eyes darkened, his jaw setting in a way that made it clear he wasn't ready to share any more. The walls went up again, just like that. The shift was subtle but undeniable. He was back behind his wall of indifference, his focus narrowing on the paper in his hands.

"We are," he said, his tone final. "But some answers come with a price."

I couldn't help it. I laughed, though it was short, humorless. "What does that mean? A price like blood? Or something worse?"

Vance met my gaze, and in his eyes, I saw the flicker of something dangerously close to regret. But it was gone in a heartbeat. "You'll find out soon enough."

I didn't know what to expect from him next. The Vance I'd come to know was a man who wore secrets like armor, who dealt in half-truths and clever misdirection. But the way he'd looked at me just then—like a cornered animal, desperate to escape his own thoughts—was something new. And it unsettled me in a way I couldn't quite place. He wasn't just a player in this game anymore; he was as tangled in it as I was.

I folded my arms across my chest, trying to gather my thoughts, to formulate a plan. The factory loomed around us, its silence now oppressive, pressing in on us from every side. Vance's words, though spoken quietly, felt like a dare. "You'll find out soon enough," he'd said, but there was something in his voice that made me think he didn't even believe that. Maybe he wasn't as sure about the endgame as he wanted me to believe.

"Well, that's not ominous at all," I muttered under my breath. He shot me a quick glance, a flash of something flickering in his eyes—amusement, annoyance, or maybe just the remnants of an old habit. I couldn't tell, but I didn't expect him to give me any more than that. He'd already given me just enough to make me want to burn the paper he'd handed me and walk out of this nightmare. But I couldn't.

I couldn't walk away now. There was too much at stake. Too many unanswered questions, and for the first time, I was beginning to feel like I wasn't just playing along with his game—I was a part of it. Whether I wanted to be or not.

"Is this your version of trust?" I asked, my voice cutting through the silence. "Because it feels like we're just building a house of cards here, and one good breeze is going to knock it all down."

His lips twitched, but he didn't smile. "Maybe. Or maybe we've already crossed the point where the wind doesn't matter anymore."

I shook my head, frustrated, angry with myself for being here, for being drawn into whatever this was. "Don't do that," I snapped. "Don't speak in riddles. Either tell me what the hell is going on, or I'm done. I'm out."

The words hung in the air between us, sharp and final. For a moment, I thought he might call my bluff, might play the game his way and make me chase after him. But instead, he exhaled sharply, his gaze sliding toward the shadows in the far corner of the room. He wasn't looking at me anymore—not really. His mind had already traveled to some distant place, somewhere I couldn't follow.

"I can't give you everything," he said, his voice low and tight, as if the words were a confession. "But I can give you this: it's not just Hale we're after. We're after something bigger. And we're not the only ones looking."

I stared at him, trying to wrap my mind around the layers of meaning buried in his words. He wasn't just talking about power or money. This wasn't a fight over territory—it was something deeper. The kind of thing that could take everything down with it, like an avalanche swallowing everything in its path.

"What are you saying?" I asked, even though I already had an idea. The weight of it settled over me, colder than the factory air. "That this isn't just about us? That we're just pawns in a bigger game?"

"Maybe," he said, finally turning to face me. There was no bravado in his expression now—just the barest flicker of exhaustion. "But the game's already started, and the stakes are higher than we thought."

It was as though the words hung there in the air, shifting and mutating with the passing seconds. There was something about the way he said it that made my heart race, something about the unspoken promise in his tone. As though, despite everything, there was still a chance for us to get out of this alive.

But deep down, I knew that wasn't true. The moment we walked into this factory, we had crossed the point of no return. There were no clean exits now, no safe paths leading back to where we came from.

"Then what do we do?" I asked, the words sounding small in the cavernous room. It was an awful question, one I didn't want the answer to. But I needed it. I needed to know what came next.

Vance's gaze flickered, unreadable as always. But this time, I thought I saw a flicker of something else in his eyes. Something raw. Something... uncertain. It was gone before I could make sense of it, replaced by the familiar hardness that had become his mask. He was good at that—burying whatever was beneath the surface. But I knew, just from the way his hands tightened around the paper in his grip, that this was bigger than anything he'd ever faced before.

"We fight," he said finally, his voice steel-lined. "We find what's left of the truth and we burn it to the ground. If we don't, Hale will. And the rest of them."

He said "the rest of them" as if he were talking about ghosts—unspeakable figures that loomed just outside the fringes of the light, always lurking, always waiting. I didn't ask him who "they" were. I didn't want to know. Whatever world he was walking in, I had already stepped far too deep into it, and there was no turning back.

But just as the words left his mouth, the faintest sound—a scrape of metal against concrete—broke the silence. My heart skipped a beat. We weren't alone.

Vance's eyes snapped to the shadows, his hand instinctively reaching for the gun at his side. His body tensed, every muscle primed for action. But he didn't move, didn't make a sound. He was waiting—waiting to see if the intruder was someone we could handle, or someone we'd have to run from.

I couldn't breathe, couldn't think. My entire focus was on the sound, the way it slithered through the room like a threat. There was no mistaking it now. We weren't alone. And the factory wasn't as empty as it had seemed.

Then, just as suddenly as it had started, the sound stopped.

And the room fell into an eerie silence once more.

Chapter 5: Dancing with Shadows

The streets had taken on a haunted quality by the time Vance and I were knee-deep in the heart of the city's underbelly, moving quickly but silently, as though we were shadows ourselves. The usual hum of city life was subdued, replaced by an eerie stillness, like the world was holding its breath. It was the sort of silence that made every footstep, every whispered breath, feel like a betrayal.

We'd slipped into this grim tango without either of us fully realizing how it happened. One minute, we were locked in an endless game of tug-of-war—him trying to get information, me trying to keep it from him—and the next, we were partners in this twisted little dance, moving side by side through alleyways that smelled of wet concrete and burnt rubber. His dark hair was slightly ruffled, the edges of his jacket fluttering in the cool wind like a flag of defiance. I, of course, looked like a mess—heels too high, skirt too short, and my hair hanging in messy waves around my face. But I didn't care. It wasn't about appearances tonight; it was about survival. And maybe—just maybe—a little bit about proving something to both him and myself.

The tension between us was palpable, thick enough that I could almost taste it. Every time our hands brushed, a shiver skittered down my spine, a sharp reminder of the dangerous line we were walking. There was something about him—something that pulled at me even as I fought against it. He wasn't what I expected. He wasn't charming or smooth in the way most men who played this game were. No, Vance was something else entirely. There was a quiet, brooding intensity about him that made everything in me want to stay a safe distance away—but, like I said, I was a moth. Drawn to the heat, even as I feared getting too close to the flame.

"You're awfully quiet tonight," he muttered, his voice low, a gravelly thing that made the air around us feel charged. We'd been walking for a while, each step careful, as though we were entering the heart of a predator's den.

I glanced at him, my lips twitching at the edges. "Maybe I'm just tired of hearing you talk."

His eyes flicked to mine for a second, and I saw that familiar flicker of amusement. "I don't believe that for a second. You're just trying to pretend you don't like my company."

I let out a soft snort, glancing away. "Keep dreaming. You're a pain in the ass."

"Sure," he said, his lips curling up in that way that made my stomach tighten unexpectedly. "But I'm your pain in the ass."

I rolled my eyes, but the words lodged themselves in my mind, sticking with me in a way that was far too disconcerting. It was supposed to be a joke, wasn't it? But there was something in the way he said it—something in his tone—that made me wonder if he wasn't so much joking as he was stating a fact.

I wanted to argue with him, to snap back, but the words died on my tongue as the shadows ahead of us shifted. Someone was there.

I tensed, my heart rate quickening. "Did you hear that?"

Vance's posture shifted instantly, his body going still like a predator sensing danger. "Yeah. Stay close."

We moved together, instinctively closing the gap between us. My fingers brushed the fabric of his jacket as we took slow, deliberate steps toward the sound. Every nerve in my body screamed at me to back off, to run in the opposite direction. But there was something else, too—an undeniable pull, a need to keep moving forward, to confront whatever awaited us in the darkness.

I couldn't tell if it was just the tension of the moment or something deeper, but I felt as though I was teetering on the edge of something important. Something I couldn't turn back from. Maybe it was the way he'd looked at me just now, that flicker of something beneath the surface. Or maybe it was the way we were moving in sync now, two people who'd once been enemies, now reduced to two halves of a whole, dancing on the same knife's edge.

The figure ahead of us finally stepped into the dim light of a flickering streetlamp, revealing a man in a long coat, his face obscured by a dark scarf. He was tall, broad-shouldered, and if I had to guess, he'd been waiting for us.

"Thought you two would show up," the man said, his voice deep and clipped, with an almost bored edge to it.

I narrowed my eyes, instinctively stepping closer to Vance. "Who are you?"

He tilted his head slightly, his eyes narrowing behind the shadow of his scarf. "Not who you think I am. But that's not really important. What matters is that I've got something for you. Something that could change the whole game."

I exchanged a glance with Vance. "What's the catch?"

"There's always a catch," the man said, as though he were delivering a simple fact. "But if you're willing to pay the price, you'll get what you came for. Or... what you didn't know you came for."

Vance shifted beside me, and I could feel the muscles in his shoulders tense. "We don't have time for riddles. Just tell us what it is."

The man chuckled, a low, hollow sound. "You'll find out soon enough. But be careful. There's more at stake here than either of you realize."

I didn't know if I was ready for whatever was coming next, but there was no turning back now. Vance and I were already in too deep, and the shadows were closing in faster than we could outrun them.

The man in the shadows took a step forward, his coat billowing slightly like a dark wave that threatened to pull us under. The pale glow of the streetlamp did little to illuminate his features, but enough of him was visible to make my skin crawl. He had the look of someone who knew exactly how much danger he could wield, someone who reveled in it, even.

I took a slow breath, my fingers curling into the fabric of my jacket as if it might offer me some kind of protection. The quiet hum of the city felt distant now, like an old memory, as if we'd slipped into another world entirely—one where the rules didn't quite apply. It wasn't just the darkness around us; it was something in the air, something thick and suffocating, that told me we were past the point of no return.

Vance stepped closer, the tension between us an invisible force that I could almost feel pressing down on my chest. He was a wall of cold resolve beside me, but I could sense the shifting undercurrents in him, the way his body reacted to the man across from us. Whatever this was, it was more than just a simple exchange. Something larger was at play, and for once, I was starting to get the feeling that I was out of my depth.

"Do you think we look like amateurs?" Vance's voice was a mix of annoyance and challenge, like he didn't want to play this game but had no choice.

The man didn't respond at first. Instead, he seemed to weigh Vance and me, his gaze drifting from one of us to the other as though we were chess pieces in a game he'd been playing for much longer than we realized. Finally, he exhaled, a sound like something ancient.

"You're playing a game, alright," he said slowly, his words deliberate. "The question is: Are you prepared for the endgame?"

I tried not to roll my eyes, but I could feel the frustration bubbling beneath the surface. Vance was right. This wasn't the time for cryptic riddles. We needed answers, not more questions. But before I could say anything, the man pushed off the alley wall with a fluid motion and stepped closer, the echo of his boots on the pavement making me shiver.

"The truth isn't always what it seems," he continued, his eyes now gleaming with something I couldn't quite place. "You think you're chasing shadows, but it's more than that. All of it. Everything you've been told. It's a game of misdirection."

His words hit me like a slap, an unsettling realization gnawing at the edges of my mind. Chasing shadows. Was that it? Were we just running after something that wasn't even real? The pieces I had—so carefully gathered, so diligently protected—suddenly seemed flimsy, like a house of cards on the verge of collapse. My chest tightened as the weight of his statement settled in.

"Stop talking in riddles," I snapped, my voice sharper than I intended. "What do you want from us?"

The man's lips twitched, like he was amused by my frustration, or perhaps he was simply enjoying watching us scramble. I could feel Vance's tension next to me, the way his jaw clenched as if he was preparing for a fight. But neither of us could afford to make the first move. Not yet. Not until we had something—anything—to use.

"You want the truth?" the man asked, and for the first time, there was a spark of something almost human in his eyes. "Here it is. Someone is watching you. Someone who's been playing both sides of this little game. Someone who knows exactly what buttons to push."

My heart skipped a beat, and I couldn't help the sharp intake of breath. My gaze darted to Vance, and I saw the flicker of something dangerous in his eyes.

"Who?" Vance asked, his voice low, barely controlled.

The man smiled, a slow, almost cruel thing. "Someone you know. Someone you trust."

The world tilted on its axis, the ground beneath my feet shifting. I stumbled, but Vance's hand shot out to steady me, his fingers curling around my arm with a strength that was almost startling. It was only then that I realized how close we'd gotten in the last few minutes, how much we were starting to rely on each other, even in the midst of our shared mistrust.

"Don't play games," I said, my voice a little shaky, even as I tried to mask the uncertainty rising in my chest. "Who's watching us? Who's pulling the strings?"

The man looked at us, his smile still stretched across his face, but there was something else now—something that sent a chill down my spine. "You'll find out soon enough. But not here. Not tonight."

My frustration hit its peak. "What the hell does that mean? You show up out of nowhere, give us cryptic warnings, and then what? You leave us hanging?"

The man's expression didn't change, but the amusement in his eyes faded, replaced by a colder, more calculating look. "I don't do favors. I'm not here to hold your hand. But if you want to play, if you want to survive, you'll have to follow the breadcrumbs. The truth's already been set in motion. And when it finally clicks for you, it'll be too late to stop it."

I could feel the weight of his words sinking in, the realization that we were in a much deeper mess than we could have imagined. The man was offering us nothing, not really, except a chilling promise: the game was already in motion, and the end would come whether we were ready or not.

Before either of us could respond, he turned, his coat swirling around him like a cloak of mystery, and vanished into the night.

I stood there for a long moment, staring at the empty space where he had been. The silence pressed in, thick and suffocating, as if the city itself had gone quiet in the wake of his departure.

"What now?" I asked, my voice barely a whisper.

Vance didn't answer immediately, his gaze fixed on the shadows ahead. Finally, he turned to me, his jaw tight, his expression unreadable.

"Now we find out who's playing both sides," he said, his voice dark and determined. "And we make them regret it."

The silence stretched between us, thick and suffocating, as we made our way through the city's winding streets. My steps were sharp, deliberate, but there was a nagging pulse in my chest that made it impossible to fully focus. Vance was still beside me, his presence a constant, like a shadow I couldn't escape no matter how many times I tried to shake him off. We'd been working together for hours now, the weight of our shared pursuit pressing down on us, and despite every attempt to hold onto some semblance of distance, there was a magnetic force between us that seemed only to grow stronger with every passing minute.

He wasn't supposed to matter. He was the enemy, the one I'd fought tooth and nail against in the past, the one whose smirk I would have happily punched off his face at any given opportunity. But somewhere in the haze of this ridiculous, dangerous mess we'd found ourselves in, I couldn't deny that the tension between us had shifted—morphed into something else entirely.

I couldn't tell if I was scared of it or drawn to it, but I couldn't ignore it either.

"You're quiet," Vance remarked, his voice slicing through the darkness. "Usually you've got some snarky comment on the tip of your tongue."

I shot him a sideways glance, trying to muster some of my usual bravado. "I'm just savoring the silence. Don't get used to it."

He smirked, his eyes glinting in the low light. "Can't help it. I've learned to cherish quiet moments with you. They don't come often."

I rolled my eyes, though a small part of me wondered how much of that was true. We'd bickered constantly back in the day, our words like weapons, but now… now everything seemed tinged with something far more complicated. I had no intention of giving in to whatever this was. No way. He was still Vance, still the same arrogant, infuriating man who'd always been one step ahead. Nothing had changed.

Except, maybe, everything.

"Do you ever shut up?" I muttered, more to myself than to him. "I swear, if I hear one more thing about 'cherishing' moments, I might just hurl myself into the nearest pothole."

He laughed, a sound that made the air around us shift. "I think it's cute when you pretend to hate me."

"I don't hate you," I said quickly, a little too quickly, and then regretted it. "I just—don't like you."

"Ah, that's it. The fine line between hate and like. I know it well."

There it was again, that flicker of something, something that couldn't be ignored. I quickly forced my mind back to the task at hand, to the danger that loomed like a storm cloud over us. Our mission was the only thing that mattered right now. The man from earlier, the one who'd practically toyed with us in that alley, was still fresh in my mind. The warning he'd given us, the promise of a game we couldn't even begin to understand, was like a heavy weight pressing down on my chest.

My pace quickened, and Vance fell in step beside me, no words between us now—only the rhythmic sound of our footsteps on the pavement.

We rounded a corner, and I froze. The street ahead was deserted, the usual din of city life swallowed by the darkness. But there was something in the air, a feeling that made my skin prickle. The hairs on the back of my neck stood up, a visceral warning that I couldn't ignore.

"We're being watched," I said, the words coming out in a rush, my voice tight with sudden apprehension.

Vance didn't speak at first, but I could feel his body go still beside me. A second later, he exhaled sharply, his hand brushing mine as he reached for something in his jacket.

"I thought we were past this," he muttered, scanning the shadows, his posture alert. "Stay close."

I didn't need telling twice. Without another word, we pressed ourselves against the nearest building, its rough brick wall cool against my back as I tried to steady my breath. The adrenaline surged through me, and despite everything—the tension between us, the fear, the uncertainty—I couldn't help the rush of exhilaration that accompanied it. There was something intoxicating about this, something thrilling in the danger, even if it meant walking headlong into whatever trap was waiting for us.

A faint sound reached my ears—footsteps, slow and measured, just around the corner.

Vance's grip on my wrist tightened, pulling me closer to him, his breath barely a whisper against my ear. "Get ready."

I nodded, swallowing hard. The steps grew louder, closer, until they stopped, just on the other side of the corner. I held my breath, the silence thick as I waited for whatever was coming next. The man from the alley, perhaps, or someone else entirely.

And then—nothing.

Just when I thought we'd been caught, the footsteps retreated, fading into the distance.

I let out the breath I'd been holding, only realizing how much I had tensed until my muscles ached. Vance didn't move for a few moments, his body still pressed against mine, his focus entirely on the empty street ahead.

"Who was that?" I finally asked, my voice hoarse.

"Someone who's been following us for a while," Vance said, his words clipped, controlled. "We need to move."

I didn't question him. I didn't need to. Whatever this was, whoever was pulling the strings, we were too far in now. No turning back.

We stepped back into the shadows, moving quickly but cautiously, as the city seemed to close in around us. Every flicker of movement, every sound, was a potential threat. I kept my eyes on the darkened alleyways, my hand still firmly gripping Vance's jacket as though it were the only thing anchoring me in this nightmare.

We'd only taken a few steps when the air shifted again—this time, something more deliberate. A figure appeared at the far end of the street, his form emerging from the darkness like a phantom, his silhouette unmistakable.

It was him.

The man who had warned us.

But this time, he wasn't alone.

And neither were we.

Chapter 6: The Spider's Embrace

I had never been a fan of darkness. It had always been that quiet kind of unsettling, creeping in from the edges of the room like a thief, stealing away comfort without warning. But this place, this cursed stone temple we'd found hidden deep in the woods, had darkness in a way that felt alive, breathing beneath the earth, waiting for the right moment to consume you whole.

The air inside was thick, pressing in on my chest as if the walls were watching, waiting. I could taste the dampness on the back of my tongue, like wet earth and ancient dust. We moved cautiously, Vance ahead of me, a silent figure in the gloom, his silhouette only a shadow against the pulsing glow that emanated from somewhere ahead. I couldn't tell if the light came from the walls, or if it simply bled into the air itself, like the very fabric of this place had been woven with magic. The symbols on the stone—arcane, twisted things—had no real shape that I could comprehend. They glimmered faintly, as if they were alive, watching us approach with intent. It wasn't the kind of magic you could tame with a simple chant or a flick of the wrist. No, this was primal, ancient, the kind of magic that had a voice of its own and wasn't afraid to be heard.

"Do you feel that?" I asked, my voice a whisper that barely made it past my lips.

Vance didn't answer right away, his sharp eyes scanning the walls like a predator hunting for any hint of movement. His dark hair fell over his brow, a few strands glistening with sweat from the heat of this place, despite the chill in the air. There was something mesmerizing about him, even now, even with everything swirling in the dark around us.

He turned to me, his gaze intense. "I feel it." He said it softly, almost as if he didn't want to acknowledge it too fully. But I could see it in his eyes, that flicker of something—something that had been growing between us since we'd first met. I didn't want to admit it, not here, not now, but I couldn't ignore the way he drew me in. Not when the magic of this place was already doing that to me.

We continued through the chamber, our footsteps muffled by the thick stone beneath us. The air was so dense with magic, with the ancient weight of whatever had been hidden here, that I could hardly breathe. And yet, there was a strange pull, something I couldn't explain, like my feet knew the path before I did. Like I had been here before in some other life, in some other world. My hand brushed against the wall, and I felt the power surge through me—hot and electric—like I had just touched a live wire. I jerked my hand back instinctively, but not before I heard the faintest of whispers.

"Stop," the voice hissed, so low I wasn't sure if it had been in my mind or if it had come from the shadows themselves.

I froze, my heart slamming against my ribs. But Vance was already several steps ahead, moving deeper into the chamber, and I couldn't see his face, couldn't read his expression. His presence, once a comfort, now felt like it was pulling me further into the storm. I wanted to call out to him, but something in the air made my tongue stick to the roof of my mouth. It was like the very space around us had thickened, becoming more suffocating with each passing moment.

The glow ahead brightened, casting harsh shadows on the stone walls. A figure stood in the center of the room, cloaked in robes that shimmered like the moon on water. At first, I thought it was an illusion, a trick of the light, but then the figure moved. It was slow at first, as if it were testing the air, then, with an almost imperceptible shift, it straightened, and I knew—without question—that we had crossed into something we couldn't come back from.

Vance stopped beside me, his presence suddenly a weight that pressed against my back. I could feel the heat of his body, the magnetic pull that had always been there, but now it was suffocating.

His fingers brushed mine, just a fleeting touch, but enough to make the hair on my neck stand on end.

"Stay close," he murmured, though his voice was tight. His usual calm was gone, replaced by something raw and unfamiliar.

I didn't know if I should trust him, or if I should run, but all I could do was watch as the figure before us moved closer, each step deliberate, each footfall impossibly soft on the stone floor. And that's when I saw it—the faint glimmer of silver threads in the air around the figure. Spider's webs, no thicker than a hair, but glistening in the low light. They stretched across the chamber, weaving between the walls, the air, the very fabric of reality.

The figure's hands raised, fingers stretching toward us, and the webs responded, moving as though they had a mind of their own. My breath hitched in my chest as the webs tightened, pulling the air around us, constricting, wrapping us up in a web we couldn't escape. I could hear the soft hum of magic, low and resonant, like a pulse that matched the beating of my heart.

"Welcome," the figure's voice was a melodic, lilting sound that made the hairs on the back of my neck prickle. "You have entered the Spider's Embrace."

I couldn't move, couldn't think, the words filling my mind, drowning out everything else. The magic was suffocating, intoxicating, and I could feel it wrapping around me, pulling me in, until the world around me seemed to dissolve into darkness, into nothingness.

I looked at Vance, his face tight, his jaw clenched as though he were fighting against something. The webs—spider's webs—were everywhere now, wrapping around his limbs, pulling him toward the figure, toward the center of this webbed nightmare. I wanted to scream, wanted to fight, but my body was frozen, caught in the same snare.

And then I heard it—beneath the hum of the magic, beneath the whisper of the webs—I heard the voice in my head again. The same voice that had warned me earlier.

It's too late. You've already been chosen.

The world had gone eerily quiet, as though the moment itself had frozen in time. The figure before us, draped in its shimmering, otherworldly cloak, seemed to draw the very air out of the room. I could barely breathe as the webbing inched closer, closer still, and I couldn't help but wonder—what was I about to walk into? My heart thundered in my chest, but my limbs felt like lead, heavy and unresponsive. Every instinct in my body screamed at me to run, to escape, but my feet were rooted to the stone floor, unwilling to move.

And then I felt it, a tug, not on my body, but on my very soul. It was like a magnet pulling me in, a force so subtle and irresistible that I couldn't help but lean toward it, just a fraction. For a moment, I thought I saw a flicker of movement in Vance's eyes, something vulnerable, something he usually kept buried so deep that I almost never caught a glimpse of it. But now, it was there, raw and exposed, and it frightened me more than any of the dark magic swirling around us.

He turned toward me then, his lips pressing into a thin line, his brow furrowed in concentration. "Don't," he said, his voice tight, almost warning, but there was an underlying desperation to it, one I wasn't sure I could ignore. "This is not the time."

I didn't ask him what he meant, though I wanted to. We were tangled in this web, caught between a fate neither of us had chosen, and every step we took only seemed to lead us deeper into the labyrinth of uncertainty. There was no escape now—not without understanding what we were really up against.

I swallowed hard, my throat dry, as I watched the figure before us stretch its hands out again, the silver threads of its web reaching out like fingers, testing the space between us. They hovered in midair, curling and uncurling as if they were sentient, aware of our every move. The magic in the room was so thick, so palpable, that I felt as though it could suffocate me at any moment. The walls, the air, even the shadows seemed to pulse with it, an unseen rhythm that I could feel deep in my bones.

"You've already been chosen," the figure repeated, its voice soft but unnervingly clear. It wasn't a question, but a statement, an inevitability that hung between us like a fog. "There's no going back now."

I glanced at Vance again, my eyes searching his face for some sign, some clue, but he wasn't looking at me anymore. His gaze was locked on the figure, his features hard, his jaw clenched tight. He was thinking, calculating, but he was also afraid. I knew that much now. I could see the tension in his shoulders, the rigid way his body stood. Vance was always so composed, always in control—but here, in this cursed place, he was like a puppet caught in the web, trying to break free but unable to.

My hand moved instinctively toward his, and when I touched him, there was a brief moment where I felt like we were two pieces of a puzzle, perfectly fitting together in a way that was both unsettling and right. I felt the warmth of his skin, the steady beat of his heart beneath the surface, and I realized how much I depended on him, how much he depended on me, even when neither of us was willing to admit it.

"Is this what you've been hiding?" I whispered, not entirely sure if I wanted the answer. "Is this what you knew?"

Vance didn't answer right away, and when he did, his voice was low, almost inaudible over the hum of magic in the air. "It's worse than you think."

That didn't reassure me. I had thought we'd been searching for answers, looking for some kind of truth, but now, in this moment, I wasn't sure I wanted to know the truth. The more I learned, the more tangled I became in this web—physically and emotionally—and the more the stakes seemed to rise with every passing second.

The figure spoke again, its voice strangely soothing, like a lullaby sung by someone who knew the darkness far too well. "The webs you are trapped in are not of my making," it said, its eyes flickering as if it were amused by our fear. "But they are yours now. And you will see them in everything. In the way your hearts beat, in the way your minds think. This is the price of fate."

I shivered. It didn't feel like a price I wanted to pay. And yet, I was here. With Vance. With this—this thing that hovered at the edge of understanding, a riddle wrapped in shadows. The webs had already claimed us, whether we liked it or not.

I felt the tug again, but this time it was stronger, more insistent, as though the web had come alive and was pulling me in—closer to the figure, closer to the magic that bound me. I struggled against it, my heart racing in my chest, but the more I fought, the tighter the web seemed to hold me.

Vance's grip on my hand tightened as if he sensed my panic. "Stop," he said again, his voice cutting through the fog of confusion that clouded my mind. "Don't fight it. Not yet."

I looked at him, my eyes wide, disbelief flooding my veins. "What are you talking about? We can't just—"

"I'm not asking you to trust me," he interrupted. "But I need you to listen. The webs are alive. They choose who they take, and once you're caught—" He paused, his voice thick with something I couldn't place. "Once you're caught, you have to understand how to play the game. Or it will play you."

I wasn't sure what he meant, but something in his words sent a chill through me. The webs weren't just traps—they were alive, breathing, growing. And as much as I hated to admit it, I knew Vance was right. This was a game—one where we didn't have the luxury of making mistakes. One where every choice could be our last.

The webs hummed with energy, a faint, vibrating pulse that mirrored the rapid beat of my heart. With every breath, I felt them pull tighter, the strands delicate but impossibly strong, winding around my thoughts, twisting their way into the very marrow of my bones. There was a deep, gnawing sensation in the pit of my stomach that made me want to scream, but the silence of the chamber pressed in on me, suffocating the sound before it could even form.

"Vance, we need to get out of here," I said, my voice shaking more than I wanted it to. I hated how it sounded—like a plea, desperate and weak—but the air itself seemed to weigh a thousand tons, pressing down on me from all sides. "This isn't just magic—it's something else. It's... wrong."

His gaze flicked back to me, his lips parting as if he wanted to say something, but then his eyes narrowed, the familiar coolness returning, masking whatever fear or doubt I'd glimpsed earlier.

"We can't leave," he said, the words clipped and deliberate. "Not unless we know how this works. Trust me, if we run now, it'll only get worse."

His voice had that familiar edge, the one that made me want to argue but also somehow made me want to crawl into the safety of his shadow. The thing was, I wasn't sure which one of us was more dangerous in this situation—him or the magic closing in around us. And maybe, just maybe, I trusted him more than I should. It was a dangerous thought, especially now, but there it was, tangled in my chest alongside the other emotions I didn't know how to untangle.

The figure at the center of the chamber continued to stand perfectly still, its hands suspended mid-air, the silver threads of its web shimmering, alive with magic. I tried to ignore the pull in my chest, the way the webs seemed to want to reach for me, drag me deeper into their embrace. But no matter how much I fought it, the feeling only intensified. The whispers from before—soft and insistent—returned, a faint murmur in the back of my mind.

"You're already part of the web," they whispered. "You always were."

I shook my head violently, trying to block out the voice, the knowledge that it was speaking a truth I wasn't ready to accept.

"What are you, really?" I said, my voice steady despite the fluttering panic rising in my chest. I forced my feet to move, taking a small step forward, my breath shallow as I finally looked directly at the figure, whose eyes glowed faintly, like two shards of the moon. "What do you want from us?"

The figure didn't respond at first. Its gaze flickered to Vance, then back to me, and in that moment, I realized it wasn't just waiting for an answer. It was studying us—probing us, measuring our worth, our potential. As if we were nothing more than pieces on a chessboard, waiting to be moved.

The air grew heavier, thicker with the magic, and I felt the pressure of the webs wrap tighter around me, like invisible hands closing in. Vance's grip on my hand tightened, as if sensing my growing panic. His eyes didn't leave the figure as he spoke, his voice low and commanding.

"You can feel it, too, can't you? The pull of the web. The thread weaving us together, tighter and tighter." His voice was like gravel, rough but steady, as though he were trying to convince himself more than me. "But this is how it works. The webs don't just ensnare us physically—they bind us in ways we can't even begin to understand."

I wanted to argue, wanted to scream that I didn't want any part of whatever strange magic was playing out before us, but my body wouldn't respond. Instead, I stood there, watching the figure—no longer human, but something else entirely—step forward. The webs stretched impossibly far, their reach extending, curling toward us.

And then the figure spoke, its voice a sharp contrast to the stillness that had previously held the chamber. It was both melodic and haunting, vibrating through my chest.

"You are not here by accident," it said, each word heavy with meaning, laced with the magic of this place. "You have been chosen, bound to the threads that tie fate itself. You, both of you, are part of the pattern. Whether you like it or not."

The words landed like a blow, and for a moment, I couldn't breathe. I turned to look at Vance, the question in my eyes. Had he known? Had he been a part of this web long before I ever stepped into it?

Vance met my gaze, his expression unreadable. He didn't speak, but I could see the tension in his shoulders, the way his jaw clenched. This wasn't just about us being here. This was about something far more dangerous, something beyond the scope of what we could have anticipated.

"We have no choice," he murmured under his breath, almost too quietly for me to hear.

But before I could ask him what he meant, the figure's hands raised again, the webs following its every motion. They moved, shifting through the air with a precision that sent a wave of dread through me. The webs seemed to come alive, wrapping around us, clinging to our skin, weaving into our very souls.

I gasped, trying to pull away, but it was like fighting the tide—futile and impossible. The webs constricted, tighter and tighter, until my chest felt like it was being crushed under the weight of a thousand invisible threads.

"You cannot escape," the figure said, its voice cold and final. "The web has been cast, and now it pulls you in. There is no going back."

And just as the webs closed in, just as I thought I would lose myself entirely, a shrill sound cut through the air—a shriek that seemed to reverberate in every corner of the room, shaking the very foundations of the temple. I turned in time to see a dark shape moving in the shadows, something that had been hiding, waiting, and now—now it was coming for us.

The figure, its glowing eyes widening, hissed, its voice thick with something akin to fear.

"No. This cannot happen. Not yet."

And then, the world exploded into chaos.

Chapter 7: Betrayal in the Web

The rain had been falling for hours, a constant drumbeat against the roof of the small apartment. The city, alive with the flicker of neon lights and the hum of distant traffic, felt impossibly far away from the space I inhabited. Inside, the air was thick, heavy with secrets neither of us wanted to speak aloud. I stood by the window, watching as the raindrops trickled down the glass, leaving streaks of water like tears too hesitant to fall. Vance had left hours ago, and yet, his absence filled the room with a presence that was more suffocating than comforting.

The door creaked open behind me, and I didn't have to turn around to know who it was. I could feel him—the weight of his footsteps, the sharpness of his silence, the electricity that buzzed in the space between us. But it was the slight hitch in his breath, the way his jacket rustled against his body, that made me hesitate. It was a familiar sound, one that had come to represent his return, but tonight, it was wrong. The steady rhythm of his movements was off-kilter, a misstep, a warning.

"You're back," I said, my voice barely above a whisper, the words hanging between us like a confession I wasn't ready to make.

He said nothing, just stepped deeper into the room. The faint odor of whiskey and cologne clung to him like a second skin, mixing with the damp earthiness of the rain. I didn't need to look to know he was avoiding my gaze, his eyes trained on the floor, the way his fingers tugged restlessly at the edge of his sleeve.

I should have told him everything then, should have demanded the truth, but I couldn't. Because the truth—his truth—was a knife I wasn't ready to feel in my own chest. It was easier to pretend, to bury the fear that sat heavy in my stomach, to ignore the gnawing suspicion that had been clawing at the edges of my mind for days.

But there was no escaping it now. The cracks were too wide, too glaring to pretend they didn't exist.

"You need to talk to me, Vance," I finally said, turning to face him. My voice shook, but I refused to let it betray me. "What happened? You've been gone too long, and you're—"

"You should've stayed out of it, Kate," he interrupted, his voice low, sharp. He wasn't angry, not exactly. It was something worse, something darker. He was scared. Scared of what he had done, of what was coming, of what I would think if I knew the truth.

I didn't move, didn't speak for a long moment, because the weight of his words pressed down on me harder than I wanted to admit. "What do you mean?" I whispered.

His eyes flicked up to mine, and I saw it then—the tremor in his gaze, the guilt that had replaced the confidence that used to shine through in every glance he gave me. The man who had once made me feel like I could do anything, conquer any fear, was now standing in front of me like a ghost of himself, a man broken by the choices he'd made.

"The deal... it's already been made. I didn't want you involved, but it's too late. The pieces are already set in motion." His voice cracked, the words jagged and jagged in a way that felt like betrayal itself. "They'll come for you next."

"Who will come for me, Vance?" I asked, stepping closer, my breath catching in my throat. "Who the hell are you really working for?"

He swallowed, his throat working as though the question physically hurt him. "I didn't want to lie to you," he said, his voice nearly a whisper. "But you don't understand what they're capable of. This isn't something I can just walk away from."

"And I'm supposed to believe you?" I demanded, stepping back. "You think I'm just going to sit here, waiting for you to fix this, again and again?"

Vance flinched, as if the words stung more than I could have known. "You don't get it, Kate. I never wanted you to be part of any of this. But now... now it's too late. There's no getting out of this mess. Not for either of us."

For a long time, neither of us spoke. The only sound was the relentless rhythm of the rain, tapping on the window like an impatient visitor.

I felt dizzy. My body was on autopilot, moving without thinking, reacting without fully understanding the weight of the decisions I was making. But deep down, somewhere beneath the sharp ache of betrayal and the anger that was beginning to take root, I understood.

This wasn't just about us anymore. This was about everything. The city. The power struggles that had been woven so deeply into the fabric of our lives. The choices we made. The things we did to survive.

I reached for the table by the window, steadying myself. The cool surface felt like a lifeline against the storm that raged inside me. "You've been lying to me," I said softly, my voice trembling. "And now... now you want me to trust you again?"

Vance didn't say anything, didn't defend himself. He didn't have to. His silence spoke louder than anything he could've said.

And as I stood there, heart in pieces, I realized something that made my chest tighten. I wasn't angry at him. Not entirely. I was angry at myself—for letting it go on this long, for allowing him to become someone I depended on, for letting myself fall into this tangled mess of lies and half-truths.

But I had to make a choice. I had to decide whether to save the city, save myself, or save the man who had once been everything to me.

I wasn't sure I could do all three. But somehow, I had to try.

I didn't know what I was waiting for—him to say something that would make sense of it all, perhaps, or some part of me wanted him to undo everything with a simple apology, something that would make everything right again. But that wasn't Vance's style. And deep down, I knew better than to expect any kind of neat resolution. He was more like the storm itself: full of chaos, unpredictable, impossible to control.

The silence stretched between us, a canyon too wide to leap across. Finally, he moved, not toward me but to the old leather chair by the window, the one where we used to sit and laugh after long days of working the streets. The creak of the chair sounded like a distant sigh, and he sunk into it with a heaviness that seemed almost too much for the worn-out leather to bear. He ran a hand through his hair, tousling it further, and for a second, I could almost see the man I used to know—the one who used to smile like the world owed him something, who had a way of turning every moment into something worth living.

But the man in front of me now was a stranger. His shoulders hunched, his eyes darkened, haunted by things he never spoke of. And it wasn't just the city that had turned him this way—it was me. It was us.

"I never wanted to drag you into this," he muttered, voice rough as if the words were strangling him. "You think I enjoy being this person? You think I like doing all these terrible things?"

I didn't answer right away. Instead, I let his question hang in the air, more out of curiosity than any real desire for an answer. Because, frankly, I had no idea what he liked anymore. What kind of man chooses to live in the shadows, in the lies, and the manipulation? What kind of man betrays everyone he's ever loved to chase after something that isn't even his to begin with?

"I don't know who you are anymore, Vance," I said quietly, finally letting the words out. There was no fire behind them, no anger, just a raw, exhausted honesty. I was too tired to scream, too tired to make him see anything. "And I'm not sure I ever did."

He flinched like I'd slapped him, and my heart twisted at the sight. It wasn't pity; it was something far more dangerous. A small part of me—one I was trying very hard to keep locked away—wanted to forgive him, to pretend like none of this had happened. But I couldn't. Not when the truth felt so much darker than anything I had imagined.

"I thought I was protecting you," he said, his voice cracking on the last word. "But now... I see that I've just made it worse. You're in more danger than I could ever have imagined."

"From who, Vance?" I asked, stepping closer, the urgency in my voice growing with every passing second. "Who's after me? What have you gotten us into?"

He looked at me then, his eyes flashing with something that was half fear, half resolve. "It's him. You're not safe, Kate. He's here, and he's—"

A sudden noise cut him off, a sharp rattle at the window that made me freeze. My heart hammered in my chest, and I felt a cold shiver crawl up my spine. My instincts kicked in, and before I could even process what was happening, I was already moving toward the door, my hand grabbing for the old baseball bat I kept leaning against the wall.

Vance didn't move.

"Don't," he warned, his voice low, like a threat wrapped in a plea. "You don't know what you're dealing with. Don't make things worse."

"I've already made things worse, haven't I?" I snapped back, my voice shaking with frustration. "You've dragged me into a mess that's too big for either of us to handle, and now I'm supposed to just sit back and wait for you to fix it?"

The rattle came again, more insistent this time, and I paused. There was something unnatural about the sound, something wrong. I wasn't a fool—I knew the difference between a tree branch tapping against glass and the unsettling, deliberate sound of someone trying to get in.

I turned to face him, my grip tightening on the bat. "Do you know who it is? Are you going to tell me the truth, or are you going to keep dancing around it?"

He swallowed hard. "It's him," he repeated, his eyes narrowing with a mixture of dread and disbelief. "The one who's been pulling the strings all along."

I took a breath, trying to steady myself, my mind racing. The dark figure I had heard whispers of, the one who seemed to be behind every shadow, every dangerous decision. "Who?"

Vance didn't answer immediately. He looked away, his jaw clenched, before he stood up suddenly, moving past me with a fluidity that made me take a step back. "I've got to go. Now."

"Wait—what do you mean you've got to go?" I asked, my voice rising in panic. "Vance, don't you dare walk away from me again. Not now. Not like this."

But he was already halfway out the door, his footsteps echoing in the hallway as he disappeared into the night. And I was left standing in the silence, the door barely ajar, the city outside still murmuring its secrets to the rain.

I was alone. Again.

I glanced at the bat in my hands, the weight of it grounding me, and I realized something in that moment. I was no longer just a bystander in this twisted game. Whatever Vance had done—whatever he was caught up in—I was now part of it. No more running. No more pretending I could outrun the darkness.

And when the door slammed shut behind me, a sharp, unmistakable sound of finality, I made my choice. I was done waiting.

It was time to take control.

I hadn't even realized I was holding my breath until I exhaled in a sharp rush, the air leaving my lungs like a balloon deflating in slow motion. There I was, standing alone in the hallway of my apartment, the sound of Vance's hurried footsteps still echoing in my ears, and the weight of everything that had just happened threatening to collapse inward on me. He was gone. He'd left me standing there with nothing but the dark, empty space he'd created in his absence.

I glanced back toward the apartment, where the faint glow of the city lights filtered through the cracks of the blinds, casting eerie shadows across the room. Nothing felt right anymore—no part of it. I was no longer sure what was real, or who I could trust.

I couldn't stay here. Not with the air thick with unanswered questions. And so, like a puppet yanked out of its tangled strings, I grabbed my jacket from the chair and shoved my feet into boots without bothering to tie the laces. The rain was still coming down in sheets, so heavy it felt like the city itself might drown under the weight of it. But the cold air against my skin felt like a wake-up call, a sharp slap of clarity in the midst of the madness.

I needed answers.

And Vance was going to give them to me—whether he wanted to or not.

I was almost out the door when the sound of a distant thud stopped me in my tracks. It was faint at first, like a far-off crash of something heavy against the ground, but the more I stood there, the more it seemed to close in on me, a drumbeat that was beginning to reverberate through the very bones of the building. My pulse quickened. Every instinct in my body told me that whatever had just happened wasn't a coincidence. My heart pounded in my chest, loud and unrelenting, and for the first time since I'd left that room with Vance, I realized that I wasn't just part of some dark game. I was the target now.

I turned back toward the apartment, every nerve on high alert, my hand reaching for the bat again, like it could somehow shield me from whatever was coming. I barely had time to step inside before the window shattered in a sudden explosion of glass. The shards sprayed in all directions, slicing through the air like the jagged pieces of my crumbling world. My first instinct was to duck, to protect myself from the flying shards, but I couldn't. I couldn't take my eyes off the figure now standing in the doorway, a shadow more terrifying than any storm.

It was him—the man I hadn't wanted to believe was real.

He was tall, too tall for comfort, with a presence that filled the room without a single word. His face was obscured in the low light, but I could make out the sharp cut of his jaw, the cold, calculating glint in his eyes that looked like they had seen too much. His lips barely moved when he spoke, but I felt the words slip through my body, each one landing like a nail in a coffin.

"Kate."

I wanted to move. I wanted to run, but the weight of his voice kept me rooted to the spot, a wave of icy fear washing over me. My mind raced, but my body refused to listen. All I could do was stare at him, the stranger who felt like a ghost and a predator wrapped in one.

"Don't look so surprised," he continued, stepping further into the room, his footsteps deliberately slow, as if to savor the moment. "You knew I'd find you. Everyone always finds you in the end, Kate."

"I don't know what you're talking about," I managed to rasp, my throat tight, my voice a fraction of the strength I had hoped it would be. I wasn't lying. I didn't know who he was, but I did know one thing: I wasn't going to let him have the satisfaction of seeing me tremble.

He chuckled, a low, dark sound that sent a fresh wave of unease through me. "Oh, I think you do. Vance told you everything, didn't he?"

My heart skipped a beat. My breath caught in my throat. Vance's name was like a punch to the stomach, and before I could stop myself, I took a step backward, my body already reacting to the sound of his voice. It was a mistake. I knew that now.

The man's eyes gleamed, a dangerous mix of amusement and something far colder. "Don't worry, sweetheart. He's still alive. For now."

The words felt like they were meant to break me, and in that moment, I almost let them. Almost.

Almost.

But something snapped inside me. That old, familiar defiance that had always bubbled beneath the surface surged to the forefront. I wasn't going to let him intimidate me. I wasn't going to let him break me. Not when I still had a choice.

"You think you've won?" I said, my voice steady now, despite the churning in my gut. "You think just because you're standing here in the middle of my apartment, in my city, that you've got control? You're wrong."

The man raised an eyebrow, clearly entertained by my words. "Oh, I'm not trying to control anything, Kate. I already control everything. And you? Well, you're just a piece of the puzzle now. Just like Vance. Just like the rest of them."

I clenched my fists, refusing to let the fear win. "I don't know who you are, but I'm not afraid of you."

A slow smile spread across his face, predatory, chilling. "You will be."

And then, before I could even register what was happening, he lunged, faster than I could react. His hand gripped my arm, yanking me off balance, and in that split second, I saw it—the gleam of something metal in his other hand, a flash of silver that reflected the dim light of the room.

A knife.

I couldn't breathe. The air felt thick, suffocating, and as his grip tightened around my wrist, I realized something worse than fear: I was running out of time.

Chapter 8: The Abyss of Doubt

The rain fell in steady sheets, each droplet a soft, rhythmic echo against the pavement. I stood by the window, my fingertips tracing the condensation on the glass, watching as the city bled into a blur of wet streets and flickering streetlights. The world outside felt distant, like I was viewing it from the wrong side of a dream, too far removed to touch, yet too close to ignore. My mind churned with thoughts of him—Vance, the man who had once made me believe that love could heal even the deepest scars. Now, all I could see was the wreckage of trust, a landscape littered with broken promises and faded glances.

The room behind me smelled faintly of lavender and dust, the remnants of a life that had felt whole only weeks ago. I couldn't shake the sense of betrayal that clung to my skin like a second layer, suffocating in its familiarity. He had kissed me as though he wanted to save me, as though every whisper and touch were threads weaving a future together. And yet, somehow, in the quietest corners of my mind, doubt had started to fester. It wasn't just the secrets he'd kept, or the things he'd left unsaid; it was the way he had looked at me with those eyes, heavy with something—regret? Fear? Or was it just the illusion of affection he had managed to craft with his charm?

I had always prided myself on my ability to read people, to see through the masks they wore. But with him, it was different. He had cracked open something inside me, something that had been carefully sealed for years. And I had let myself believe in the fairy tale, even when the signs of impending disaster had been staring me in the face. But now, I was standing at the edge of a cliff, looking down into the abyss, the wind whipping through my hair as I questioned everything I thought I knew.

The door behind me creaked open, and my heart gave an involuntary lurch. I didn't need to look to know who it was. Vance's presence was like a storm moving through the room, a force that disrupted everything it touched. He was always so damn good at that—disrupting. He filled every space, every silence, with the weight of his own uncertainty. His footsteps were quiet, deliberate, yet they seemed to echo louder than any words could. The tension in the air thickened, wrapping around us like the vines of some dark, unyielding tree. I felt him before I saw him, the way the temperature seemed to shift in his presence, the way my pulse quickened despite myself.

"Are you going to stand there all night, or are you going to let me in?" His voice was rough, as though he had been holding something back for far too long. I could hear the trace of frustration in it, the edge of something raw.

I didn't turn to face him. Not yet. Part of me wanted to savor the distance between us, to keep the space as a shield, a way to avoid confronting the truth I was afraid to acknowledge. The other part of me—a much smaller part—longed to throw myself into his arms, to believe that everything could go back to the way it had been. But that part of me was shrinking, fading, leaving behind only the cold reality of what had been done.

"I don't know what you want from me, Vance," I said, my voice barely more than a whisper. The words felt foreign, as if they belonged to someone else entirely, someone who wasn't still desperately clinging to the remnants of a dream.

"I want you to look at me," he replied softly. "I want you to see that I'm here, and that I'm sorry. You think you're the only one struggling with this?"

At the sound of his voice, I turned. And there he was, standing in the doorway, his face drawn and tired, his eyes shadowed with something I couldn't quite place. I hated myself for the flicker of something soft that stirred inside me. It was so easy to fall back into old patterns, to let his presence soothe the ache that had settled deep in my chest. But the ache wasn't for him, not anymore. It was for the girl who had believed in him, who had given him the benefit of the doubt time and again, only to be left with nothing but pieces of a story she hadn't been told.

"I didn't ask for your apology," I said, the words cutting through the quiet like a knife. "I didn't ask for any of this. You came into my life with all your promises, all your damn perfect words, and now I'm left trying to figure out who you really are."

He stepped closer, and I felt the heat of his body, the undeniable pull that had once made me forget myself. "You think I don't regret it?" His voice was rougher now, desperate. "You think I don't regret every moment I kept my distance? Every second I let this go too far? I wanted you. I still do."

I swallowed, trying to quell the storm that had started to rise in my chest. "You want me, but you don't trust me. That's the problem. And I don't know if I can fix that."

His face twisted, a grimace of frustration and something else—pain, maybe. I wasn't sure. "I didn't ask you to fix it. But I'm asking you to stop running. You don't have to carry this alone."

And there it was, the trap I had been walking around for days, never quite daring to fall into. The moment I had feared. The truth that had been waiting, hiding in the wings, ready to unravel everything I thought I understood.

"I don't know if I can be what you want me to be," I said, the words slipping out before I could stop them. "And I don't know if I can be what I want to be with you."

For a long time, neither of us said anything. The silence between us was thick, suffocating. It was a silence that spoke louder than anything we could have said, a silence that echoed with the weight of choices made and the paths we hadn't yet walked. I wasn't sure if it was the rain or the moment, but something inside me cracked, just a little.

The rain continued to fall in a steady, unrelenting cadence, a constant reminder of how little control I had over anything anymore. It beat against the windows like an old, forgotten song, a rhythm that should have been comforting but instead only deepened the feeling that something was unraveling. The dim glow of the streetlights barely cut through the curtain of water, casting long shadows that crept across the room. The clock on the mantel ticked away in the background, each second dragging me closer to the realization I wasn't sure I was ready for.

I couldn't look at Vance anymore. Not the way I used to. Not with that same unguarded longing, that same soft hope that had once made me feel like I could trust him with every piece of myself. Now, all I could see was the distance in his eyes, the way he kept reaching for something in the air between us, only to come up empty. He'd been right about one thing—he hadn't asked me to fix anything, but what he didn't realize was that I didn't have the strength to fix it anymore. Maybe I never did.

The silence stretched between us like a physical thing, heavy and unyielding. He shifted on his feet, just a fraction, but it was enough to tell me he wasn't ready to walk away. Not yet. That was the thing with Vance—he never left until you pushed him. And I wasn't sure I had the heart to do that.

"I don't know what you want me to say," I finally muttered, my voice trembling despite my best efforts to sound composed. "We can't keep pretending everything's fine when it's not."

"I'm not pretending anything," he said, the edge in his voice like the distant rumble of thunder. "I'm just trying to get you to see that I'm still here. And I'm sorry. God, I'm so sorry for everything I've done to you."

I wanted to believe him. I wanted to fold myself into him like I had done so many times before and pretend that the past was a shadow we could leave behind us. But the weight of my own doubt kept me tethered to the present, where the truth refused to let me go.

"Sorry doesn't fix it, Vance," I said quietly, but the words came out sharper than I expected. "Sorry doesn't make up for the lies. Sorry doesn't erase everything we've been through."

His face darkened, a flash of frustration crossing his features. "You think I don't know that? You think I don't feel the weight of what I did every single day?"

I wasn't sure if I believed him. Maybe he felt it, but was it the guilt of a man who had been caught, or was it something deeper? I didn't know anymore. I was so tired of guessing, so tired of wondering if he was telling me the truth or if I was just a character in some story he had written for himself.

"You keep saying that," I said, a bitter laugh escaping my lips before I could stop it. "You keep telling me how sorry you are, but you never actually say what you're sorry for. You're sorry for what you got caught doing, or sorry for what you didn't get to finish?"

His eyes narrowed, his jaw tightening in that familiar way I had once found endearing but now found infuriating. "You think I'm that shallow? You think I only care about myself?"

"I think you only care about keeping yourself in one piece," I shot back, my voice growing stronger despite the tremor in my hands. "You've been lying to everyone—yourself, me, hell, even your own damn reflection—and now you're trying to act like you've had some big epiphany. But you haven't. You just don't want to lose me."

His expression faltered for the briefest of moments, and I saw something that almost made me hesitate. Almost. But the anger I'd been bottling up inside me for weeks spilled out all at once, too fierce to ignore. "I'm not your safety net, Vance. I'm not the person you get to run to when everything else falls apart. I don't want to be some... some backup plan for a man who can't even be honest with himself."

The words hung between us like smoke, choking the air with their rawness. For a long moment, neither of us moved. I thought I might have finally pushed him away, that I might have finally broken free of this loop of lies and half-truths. But when he spoke again, his voice was quieter, strained, like he was on the verge of something he didn't want to admit.

"I never wanted you to be a backup plan," he said, his words low but unmistakably sincere. "You've always been the plan. The only one."

Something in my chest tightened, but I couldn't bring myself to trust it. Not yet. Not after everything.

"Then why didn't you tell me the truth from the start?" I asked, my voice barely above a whisper. "Why didn't you trust me enough to be honest?"

He let out a slow breath, running a hand through his hair as though he was trying to scrub away the words. "Because I was scared," he admitted, the vulnerability in his tone startling me. "I was scared that if I told you everything, you wouldn't look at me the same way. And the truth is... I wasn't ready to lose you."

The confession landed like a heavy stone, sinking deep into my gut. I wanted to say something, wanted to push him away once and for all. But the words tangled in my throat, and I couldn't speak past the knot of emotions swirling inside me. The truth was, I was just as scared as he was. Scared of losing him. Scared of losing myself in this mess of uncertainty. And most of all, I was scared that no matter how hard I tried, I couldn't fix what was already broken.

I took a step back, not away from him, but into the quiet that stretched between us. "I don't know how to fix this, Vance. I don't even know if I want to try."

His face twisted, a mixture of desperation and something deeper, darker, that I couldn't quite place. "I don't need you to fix it. I just need you to be here. With me. Whatever it takes."

I couldn't answer him. Not right away. The weight of what he had said, the honesty in his eyes, left me raw and vulnerable. And I wasn't sure if I was strong enough to face whatever came next.

The air in the room was thick, suffocating with the unsaid, with the truth that had been skirted around for too long. I felt like a walking contradiction, my heart pounding for him while my mind screamed in protest. I had promised myself I wouldn't go back to the person I was before him—the version of me who trusted without question, who believed in happy endings without the need for proof. Yet here I was, caught between wanting to believe his words and the undeniable evidence of how far he had gone to lie to me.

Vance took a step forward, his face unreadable, the muscles in his jaw working as if holding back everything he wanted to say. I could feel his gaze on me, but I refused to meet it. I wasn't ready to look at him, not with the vulnerability I knew was still there, lurking beneath all the doubt. The silence stretched between us like a chasm, one I didn't know how to bridge, one I wasn't even sure I wanted to cross.

"I didn't come here to beg," he said quietly, his voice more a confession than an accusation. "But I guess that's exactly what I'm doing."

I didn't answer immediately. Part of me wanted to tear into him, to remind him of all the things he had done wrong, to make him feel the weight of everything he had cost me. But I had already screamed until I couldn't anymore, and nothing had changed. We were still standing on the edge of the same cliff, and no matter how hard I tried to ignore it, I couldn't deny that I was still tethered to him, anchored by something stronger than my anger.

"You've already begged," I finally said, my voice thick with the years of unspoken frustration. "And you'll keep begging, won't you? You'll keep coming back, trying to fix something that's already broken. But I don't know if I can do it anymore, Vance. I don't know if I can keep pretending I'm okay."

He seemed to shrink under my words, as though each syllable had stripped away a layer of the façade he'd been holding up for so long. "I never wanted to make you feel like you had to pretend. I never wanted you to carry this alone."

I couldn't help it—something inside me cracked. I shook my head, a laugh escaping my lips, bitter and raw. "You think I haven't been carrying this alone? You think I haven't been questioning every word I've ever said to you, wondering if I was just some fool?"

The walls I had built around myself started to crumble, brick by brick, and I felt an overwhelming sense of loss, of wanting something I wasn't sure I could have anymore. I wanted the man who had held me in his arms and whispered that we were a team. But that man wasn't standing in front of me. The man before me was a stranger, someone I couldn't quite reconcile with the version I had fallen for. And yet, here he was, still offering me pieces of himself, as if I were supposed to pick them up and glue them back together into something whole.

"Maybe I was a fool too," he said, his voice quieter now, more vulnerable than I had ever heard it. "But I was never pretending to be perfect. I just didn't know how to fix what I'd broken."

The words landed like a punch to the gut, and for a moment, I couldn't breathe. It wasn't the apology itself that hit hardest, it was the truth in his voice. The truth that he knew. He knew what he had done, and he was still here, still asking for forgiveness, still hoping I could somehow find a way to love him again. And that was the worst part. That even after everything, there was a part of me that wanted to forgive him. There was a part of me that wanted to let him back in.

But I couldn't. I wouldn't.

I took a deep breath, gathering the strength to speak through the lump in my throat. "You don't get to make me feel like I'm the one who's at fault here. You made your choices, Vance. You can't just erase them with a few words."

He flinched, but he didn't look away. "I don't expect you to forgive me. But I am asking you to believe that I'm trying. Believe that I'm still trying to be the man you saw in me."

There it was, the heart of the matter. It wasn't about apologies or mistakes—it was about the shattered image of the man I had once believed in. I had built him up in my mind, had woven our future with threads of hope and passion. And now, standing in front of me, he was nothing more than a ghost of the person I had loved.

"I don't know who you are anymore," I said, the words tasting bitter as they left my mouth. "And maybe that's the hardest part. I don't even recognize the man who stands here asking me to believe in him."

His eyes hardened, the vulnerability flickering out like a candle in the wind. "I've never stopped being the man you loved," he said, his voice low and controlled, as though he were holding something back. "I've just been waiting for you to see it. To see me."

I took a step back, my heart pounding. The room felt smaller, as if it were closing in on me, the weight of his words pushing me toward a decision I wasn't sure I could make. My thoughts were scattered, my emotions all tangled up in a knot I couldn't unravel. But then, just as I was about to speak, to tell him that I couldn't go back, there was a knock at the door. It was sharp, insistent, and it cut through the tension like a knife.

Vance's gaze flickered toward the door, his jaw tightening, but he didn't move. Neither of us did. We both stood there, waiting, as if whatever was on the other side might hold the answer we had both been searching for. But neither of us knew what would happen when that door opened. Neither of us could have predicted who would be standing there.

Chapter 9: The Reckoning

The air was thick with the scent of rain, heavy clouds hanging low above the city like an unfinished promise. The streets were a labyrinth of wet cobblestones, slick with the remnants of a storm that had passed through hours earlier, leaving nothing behind but a damp chill that clung to my skin. I could feel the weight of the night in the marrow of my bones, the silence of the city pressing in around me, suffocating in its intensity. It was the kind of quiet that preceded something monumental—something irreversible—and I stood on the edge of it, my heart racing.

Vance stood beside me, his gaze fixed on the dark horizon, where the skyline of Crescent City pierced the sky like jagged teeth. His broad shoulders seemed even more imposing in the fading light, casting long shadows on the ground. I had never seen him so still, so consumed by whatever was happening inside his mind. His hands were clenched at his sides, the muscles in his jaw twitching slightly, as if he were trying to fight against the truth that had just been laid bare between us.

We hadn't spoken since the moment the revelation hit, the truth about my role in everything that had led us here, to this moment. A part of me still couldn't believe it, but the other part—the part that was finally awake after years of being dormant—understood. It was like a sudden, fierce spark that had ignited something inside me, a fire I couldn't extinguish even if I tried. And I wasn't sure if I even wanted to.

I glanced at him, but he didn't meet my eyes. His silence was suffocating, so I decided to break it, even though I knew it would be anything but easy.

"You don't have to do this," I said, my voice unsteady, betraying the calm I was trying to project. "You don't have to fight this battle. I can take care of it. I always have. This city, this life, it's mine to bear."

He turned to me then, the intensity in his gaze pinning me in place. There was something unspoken in the way he looked at me—something that stirred a storm of emotions I hadn't been ready to face. He was always so guarded, so meticulous in hiding the depths of his feelings. But in that moment, the walls he had built around himself cracked, just enough to let me see the truth of what lay beneath.

"I've seen you fight before," he said, his voice rough but steady, like he was drawing strength from the very thing he hated most. "And I've seen what it does to you. You don't have to keep carrying it alone, you know."

The words hit me harder than any blow could. There was a vulnerability in his voice that made my stomach twist, but it wasn't the kind of weakness that would make me pull away. No, it was the kind of vulnerability that anchored me to him in a way that felt like a promise—one I wasn't sure I was ready to accept.

"I'm not alone," I whispered, barely believing it myself.

"You are," he replied, his voice soft, but there was no mistaking the conviction behind the words. "At least, you have been. But you don't have to be anymore."

I swallowed hard, the lump in my throat making it difficult to speak. For so long, I had been the one who kept everyone at arm's length, who shut out anyone who might have cared, convinced that I was better off alone. But now, standing there with him, the weight of his words settled over me, as if they were a tether, pulling me toward something I couldn't quite name.

The wind picked up, sending a chill through my body, but it wasn't the cold that made me shiver. It was the look in his eyes—something that lingered there, something raw and real that neither of us had ever dared to confront. And as the storm clouds loomed darker above us, I knew that the battle wasn't just outside anymore. It was within me.

"I can't promise you anything," I said, forcing the words past my lips, even as they trembled. "Not yet. But I will fight with you. Not because of some shared destiny, not because of some grand plan, but because I want to. I don't know what's waiting for us on the other side, but I'm not running anymore. Not from you, not from this."

The air between us crackled with an electric tension, the kind that came when two people dared to speak the truth of what they had been avoiding. His hand reached for mine then, tentative at first, as though he wasn't sure if I'd pull away. But I didn't. I let him take it, letting the warmth of his touch seep through the barriers I had so carefully constructed around myself.

"Then let's not waste time," he said, his voice resolute, a steel edge creeping into it that hadn't been there before. "Whatever happens, we face it together."

And in that moment, as we stood there on the edge of the city, the rain beginning to fall again in soft, steady sheets, I knew that there was no turning back. We were bound by something deeper than the fate of Crescent City, something that went beyond the chaos and darkness closing in around us. It was something raw and untamed, something that felt more like a beginning than an end.

I squeezed his hand, my grip tightening as if to reassure him, or maybe myself, that this was the only way forward. The storm outside was nothing compared to the storm brewing inside me, but for the first time in my life, I wasn't afraid of what was coming. Together, we would face whatever waited in the shadows, and whatever it was, we would face it head-on.

The city waited, its dark streets whispering the same words over and over again: Reckoning.

The city's pulse was unmistakable now—alive, quivering with something more dangerous than the usual undercurrent of fear. The kind of energy that shivered through every cracked street and crooked alley, settling in the very bones of Crescent City. There was a nervousness to the air, like the whole place knew something was coming, but nobody wanted to name it. It was a breath held too long, an inevitable thing, and all I could do was watch it unfold. With Vance's hand still in mine, I knew that I was no longer just a passive witness to this twisted game of fate. I was in it now. Fully, irrevocably. And there was no turning back.

His presence beside me was both a comfort and a reminder of everything that had gone wrong and right. We were tangled in a history neither of us fully understood, bound by secrets and regrets too heavy to carry alone. And yet, here we were, standing on the precipice of something far worse than either of us had anticipated. The truth, as it had a tendency to do, had a habit of exposing things at the most inconvenient times.

I felt the weight of Vance's gaze before I even turned to look at him, his face a mask of unreadable emotion. The tension between us, like static, crackled in the space where words failed to fill. My heart beat out a steady rhythm, thudding in my chest as though it had a life of its own, pushing me forward even when my legs wanted nothing more than to fold beneath me.

"You know, I could still leave," I said, the words coming out too quickly, too easily, but I couldn't stop them. "I've done it before. The whole 'disappear without a trace' thing. It's not as hard as people think."

Vance turned to me, his jaw tight but his expression softening just enough to betray something beneath the steel. "And where would you go?" he asked, his voice laced with a quiet amusement that didn't quite mask the gravity of the situation. "You're not the type to run."

I smirked, the corners of my mouth twitching upward. "No. I'm not." But for a moment, I allowed myself to wonder just how much longer I could keep up this facade of being invincible. How long could I pretend that I wasn't already a step away from being swallowed whole by this city, by the secrets I kept buried inside it?

We didn't speak again as we moved deeper into the shadows of the city. The faint glow of distant streetlights barely illuminated the path, the darkness wrapping around us like a blanket of cold, the only sounds the soft scrape of our footsteps on wet stone. It was a quiet kind of chaos—the kind that threatened to consume everything in its path. A world teetering on the edge of something explosive.

Vance's hand brushed against my own once more, a quiet reassurance I wasn't sure I deserved. His touch grounded me in the here and now, reminding me that there was something to hold on to, something worth fighting for in the middle of all this madness. It was a fleeting comfort, though, because I knew better than to trust in the easy promises of fleeting moments. In a city like this, even the most fleeting comforts came at a price.

"There's no going back," he said softly, as though reading the thoughts that had been twisting in my mind. "I hope you know that."

"I do," I answered, though the words felt like a confession. "But it's not about going back. It's about moving forward. I've never been good at standing still."

Vance's laugh, deep and rough, surprised me. He hadn't laughed in days, and I hadn't realized how much I'd missed the sound of it until now. "You've got a hell of a way of doing that," he said, shaking his head. "Always charging forward, never looking back. What happens when you run out of road, huh?"

I shrugged, though my heart raced as the distance between us and the danger ahead grew shorter. "I guess I'll have to find a new road."

He stopped walking, pulling me to a halt with him. The movement was so sudden that it threw me off balance for a moment, and I looked up at him, startled. But he wasn't looking at me. His gaze was locked on the street ahead, his expression sharpening as if he were seeing something I wasn't. His lips parted, and I could see the tension in his body, the way he was holding back whatever he'd been ready to say. I didn't need him to say it out loud; I could feel it in my bones—the approach of something inevitable, something we'd both been avoiding.

"Vance," I said, my voice barely above a whisper, the weight of the moment pressing down on me. "What if we're not enough? What if we can't stop it?"

He turned back to me, his eyes dark with a mix of determination and something far more vulnerable. "We will be. You and me. We've got more than enough to take this down. We just have to stop thinking we're alone in it."

I met his gaze, holding it long enough for the gravity of his words to sink in. And for the first time in a long while, I felt the pieces falling into place, all those moments we had brushed past each other, all the things left unsaid, starting to form a whole. A promise, perhaps, or something even greater.

"There's no turning back," I repeated, my voice steadier now, stronger. "But that doesn't mean I have to do it alone."

Vance nodded, his expression unreadable but his grip on my hand tightening just a little more. I didn't need him to say anything more. We were in this together, and for better or worse, there was no more room for fear.

The streets ahead were dark, the shadows stretching long and ominous, but they no longer seemed as threatening. Not when I had Vance at my side. We would face whatever came next. Together. And maybe, just maybe, we'd win.

We moved deeper into the heart of Crescent City, and it wasn't long before the quiet gave way to something more sinister. The streets grew narrower, the air thicker, as if the city itself was closing in around us. My senses were heightened—every creak of the cobblestones beneath our feet, every distant flicker of light in an alley, every gust of wind that carried with it the faintest hint of something burning. It wasn't just the storm overhead now—it was something far darker. Something that had been lurking at the edge of my awareness, creeping closer with every step we took.

I didn't have to look at Vance to know he felt it too. The tension between us wasn't just a product of our shared history or the dangerous path we'd chosen—it was the tangible weight of everything that was about to collide. The final confrontation loomed ahead, just beyond the next corner, and with it, the kind of reckoning neither of us had truly been prepared for.

"Are we sure about this?" I asked, my voice barely louder than the hum of the city, unsure if I was questioning him or myself.

Vance's stride didn't falter. He was the picture of calm, his face shadowed in the dim light, but I knew better than to mistake his silence for certainty. Vance had never been one to express doubt aloud, but I could feel it in the way he held his shoulders tight, in the way his hands clenched at his sides when they weren't wrapped around mine. He was just as much a prisoner to this twisted fate as I was, despite all the walls he'd built up to protect himself from it.

"We don't have a choice," he replied, his voice steady but edged with something I couldn't quite place—anger, frustration, or maybe fear. Fear was the one thing he didn't allow himself to show, but there was always a flicker in his eyes when he was on the edge of something. Something big. "We're already in it. It's too late for hesitation."

I nodded, even though every part of me wanted to turn and run the other way. But I didn't. Instead, I walked with him, our steps in sync as we approached the old district—an area of the city that hadn't seen sunlight in decades. The buildings here were like tired, forgotten monuments to a past that the city preferred to bury, their once-grand facades now crumbling into shadow. The air smelled of old wood and damp stone, with an undertone of something metallic, like blood that had been left to dry for too long.

The entrance to the old temple was nothing more than a gaping hole in the side of one of the buildings, the remnants of an archway crumbling into nothing. The place felt alive, as if it had been waiting for us, watching, biding its time. I hesitated on the threshold, the hairs on the back of my neck standing on end.

"This is it," I whispered, my voice a little unsteady.

Vance didn't say anything, but his hand found mine again, this time his fingers slipping between mine, the warmth of his touch grounding me in ways I hadn't realized I needed. In a world where nothing felt certain, where every decision had led us here, his hand was the one thing I knew I could trust.

The inside of the temple was a maze of shadows, the flickering of torchlight revealing faded murals on the walls—scenes of battles long past, gods and monsters locked in eternal struggle. But it wasn't the images that caught my attention. It was the deep, echoing silence that surrounded us, thick and oppressive. It was the kind of silence that made you think you weren't alone, even when you knew no one else was there.

"Do you hear that?" I asked, my voice low, instinctively glancing around as though I might catch a glimpse of whatever was watching us.

Vance's grip tightened on my hand, his eyes scanning the room with a sharpness that belied his usual cool composure. "I don't hear anything," he said, his voice taut. But I knew he felt it, too—whatever had made the air feel as if it were vibrating with something too ancient to comprehend.

We stepped further into the temple, and that's when I saw it—the altar at the far end of the room, bathed in a strange, unnatural light. It was a simple thing, made of stone, but there was something about it that felt... wrong. Like it was meant to be the center of something far darker than I had ever imagined.

A soft scraping sound echoed behind us, making my blood run cold. I whirled around, but there was nothing there—just the same walls, the same shadows. Vance stiffened beside me, and I could see the tension in his jaw as he fought to remain unfazed. But it wasn't fear I saw in his eyes—it was something else. Something deeper.

"I think we've overstayed our welcome," he muttered under his breath, more to himself than to me.

Before I could respond, a voice—a low, guttural whisper—breathed from the darkness. It was the kind of voice that didn't belong in this world. "You're too late."

The words came from nowhere, but they felt like they were coming from everywhere at once. My heart stuttered in my chest, and I turned, but again, there was nothing.

I could feel the air pressing in on me, a weight so heavy it was suffocating. And then I saw it—a figure, cloaked in shadows, standing near the altar. For a moment, I thought my mind was playing tricks on me, but then I saw the faint gleam of metal, the glint of something sharp, and the sudden, piercing realization hit me like a tidal wave.

"You've been here all along," I whispered, the truth seeping into my veins, spreading through me like fire.

The figure stepped forward, revealing itself in the dim light, and for the first time in years, I understood what it meant to truly fear the unknown.

And then, with a voice like the crack of a whip, it spoke again.

"You didn't think you'd get out of this alive, did you?"

Chapter 10: Shadows of the Past

The rain had been falling for hours, a steady, relentless tapping against the windows. I could hear it over the hum of the refrigerator, the creaking of the wooden beams in the walls, and the soft thud of my own heartbeat. It was a sound I used to find soothing—a kind of lullaby that helped me forget. But tonight, it only served to remind me of everything I was trying to outrun.

The diner was empty, save for the faint glow of the neon sign outside casting pale shadows across the floor. I pulled the last of the coffee into my mug, watching the dark liquid swirl in a quiet spiral. It was as if the world had gone on pause while I stood still, trapped in the space between what had happened and what I couldn't bring myself to face.

Vance. The name was a bitter pill, but it was nothing compared to the taste of betrayal that had lingered in my mouth ever since. He had always been my anchor, the steady hand pulling me from the wreckage of my own decisions, the voice in my ear that kept me from falling into the abyss. But that night... that night, everything I thought I knew about him shattered like glass, and I was left standing in the debris.

His betrayal had left more than a mark on me; it had splintered something deep inside. And the worst part? I had seen it coming. I just hadn't wanted to believe it. The signs were there, clear as day—Vance's secrets, the lies that dripped from his smile like poison. I'd ignored them. I'd told myself I was imagining things, that my paranoia had taken over, but the truth had unfolded before my eyes, each moment worse than the last.

My fingers curled around the handle of the mug, knuckles white. How could I have been so blind? How could I have been so stupid to trust him? There was a bitterness that rose in me, something darker than I could have expected, and it made me sick to my stomach. I was ashamed of how easily he had taken me in, of how I had let myself believe in him, despite all the warning signs.

The diner door swung open with a screech, the bell above it jangling in protest. I didn't need to turn around to know who it was. I could feel him before I saw him, the air shifting in his wake, like a storm rolling in.

"Still hiding in here, huh?" Vance's voice was low, teasing, but it didn't carry the usual warmth I had once associated with it. It was flat, almost detached, like he wasn't really there, just a shadow of himself. I didn't look at him. I couldn't. Not yet.

He stepped closer, the sound of his boots against the worn linoleum floor steady and familiar, like a rhythm I used to love. I had always found comfort in the way he moved—confident, strong, purposeful. But now, all I felt was the weight of the silence between us.

"You're really going to pretend like you don't have anything to say to me?" he asked, a soft edge of frustration creeping into his tone. His voice was like velvet, smooth and easy, a weapon in disguise.

I finally met his gaze, my eyes burning with a fury that I didn't know I had the capacity for. "What do you want, Vance?"

He stood there for a moment, silent, studying me. His jaw tightened as if he were fighting to say something, but the words never came. He knew what he had done. And that, more than anything, infuriated me. The fact that he had the audacity to look at me like he was the wronged one, like he had no idea why I was this angry, it was beyond infuriating.

"I need you to listen," he said, his voice finally breaking through the tension. There was a crack in it now, something raw, something human. But I wasn't ready for it. Not yet. Not after everything.

"I listened to you once, Vance. You don't get to ask for that again. Not after everything," I shot back, the words cutting through the air like shards of glass.

His face softened, just a fraction, but it was enough to make my heart skip. I couldn't deal with the softness. Not from him. Not after what he'd done.

"Please," he whispered, his voice low enough that it almost seemed to tremble. He closed the space between us, but I stood rooted to the spot, unwilling to let him erase the distance with the same ease he had erased my trust. "I didn't mean for you to find out like this. I didn't mean for you to get hurt."

I wanted to scream, to tear the words from him until they no longer made sense, until they were nothing but a jumble of meaningless sounds. But instead, I swallowed, hard.

"Is that supposed to make it better? Because it doesn't. I'm not some naive girl, Vance. I'm not stupid enough to fall for your lies anymore."

He flinched, the movement so subtle that if I hadn't been watching him so closely, I would have missed it. His eyes darted away for a moment, as if the weight of what I had said was too much to bear. When he spoke again, his voice was barely a whisper, but it felt like it carried the weight of the world.

"I never meant to lie to you. I just—" He paused, searching for the right words, and for a moment, I saw the man I used to know, the man who could make me feel safe. But that man was gone, replaced by a stranger who had betrayed me in ways I still couldn't fully understand.

"You just what?" I asked, my voice tight, my hands clenched around the mug until my fingers ached.

But he didn't answer me. Instead, he just stood there, as if he were waiting for me to somehow make it all okay again. But I knew better. It wasn't something I could fix. Not anymore. Not after everything.

The air in the diner felt thicker than it had moments ago, charged with a quiet kind of tension that hummed under my skin.

Vance hadn't moved. He was still standing there, his presence filling the space like an unwelcome guest who refused to leave. I could feel the weight of his eyes on me, but I refused to look up. Not yet.

Instead, I focused on the mug in my hands, the heat of the ceramic against my fingers, the bitter taste of the coffee now cold on my tongue. I could almost hear the seconds ticking away, one after another, stretching the silence between us into something unbearable. My heart pounded as I fought to keep it together, to not let the flood of emotions—anger, hurt, confusion—consume me.

Vance shifted, just slightly, and I finally looked at him, if only for a moment. His expression was unreadable, the same steady, calm mask he'd always worn. The mask I had trusted. And the one that, now, I knew I could never trust again.

"I came to apologize," he said quietly, each word drawn out like it took effort. His voice was still smooth, still familiar in a way that made it impossible to ignore. But there was a rawness beneath it, a fragility I hadn't expected. "I didn't handle things well. I know that. I should've told you the truth, from the start."

I laughed, though there was no humor in it, just a brittle edge. "You think this is about the truth? You think telling me the truth would've made this okay?" My voice broke on the last word, and I hated it. Hated that I could still care about him after everything.

Vance's gaze softened, just a fraction. It was the kind of look that used to make me melt, but now it only made me angry. The pity. The understanding. The apology that came too late. I wanted to tell him that I didn't need his pity, but the words felt stuck in my throat. How could I explain that I was beyond his apologies, beyond the moment when things could be fixed with just a few kind words?

"I never meant to hurt you," he continued, his voice dropping lower as he took a tentative step toward me. I stiffened, but he didn't seem to notice. "I never meant for any of this to happen."

"Then why did it?" I asked, my voice suddenly tight with something sharper than just anger. It was desperation, the kind that clawed at my insides, the need for something—anything—to make sense of the mess he had created. "Why did you let it happen?"

His brow furrowed, as though the question took him by surprise. He opened his mouth, then closed it again, as if he couldn't quite find the words. I watched him, my chest tightening with a mix of bitterness and sorrow.

"Sometimes... sometimes we think we're doing the right thing," he began, his eyes dark with something I couldn't place. "We think we're protecting the people we care about, but we end up hurting them worse than we could've imagined."

There was a long pause, during which all I could do was stare at him, hoping that somehow he would explain it all. Make it right. But he didn't. Not with words. Not with anything.

"I can't fix this, can I?" Vance asked, his voice barely audible now, a thread of vulnerability creeping through the cracks.

"No," I whispered, the word a stone that sank into my chest. The finality of it hung between us like a cloud, thick and suffocating. "You can't."

He nodded, as if he already knew the answer, and yet he was still standing there, still waiting for something from me. As though there were some magical moment when everything would click back into place, when the puzzle pieces of our broken relationship would snap together and make sense again.

But there was no such moment. No magic fix. There was only the weight of the past between us, a rift too wide to close with apologies or promises.

Vance opened his mouth, but I held up a hand, the gesture stopping him before he could speak. "Don't. I don't need to hear it anymore."

He froze, and for a second, I thought he might argue. But then his shoulders slumped, and his eyes dropped to the floor. The fight left him as quickly as it had come, replaced by a weariness I hadn't seen before. I almost didn't recognize him—this man who had always been so strong, so confident. Now, he was like a shell of the person I had once known, worn down by guilt and regret.

"I don't want your guilt, Vance," I said, my voice stronger now, more certain. "I don't want your regret. I want... I want to stop feeling like I'm drowning every time I think about you."

He didn't reply, but there was a flicker in his eyes, something that said he understood all too well. We were both drowning, in different ways.

"I should go," he said finally, the words hollow, like he was just trying to make sense of what had happened, too.

I nodded, not trusting myself to say anything else. There was nothing left to say, anyway. He had done enough talking. Now it was time for him to leave.

As he turned and walked toward the door, I could feel the air shift, a sense of finality settling in the space between us. The door creaked open, the bell chiming with a softness that felt like a goodbye. Vance paused just before stepping outside, his back still to me, and then, without turning around, he spoke one last time.

"Take care of yourself," he said quietly. And then he was gone.

The door swung shut behind him, and for a long moment, I just stood there, staring at the spot where he had been. A part of me wanted to run after him, to shout at him, to demand answers, to somehow make him feel the hurt I was carrying. But the other part—the part that was still grieving the loss of the person I had thought he was—told me to let it go. To move on.

But how? How did you move on from someone who had once been everything to you, and now... nothing?

The hours slipped by in a haze, the weight of Vance's absence settling over me like a heavy fog. I couldn't escape it, couldn't shake the feeling that something was slipping through my fingers, like sand. Even as the clock ticked on, I found myself drifting in and out of memories—some warm, some sharp, like thorns buried deep under my skin.

Crescent City had always been a place that had a way of getting under my skin. The salty air, the mist rising off the bay in the early mornings, the way the streets seemed to hum with the secrets of its people. It was the kind of town where everyone knew everything, and yet no one knew a thing. The perfect breeding ground for the kind of mess Vance and I had gotten ourselves tangled in. But now, even the familiar sights—the busy cafés with their clattering cups, the worn sidewalks lined with weathered houses—felt foreign.

I found myself wandering aimlessly through the streets, a ghost of myself, unsure of what I was looking for. Maybe I was searching for answers, for some piece of clarity I could hold on to. Maybe I was looking for something to give me a reason to move forward. But every corner I turned, every shop I passed, only seemed to make the world feel smaller, more confining, like the walls were closing in.

I passed by the bakery, the scent of warm bread wafting through the air, and it reminded me of mornings spent with Vance. The two of us huddled in the corner booth, sipping coffee, laughing over the trivialities of our lives. I could almost see us there, the sunlight pouring in through the windows, the sound of the bell above the door jingling as new customers walked in. I had never thought those moments would end, never thought they would become something I would look back on and wish I could forget.

But time had a way of changing things.

"Hey."

I froze, the sound of the voice like a sudden crack in the air, pulling me out of the fog. It wasn't his voice. It couldn't be. But still, the hairs on the back of my neck stood at attention as I turned around slowly.

The man standing before me was unfamiliar, but there was something about him that made me feel... uneasy. He was tall, with dark hair that fell just above his collar, and eyes that held an unsettling intensity. There was a sharpness to his features, a lean, almost predatory look that made my pulse quicken.

"I'm sorry to intrude," he said, his voice smooth but carrying an edge I couldn't quite place. "But I think you might be the person I'm looking for."

I didn't respond immediately, just studied him. My instincts told me to walk away, to turn and leave, but something—something in the way he looked at me—kept me rooted to the spot. There was a weight in his gaze, like he was measuring me, deciding if I was worth the effort.

"I'm sorry, do I know you?" I asked, my voice more clipped than I intended. The unease in my chest had blossomed into something deeper now, like a knot tightening around my ribs.

He smiled, but there was no warmth in it, just a coolness that sent a shiver down my spine. "I think you do. At least, I know you know someone who knows me."

I frowned, trying to place him, but I came up empty. The connection was lost, just out of reach. And yet, I felt like I had seen him before—somewhere, sometime. My mind raced, searching for any link, any scrap of memory that would explain why his presence made the hairs on my arms stand on end.

"I'm afraid I don't understand," I said, my voice growing tighter with each passing second. "Who are you?"

He took a step closer, and for a brief moment, I thought about running. But something in his eyes stopped me—something that made me freeze, as if my feet were cemented to the ground. His gaze was sharp, calculating, and it unnerved me more than I cared to admit.

"My name is Kieran," he said, his tone light but there was an undercurrent of something darker. "And I'm looking for someone."

I swallowed, the pit in my stomach deepening. There was no way I was going to ask him who he was looking for. Because I already knew. The question burned in my throat, but I kept it back. I wasn't ready for the answer.

"What does this have to do with me?" I finally managed to ask, trying to keep the tremble out of my voice.

He didn't answer immediately. Instead, he looked at me, really looked at me, as though he was studying every nuance of my face, every flicker of emotion. It was like he was waiting for something—a crack in my composure, a sign that I was more than I appeared.

"I think you know exactly what this has to do with you," Kieran said, his smile widening ever so slightly. "You see, there are people who would do anything to keep certain things quiet. Secrets, old wounds. People like me, we're good at finding those things. And you, my dear, have been holding onto something for a long time."

I felt the color drain from my face as the words sank in. My heart hammered in my chest. How did he know? How could he possibly know what I had kept buried for so long?

Before I could respond, Kieran's eyes flicked to the side, and the moment of tension between us seemed to snap. "I'm sorry," he said, almost too casually. "I didn't mean to keep you. Just a misunderstanding."

But I knew better. The smile never quite reached his eyes.

And as he turned and walked away, I felt the weight of his presence still hanging in the air, like a storm cloud waiting to burst. I knew, without a doubt, that this was only the beginning. Something had shifted, something dark and dangerous, and it was heading straight for me.

I turned to leave, but as I took a step forward, a shadow moved across my path.

It was Vance.

His face was pale, his eyes wide with a mix of disbelief and... fear. "Get out of here," he said urgently. "Now."

Chapter 11: Entangled Hearts

The floorboards of the safe house creaked beneath my boots, the only sound in the stillness of the dimly lit room. The air was thick with dust, a mix of old wood and metal that clung to my skin, seeping into the cracks of my senses. It wasn't much—a couple of faded sofas, a table scarred by time, and walls that had absorbed too many secrets. But it was ours for now, a place to hide from the world that was closing in around us. A refuge, of sorts, though I knew the safety it offered was fleeting.

Vance stood by the window, his back to me, his profile sharp against the broken light streaming through the thin curtains. The weight of the silence between us hung like a fog. Every so often, I caught a glimpse of his fingers, drumming lightly on the windowsill, and I had the sudden, unsettling sense that he wasn't just thinking. He was waiting. For what, exactly, I couldn't say.

"You look like you're about to burst," I said, my voice almost too casual, as though I didn't care, even though I did. My mouth was dry from too much quiet, too much waiting. "Any particular reason?"

His head turned just enough for me to see the sharpness in his eyes. There was something in them—danger, suspicion, or maybe something more—something I couldn't quite place, but it didn't make me feel safer. His mouth twitched like it was trying to decide whether to offer a smile or a warning, then settled on neither.

"You've been looking at me like that for hours," he muttered, his voice gruff but not unkind. "Waiting for me to make a move. Waiting for something to happen."

I shrugged, but my heart thudded uncomfortably against my ribs. He was right, of course. I had been watching him, every tiny shift in his posture, every movement of his jaw, trying to read something into him that maybe wasn't there. He was a locked door I couldn't get open, a puzzle that refused to be solved. And the more I tried, the more I realized how much I didn't understand.

"Guess I'm just getting antsy," I said, leaning against the cracked wall to give myself something to do, to distract from the tightness of my chest. "Waiting for something to happen." My eyes flickered to the corner of the room where a small, half-empty bag of supplies sat, its contents a reminder of how close we were to running out of options.

"You're not wrong," he said after a long pause, his gaze narrowing as if weighing whether or not to tell me more. He turned from the window, his footsteps measured as he crossed the room and stopped just in front of me. His proximity made my breath catch. There was something magnetic about him, something I couldn't explain—maybe it was the air of danger, the sharpness of his instincts, or the way he carried his past like a shadow that never fully left him.

I didn't know what it was, but whatever it was, it pulled me in, as much as I tried to resist.

"We've got a choice to make," Vance said softly, his voice low enough that it felt like he was speaking to no one else but me. "Either we keep running, keep hiding, or we do something about it. We face this head-on. We take them down."

The weight of his words sank into me, settling like a stone in my stomach. His words were simple, yet I knew they came with a price. Vance wasn't the type to make idle promises. His eyes held a certainty I both feared and envied.

"And what's your plan, exactly?" I asked, not because I didn't believe in him, but because I needed to hear him say it out loud. To know that there was something more than just fighting our way through this mess. I needed to know that there was an endgame, a way out of the chaos that had become our lives.

"Don't worry about the details," he replied, a slight edge creeping into his voice, something like a challenge. "Just trust me."

I opened my mouth to respond, but nothing came out. I wasn't sure if it was because I trusted him or because I didn't want to trust him, but I couldn't deny that his words stirred something deep inside me. Something that I wasn't ready to confront yet. Not while I still couldn't shake the feeling that our past—my past—was a shadow, stretching longer and darker with every step I took toward him.

He must have noticed my hesitation because his eyes softened, just a fraction, before the walls came back up. "Look, I know you're not exactly a fan of me right now," he said, his voice quiet but blunt. "But you don't have to like me to fight with me. You just have to decide if you're ready to face it all, the good and the bad. Because once we take that step, there's no going back."

I wanted to say something, anything, but the words caught in my throat. Because, deep down, I knew he was right. I had been running from my past for so long, hiding behind walls I had built and convinced myself were enough. But I also knew that Vance wasn't the type to let things be left unfinished.

And that was what scared me the most.

The crackling tension between Vance and me had a life of its own. It was subtle, a pulse that thrummed in the silence, the kind of energy that made everything feel too loud even when nothing was being said. The flicker of the low light from the single bulb hanging above us danced across the walls, making everything seem slightly more surreal, as though we were both trapped in some half-dreamed version of reality.

Vance had turned back to the window, his gaze fixed outside, beyond the grime-covered glass, as if the world he sought was just out of reach. His shoulders were tense, his hands steady, though the rest of him appeared coiled like a spring. I could almost hear the thoughts rolling behind his eyes—calculating, strategizing, and yet, something else. Something deeper. It gnawed at me.

"So," I said, breaking the silence, my voice cutting through the stillness like a knife. "We're either running or we're fighting. That's the plan?"

He didn't respond right away. I knew he was trying to gauge whether I was mocking him, or if I was genuinely interested. It wasn't often I took things seriously—not in this world, not anymore—but there was something about the weight of his quiet that made me want to understand him more, even if it meant wading through the mess he carried with him.

He turned slowly, finally meeting my gaze with that look—part challenge, part something softer I couldn't name. "I don't know about you," he said, his voice low but steady, "but I don't have a habit of running from my problems. Especially not when they come knocking at my door."

I narrowed my eyes, trying to read him. "You've never been one for subtlety, have you?"

A slight smirk tugged at his lips, the first sign of any real emotion breaking through the hardened exterior. "Guess not. You'd have figured that out by now."

I leaned back against the table, trying not to let my pulse race too quickly. Being around him made everything feel sharper, more urgent. The quiet was louder when he was near, and I wasn't sure if it was because I wanted him to say more or because I was afraid of what he might say.

"You know," I said, pushing my fingers through my hair in an effort to appear calm, "there's a difference between facing your demons and being stupid. Not sure if you've figured that out yet."

Vance's eyes flicked over me like he could see straight through the walls I'd built. His gaze softened for the briefest of moments, but the hardness quickly returned. "I don't do stupid," he replied quietly, "not unless it's absolutely necessary."

His words hit me differently than I expected, a quiet challenge wrapped in understanding. We had both been running for so long, our lives filled with nothing but survival. The notion of 'stupid' was almost foreign to us—every decision, every move had to be calculated, every risk measured.

"I don't know if I'm ready to stop running," I admitted, surprised by the honesty that came out of my mouth, like it had been waiting for the right moment to slip past the careful control I'd maintained. "And I sure as hell don't know if I can trust you."

He raised an eyebrow, his lips curling into something that might have been amusement, but I couldn't quite tell. "Trust's a funny thing, isn't it? You don't give it away easily, but when you do, it's a hell of a thing to break."

I took in a sharp breath, the air suddenly thick around me. Trust had never come easy for me. Not after everything that had happened. Not after everything I'd lost. The people I'd loved, the promises broken. But Vance... Vance wasn't like anyone else. I hated that thought. I hated that it was creeping its way into my mind, tugging at me when I wasn't looking.

"I'm not ready to believe in second chances," I said, almost as much to myself as to him. "I've seen too much to think things can just... work out."

He stepped closer, but not too close—his presence still magnetic, but distant enough to keep me from retreating. His eyes, dark and steady, held mine with an intensity that made my pulse quicken. "And what if this time, it's different?"

I shook my head, unable to answer. The truth was, a part of me wanted it to be different. A part of me wanted to believe in something other than the shadows of the past, wanted to believe that there could be more than just survival and escape. But the other part—the part that had been hardened by loss and betrayal—kept me from getting too close.

I turned away, needing space, needing to breathe without feeling like I was drowning in him. "We can't afford to think like that," I muttered, my voice shaky despite myself. "We can't afford to care."

His hand on my arm was so sudden, so unexpected, that I froze. The touch was light, almost tentative, as though he were testing the waters. It made everything feel too real, too intense, and I pulled away almost instinctively. "Don't," I said, my voice tighter than I meant it to be. "Don't make this harder than it already is."

Vance's expression didn't change, though something flickered in his gaze. "I'm not trying to make it harder," he said softly. "I'm just trying to make sure you don't make the same mistake I did."

I swallowed hard, the weight of his words pressing down on me like a heavy, unspoken promise. "What mistake is that?" I asked, but I knew. Deep down, I already knew.

I tried to ignore the way his words hung in the air, thick and heavy like smoke. His gaze was unwavering, and I suddenly found myself wondering just how much of the past he'd let me in on. Not that I was eager to hear more about the ghosts that seemed to follow him, but there was something compelling in his silence—something that told me more than any confession ever could.

"I don't need your mistakes, Vance," I said, the words coming out sharper than I intended. It wasn't just a denial of his past; it was a denial of everything he made me feel. He wasn't the kind of man who needed saving, and I sure as hell didn't need to be saved. Not by him. Not by anyone.

His lips quirked, the smirk fleeting, and I could almost see the battle waging behind his eyes. "You sure about that? Because it seems to me you've been running from your own long enough to forget how to face it head-on."

I recoiled, but my skin prickled at the accuracy of his words. Damn him. I wasn't the kind of woman who let people under her skin—not without a fight, anyway. And yet, there it was. The way his words cut straight through my armor, the way his presence unsettled the carefully constructed walls I'd spent years building.

"I didn't ask for your opinion," I muttered, moving past him to the table, needing the distance. The space between us felt like a lifeline, something solid I could hold on to. But Vance wasn't the kind of man who stayed at a distance for long. I could feel his eyes on me, boring into my back like a presence I couldn't escape.

I wanted to turn and face him, tell him everything, maybe even beg him to stop making this harder than it had to be, but I couldn't. My pride—more fragile than I cared to admit—wouldn't let me. Instead, I busied myself with the contents of the bag, pretending that sorting through supplies was more important than the raw tension building between us.

"You think you're the only one with ghosts?" he asked, his voice softer now, a note of something deeper threading through his words. He stepped closer, but I didn't turn to face him. His approach was like the tide—slow, inevitable, and relentless.

I clutched the edge of the table, my knuckles turning white, as if the solid wood could somehow ground me. "What do you want me to say, Vance? That I'm ready to dive headfirst into whatever this is between us?" I laughed bitterly, though the sound was too hollow. "I'm not. And you don't get to pretend that this—" I gestured between us with a flick of my wrist, "—is some kind of fairy tale where everything works out in the end."

His steps stopped just behind me, and for a moment, we stood there in the quiet, the space between us electric with unspoken things. I could feel the heat of his presence, his breath a whisper against my ear. "I never said it was a fairy tale," he murmured, his voice low, rough in a way that sent a shiver down my spine. "But I also never said it was over."

I closed my eyes, frustration burning in my chest. He was right. It wasn't over. None of it was. My past was right there, lingering like a shadow just out of reach, and no matter how many times I turned away, it kept following. It wasn't just about Vance. It wasn't just about him or me. It was about the world we lived in, the one that had shaped us into the people we were today. And if I was honest with myself, I didn't know how to escape it anymore.

"You're wrong," I said, my voice tight with the weight of it all. "There's no going back. Not for me. Not for either of us."

Vance's hand settled on the edge of the table beside me, close enough that I could feel the heat of his skin. "Then what do you want, huh? Tell me what it is you're running from, and maybe—just maybe—I'll help you face it."

I turned to him then, my eyes locking with his. The defiance in my chest waged war against the raw honesty in his, and for a moment, I was caught between wanting to push him away and needing him closer. "You don't get to be the one who fixes things, Vance. I'm not broken."

His lips parted as if to argue, but the words never came. Instead, he closed the gap between us, his expression unreadable. It wasn't a question or a plea—it was something else, something that felt like a promise. A promise that didn't belong to anyone but us.

I didn't step back, even as every instinct in me screamed to do so. The tension between us was so thick, I could taste it in the air. I could feel the weight of the choices, of what it would mean if I let this—whatever this was—continue.

"Stop," I whispered, though I wasn't sure who I was saying it to—him or myself.

His hand brushed mine, light, almost hesitant. But it was enough to send a spark through me. "You don't get to tell me to stop," he said softly, almost like a confession. "Not anymore."

Before I could respond, a loud crash sounded from the direction of the door, breaking the moment in an instant. My heart skipped a beat as the door splintered open with a force that sent the walls shaking. The figure that filled the doorway was all dark shadows and danger, but the cold recognition in my chest stopped me from moving. It wasn't just anyone.

It was someone from my past. Someone who wasn't supposed to be here.

And that's when I realized that whatever was happening between Vance and me—it was only just beginning.

Chapter 12: Whispers of Danger

The air was thick with the stench of damp stone and forgotten promises. The city had its own pulse, a low, rhythmic hum that reverberated through the cobblestones beneath my boots. I could hear it in the echo of my steps, in the creak of the rusted street lamps, and in the distant rattle of a carriage's wheels. But tonight, it was different—darker, as if the very walls of the city had swallowed every bit of light. Vance's hand brushed against mine, warm and steady, though I could sense the tension in his every movement. We didn't speak, not with words anyway. The silence between us was a language all its own, one I wasn't sure I understood anymore.

He turned sharply down an alleyway, his footsteps quickening, and I followed, not daring to ask where we were going. The message had been clear enough. It had come, not in the usual cryptic scrawl that haunted our lives for months, but in something far worse: a single word, carved deep into the wood of our door. "Soon." The carving had been fresh, the ink still wet, as though the hand that did it had only just disappeared into the shadows. It made my skin crawl, and every fiber of my being screamed that something terrible was just around the corner.

The narrow street opened into a small courtyard, its stone fountain dry and cracked, the once-pristine tiles now chipped and weathered. A breeze stirred the dead leaves scattered across the ground, making them skitter like whispers in the night. I could feel the weight of Vance's gaze on me, though I didn't dare meet it. He knew as well as I did that there was no turning back now. We had been played, and the puppet strings were tightening.

"What do we do now?" My voice cracked, and I hated how weak it sounded. I wasn't weak. I couldn't afford to be weak. Not when I knew the truth. The truth that gnawed at my insides like a hunger that couldn't be satisfied, a truth that had been buried for far too long.

Vance's lips pressed into a thin line, and he finally stopped, turning to face me. His eyes were unreadable in the dim light, and for a moment, I felt the old familiar stir of fear rise in my throat. The kind of fear that comes not from the unknown, but from the things you refuse to acknowledge. The things you don't want to face.

"We keep going," he said, his voice quiet but firm. "We face it head-on. Whatever 'soon' means, we're ready for it."

I wasn't so sure about that. There had been too many games, too many moves made in the shadows, and I felt like we were mere pawns being pushed around on a board too vast for us to control. I glanced at the narrow streets that wound their way like veins through the city, each one leading deeper into the unknown.

"Are you sure?" I asked, stepping closer, my breath shaky. "Because it's been a long time since I've been sure of anything."

His hand shot out, gripping my wrist with an intensity that surprised me. His fingers were cold against my skin, and I could feel the pulse of his heartbeat, fast and erratic. For a brief moment, the world seemed to stop, the sounds of the city fading into nothingness. It was just us—caught in this dangerous game.

"I'm sure," he replied, the words cutting through the silence like a knife. "We have no choice. They're waiting for us." His voice dropped lower, laced with a grimness that made my stomach tighten. "We either face it, or we let it consume us."

I nodded, though a part of me wanted to pull away, run until I couldn't hear the sound of his voice or feel the weight of his presence. But I didn't. I stayed. Because somewhere deep inside, I knew he was right. The enemy wasn't just a faceless figure hiding in the shadows. No, they had found us long before we'd ever known they were there. They were part of this world, part of us. The real enemy had always been the doubt—the fear that maybe, just maybe, we weren't as untouchable as we thought.

We continued walking, the alleyways becoming narrower, the shadows deeper, until the world felt like it was closing in on us. The silence pressed in, thick and suffocating. I could almost feel the eyes watching, waiting for us to slip up, to show a moment of weakness. The city felt alive, and it was breathing down our necks, its pulse quickening in time with mine.

Then we turned a corner, and there it was—the building. A towering structure, its windows boarded up, its iron gates rusted shut. A place that had once been vibrant, full of life and noise, now a hollow shell. It stood at the heart of the city like a monument to everything that had gone wrong.

Vance stopped in front of it, his posture tense as if he were bracing for an impact. The building felt alive in a way that made the hairs on the back of my neck stand up. There was something ancient about it, something old and angry that whispered from its crumbling walls. I could almost hear the echoes of lost voices.

"Are you ready?" Vance's voice was steady, but his eyes flickered with something I couldn't quite place. Maybe fear. Maybe something else.

I took a breath, one that felt like it would shatter me if I let it. The truth was, I wasn't ready. Not by a long shot. But there was no other choice now. The time had come, and there was no going back.

"We'll see," I said, my voice barely a whisper. But as we stepped forward, I knew. Deep down, I knew the real battle was just beginning.

We stood at the edge of the forgotten building, its iron gates hanging limply as though the structure had grown weary of holding anything in. It loomed like a memory, something half-remembered but never fully understood. The air was still, the city beyond us alive with the usual hum of life, but this place felt separate—like an echo of something that had already passed. My feet moved of their own accord, drawn toward the mystery that waited just beyond the rusted doors.

Vance was ahead, his pace unwavering as always. His presence, steady and sure, was a comfort, but it also made me wonder how much of his confidence was a mask, one he wore because he had to. He had the skill of making everything seem simple—uncomplicated. But I knew better. Behind his calm façade, I could hear the anxiety that gnawed at his silence. The tension that lay beneath his words. It wasn't the kind of tension that could be kept at bay by mere bravado.

As we approached the building, I could feel the weight of its history pressing against me, as though the walls themselves remembered things better left forgotten. There had been a time when the place had been alive with laughter, music, and all the things that made a city feel human. Now, it stood in desolation, a monument to something darker, and the shadow of that darkness followed us, whispering against the back of my neck.

"Do you feel it?" I asked, my voice a low murmur, but even I could hear the tremor that ran through it. There was something about this place, something that twisted in my gut, a presence that lingered like an unspoken promise. I wasn't sure what that promise was, but I knew it wasn't good.

Vance didn't answer right away. Instead, he reached forward, his hand brushing against the gate. It groaned in protest, a sound too loud in the stillness, like the building itself was waking up, reminding us that it had been waiting for us. That we had been expected.

"It's worse than I thought," he said, his voice clipped. "But we're in this now. There's no turning back."

I nodded, though my heart raced in defiance of logic. There had to be a way out. There always was. But the longer we stood there, the more I realized that running had never really been an option. Not now. Not anymore. The city had already marked us, and there was no point in pretending otherwise.

Vance pushed the gates open, the hinges protesting as they swung wide, inviting us into the belly of the beast. Inside, the remnants of its former grandeur lay scattered about like forgotten dreams. Stained glass windows that once shimmered with vibrant colors now stood cracked and dull, the light outside filtering through them in fractured beams, creating rainbows of dust. The air was thick, heavy with the scent of mildew and decay. Each step I took disturbed the silence, the sound of my shoes scraping across the floor too loud, too intrusive in the vast emptiness.

There was no sign of anyone. Not yet. But the stillness felt alive, the kind of alive that made every shadow stretch just a little too far. We moved deeper into the building, our footsteps echoing in the hollow spaces between the broken walls. The temperature dropped, and I pulled my coat tighter around my shoulders, the fabric offering little protection against the creeping chill.

The hall stretched before us, dimly lit by flickering sconces that cast ghostly shadows. The farther we went, the more I felt as though we were descending, not just into a building, but into something far worse—into a place where time and memory twisted in on themselves.

"Do you hear that?" I whispered, my pulse quickening as a faint sound reached my ears, too quiet to make sense of. A scraping. A scuffling. It wasn't the wind, though the breeze had picked up around us, making the abandoned structure sigh and groan. It was something else. Something alive. Something waiting.

Vance froze, his posture changing, his hand instinctively reaching for the gun tucked beneath his jacket. He didn't need to speak. I knew what he was thinking. We weren't alone.

"We should go," I said, stepping back, my instincts screaming for us to leave. "We're not ready for this."

His gaze met mine, and for the first time since we'd entered, I saw the doubt in his eyes. It was a brief flicker, quickly smothered by resolve, but it was there. And it terrified me. Not because I didn't trust him, but because I knew, deep down, that even he wasn't sure anymore. Not of the city. Not of the people who controlled it. And certainly not of what we were walking into.

"Too late for that," he said, his voice low. "We've been marked. Running now won't change anything. We have to finish it."

The truth of his words sank like a stone, and I nodded in resignation. We had come too far, walked too many miles down a road that no longer led to safety. It was a strange kind of surrender, knowing that the fight was no longer about winning or losing. It was about survival. And I wasn't sure who was more dangerous—our enemy, or the fears we'd hidden from ourselves.

We pressed on, and the walls seemed to close in, narrowing with every step. The shadows thickened. The air became heavy, like we were walking through water, the weight of it pressing down on us. Each breath was harder to take, each step felt more sluggish. There was a pressure in my chest, a tightness that had nothing to do with the atmosphere and everything to do with the reality I refused to acknowledge.

I was afraid. Not of what lay ahead, but of what I had already known deep inside me. This wasn't just about fighting back anymore. It was about confronting the truth—about myself, about Vance, and about everything we'd built up until this point. And I wasn't sure I was ready to face it.

The sound grew louder, sharper, and I realized, with a sickening certainty, that we were not alone. Whatever waited for us in the darkness had been waiting a long time.

The sound grew louder, a rhythmic scraping that seemed to crawl along the walls, threading through the cracks in the stone like a living thing. I could feel the hairs on my neck stand up, the weight of the air thickening with every inch we moved forward. My hand trembled at my side, and for a moment, I was sure I could hear my own pulse, a frantic drumbeat drowning out all the other noises. The shadows in the room twisted in unnatural shapes, bending in ways that couldn't be explained by the flickering light. And then I saw it.

The figure emerged slowly, its shape indistinct at first, a blur of movement in the corner of my vision. I blinked, trying to make sense of what I was seeing, but it felt like the space between us was stretching. The figure wore a cloak—dark, heavy—and the fabric swirled around it like a pool of ink, absorbing every speck of light. Its face was hidden, but I felt its eyes on me. Cold, unblinking. They seemed to reach out, even though there was no discernible way for them to do so.

Vance stiffened beside me, his posture suddenly rigid. I didn't need to look at him to know that we both understood the same thing: this wasn't just some random encounter. It wasn't a trap set by the city's usual players. No, this was different. This was personal.

The figure moved closer, its footfalls barely audible on the cracked floor. The sound of its breath—if it even breathed—seemed to fill the space, impossibly loud in the heavy silence. My heart hammered in my chest, and I instinctively took a step back, my boots scraping against the floor, the sound sharp and unnaturally loud. But the figure didn't seem to notice. Or perhaps it didn't care.

"You came," the voice whispered, its tone hollow, almost like it came from far away, like it was carried on a breeze that only it could feel. "I wondered when you'd show up."

I wasn't sure if the voice was mocking or simply stating a fact. Either way, it made my stomach churn.

"We're here," Vance replied, his voice low but steady, the calmness in it betraying the tension that gripped his body. He moved slightly in front of me, a subtle gesture to shield me, though I wasn't sure it would do much good. "What do you want?"

The figure's cloak shimmered, rippling with an unnatural grace, as if the fabric itself had a life of its own. It took another step forward, and I could see its hands now—long, pale, fingers that seemed to stretch out like the limbs of something that belonged to a different world. They hovered, almost gently, over a small object in the figure's grasp. A book, bound in leather so dark it seemed to absorb the light around it.

"You don't understand," the figure said, its voice a low hiss that seemed to echo off the walls, amplifying with every word. "You never understood. You think you're playing a game, but you're not. The pieces were set long before you ever walked into this city. Before you ever crossed paths with me."

I could feel the chill in its words, the weight of them pressing against my chest. It wasn't just the figure's presence that felt suffocating—it was everything it said. Everything it implied.

"Who are you?" I asked, my voice louder than I intended, a little more brittle than I would have liked. But I couldn't help it. The fear clawed at me, tightening around my throat, making it hard to breathe. I had to force myself to take a deep breath and steady myself, trying to regain some semblance of control.

The figure tilted its head, and for a moment, I could almost feel a grin—cold, amused—curling beneath the hood. "Oh, that's the question, isn't it?" it said, its words curling around me like smoke, too slippery to hold onto. "Who am I, indeed?"

The pause stretched on, thick and heavy, the silence amplifying the tension in the air. And then, in the most unnervingly casual way, the figure simply shrugged. "It doesn't matter, really. I'm just the one who's been waiting for you. The one who's been watching. I'm the one who's seen the truth."

A cold shiver ran down my spine. "What truth?" I asked, though I wasn't sure I wanted to hear the answer.

"The truth about you," it said softly, as though speaking to a child, something almost tender in the way it said it. "The truth about the choices you've made. About the path you've been walking without ever realizing where it leads."

Vance stepped forward, his jaw clenched, his body tense. "Stop playing games. What do you want?"

The figure's laugh came next, a soft, almost melodic sound, like the distant chime of wind against glass. "Games?" it echoed. "Oh, this is no game. This is far from it. And you? You're simply the last piece. The one who decides how the game ends."

I had no idea what it meant, but every fiber of my being screamed that whatever it was, it was bad. Very bad. The chill that crawled up my spine deepened, spreading through my limbs until I was frozen in place. Something was coming, and we weren't ready for it.

"Don't listen to it," Vance said sharply, his eyes flicking toward me, his gaze suddenly fierce. He stepped closer, but the figure's hand shot out, faster than I could blink, blocking him with a force that sent a ripple of energy through the air.

"Careful," it warned, its voice no longer soft but full of something darker. "You don't want to make me angry. I've waited far too long for this moment."

I wanted to shout at Vance to stop. To turn around and run before we were pulled into whatever nightmare this was. But my voice caught in my throat, paralyzed by the fear that churned inside me.

Suddenly, the figure dropped the book, letting it fall with a thud that seemed to reverberate through the room. My breath caught as it landed, and before I could react, the lights around us flickered. The building groaned again, the sound louder this time, as though something deep within it was waking up.

And then, in the blink of an eye, the figure was gone. Just vanished. Leaving us standing there in the dark, the air still vibrating with the echoes of its presence.

"Vance?" I whispered, barely able to form the words.

But there was no answer. Only the sound of the city outside, creeping back into the silence.

Something was wrong. Very wrong.

And we were running out of time.

Chapter 13: A Web of Choices

The alley smelled of rain and exhaust fumes, a strange, metallic tang that clung to the air as though the city itself was holding its breath. My boots slid over slick cobblestones as I kept my pace steady, my heart pounding with the sound of an impending storm. The night had turned colder in the last hour, and the thick humidity had condensed into a suffocating fog that seemed to wrap itself around my body, making the night feel both claustrophobic and fragile. I wanted to believe this was just another city night, like all the others—quiet, too quiet—but something about the way the shadows lingered felt different.

Vance was ahead of me, a shadow within the fog. The tension between us crackled, a web of unspoken words hanging thickly in the air. If only it were just that simple—words. We'd fought side by side, hours of blood and sweat together, and yet here we were, two people still circling each other like hesitant animals, neither one willing to make the first move. His movements were sharp, his posture rigid as though he could see something I couldn't. I didn't like it.

"You're sure about this?" I asked, trying to sound nonchalant, though my voice betrayed a nervous edge. The alley felt too small, the walls too close, and the sudden feeling of being watched didn't help.

"I'm sure," Vance replied, but his voice held a tension that mirrored mine. His eyes were narrowed, scanning every corner, every crack in the walls, but I could tell there was something more beneath the surface. Something else lurking there, something he wasn't telling me.

We moved forward, the only sounds now our footsteps, the occasional creak of metal, the low hum of the city that never truly sleeps. A sharp crack of a twig to our left made me stop dead in my tracks, my breath catching in my throat. The world seemed to slow down as the hairs on the back of my neck stood up. I looked at Vance, but he was already ahead, his hand outstretched to me, his face grim.

"I knew it," he muttered under his breath, barely loud enough for me to hear.

Before I could respond, a figure emerged from the fog, tall and menacing, the sharp outlines of his body seeming to cut through the air. He was cloaked in shadow, his features concealed beneath a mask of black. The city's dim lights glinted off the edge of his blade as he took a step forward, his boots making no sound against the wet pavement.

And then there was another figure, and another. We were surrounded.

"Nice of you to join us," Vance said, his voice dripping with sarcasm, though his hand was already on the hilt of his sword. He didn't flinch, didn't give any indication of fear, but I could feel the tension in his shoulders, the way his muscles coiled in preparation.

"Get out of here, Vance," the leader of the group growled, his voice low and threatening. "This doesn't concern you."

Vance gave a hollow laugh. "Oh, I beg to differ," he said. "I think it concerns both of us. And if you want her, you'll have to go through me."

The words hung in the air for a moment, as though the world had paused to take them in. The group of men shifted, their eyes narrowing, calculating their next move. I felt my pulse quicken. The odds were against us—five to two, and we were standing in an alley with nowhere to go. It wasn't a fight we could win.

But we had no choice. None of us could afford to back down.

I moved to stand beside Vance, my back straight, my hands trembling slightly as they gripped the small blade I kept hidden beneath my coat. I'd never been much of a fighter—not like him. He had a confidence in his movements, a cold precision that made him dangerous. But me? I was just surviving. Surviving and trying to stay one step ahead.

The leader of the group smiled, a smile that sent a chill down my spine. "You're making a mistake," he said, his voice dripping with menace.

Vance didn't reply. He simply nodded toward me, and I understood. This was it. The moment where everything would change.

I lunged, not because I thought I had any real chance of winning, but because I had to. A sharp ring of metal as my blade clashed against his, the impact rattling up my arm. But I didn't hesitate, didn't pull back. I couldn't afford to.

Vance was already moving beside me, his own sword a blur of motion as he engaged the others. His strikes were swift and sure, like a dancer in the middle of a well-rehearsed routine, each movement fluid and effortless. But his eyes—his eyes told a different story. They were cold, calculating, filled with the same fierce determination that had kept him alive for years.

I swung again, and this time, I felt the cold kiss of steel against my side. Pain flared, sharp and immediate, but I didn't stop. I couldn't. Not with them closing in, not with Vance so close, his presence both a comfort and a danger I couldn't quite figure out.

"Move!" Vance shouted, shoving me aside as one of the attackers tried to bring down his blade on me. The force of the push sent me stumbling, but I caught myself before I hit the ground.

My chest heaved, the fog of the alley suddenly feeling suffocating. My body ached, my muscles screaming in protest. But we had to keep moving.

Then, in the chaos of it all, something shifted. Something inside me. I wasn't just fighting to survive anymore. I was fighting for him, for us. I wasn't sure when it happened, but somewhere between the clash of steel and the taste of blood in my mouth, I realized that I was trusting him. Trusting him with my life. Trusting him in a way that I had never trusted anyone before.

And that—more than anything—was the most dangerous choice of all.

The world around us was a blur of motion—blades slicing the air, bodies twisting and turning, desperate to find purchase in a desperate dance. I could hear the sound of steel meeting steel, the harsh rasp of breath from both sides, the pounding of my heart in my ears. My grip on the dagger was slick with sweat, the handle biting into my palm, but it was the only thing keeping me grounded, keeping me from slipping into pure panic.

Vance was a shadow beside me, his every movement seamless, like the practiced stroke of a skilled artist painting his way through chaos. I envied that. The way he moved, controlled and sure, while I was a little less polished—more like a child playing dress-up with a weapon I barely knew how to use. But I fought anyway. Because I had to. Because I didn't have the luxury of hesitation.

"Watch your left!" Vance shouted, his voice cutting through the cacophony. I barely had time to react before I was throwing myself to the side, narrowly avoiding the blow that would have cleaved my ribs. The sharp whistle of the sword missed me by inches, and I landed hard on the ground, the damp stones biting into my elbows. My breath escaped in a rush, but I didn't have time to savor the panic.

I rolled back to my feet in one fluid motion, only to find that my attacker was already on me, his grin too wide, too eager. He was a large man, with thick arms and an even thicker neck, the kind of brute who relied on his strength rather than his wits. The kind of brute I hated.

"Not so fast," I muttered, my voice a rasp, as I sidestepped his next swing and rammed the dagger into his side. The man howled, a sound more surprised than pained, before he collapsed to his knees.

I didn't give him a second to recover, kicking the knife further in and pulling back with all the force I could muster.

Vance's voice was back in my ear almost instantly. "Move, now!" He didn't wait for me to respond before he grabbed my arm and yanked me into a roll, just as another figure came lunging toward us. I followed the instinct to move, my body obeying his command without question, as if somehow we'd become one in that brief, frantic moment of survival.

We were a tangled mess of sweat, blood, and adrenaline, both of us relying on the other's instincts to stay one step ahead of death. But even then, as our attackers closed in like the shadows themselves, something else began to seep in—the thrum of something more than just survival. It was a low burn in my chest, an unfamiliar pull that twisted in time with the rapid beats of my heart. The way his hand gripped mine when he pulled me back, the way his shoulder brushed mine as he shielded me with his body. I had been fighting with Vance for so long, side by side, but in this moment, something flickered between us, something undeniable.

It wasn't just trust. It was a shared purpose, a shared fight. He was my tether to the world as much as I was his. I knew this now. It had always been there, but the weight of it was heavier than I could have ever expected.

But there wasn't time to think about it, not with the enemy pressing in on all sides. I swung the dagger again, barely missing another blade that came at me with the force of a falling tree. My feet slipped on the wet stone, and for a moment, everything went silent—a strange, deafening quiet that seemed to stretch out of time itself.

And then, just as quickly, the world crashed back in with a jarring thud as I collided with a wall of muscle. I braced myself for the impact, but instead, I found myself falling into the warm, solid embrace of Vance's body, his arms steadying me in a way that had nothing to do with fighting. It was an odd, intimate moment—one that shouldn't have made sense in the middle of a battle. His lips brushed against my ear as he whispered, "Get it together."

I wanted to laugh, to pull away and pretend I wasn't shaking inside. But instead, I nodded, forcing myself to focus as I broke free from his grasp, ready to face the next wave of attackers.

The tide of the fight was turning. The shadows that had been looming over us since the ambush were no longer just an external threat. They were creeping into my mind, too, turning my thoughts into knots of doubt. How long would we keep fighting? How many more would we have to take down before they realized we were more than just two outnumbered individuals?

I could feel the hesitation creeping into my limbs. It was the weight of choice pressing on my chest. My heart thrummed erratically, a rhythm of terror mixed with something else—something that felt like the last piece of a puzzle slotting into place.

The men in front of us didn't pause, didn't hesitate, but for the first time, I wondered if maybe they had the right idea. It would be so much easier to let them win. To fade into the shadows they promised, to stop fighting and just accept that this was how things would end.

But then I caught Vance's eye across the fog-filled street. His jaw was set, eyes burning with an intensity that could have set the world on fire. He wasn't ready to stop. He was fighting for something—someone—and even if I didn't understand it fully, I knew that whatever it was, it mattered.

And so, with a deep breath, I steadied myself, gripping my dagger tighter, and rushed into the fray once more.

If there was a way out of this, if there was any chance of survival, we would find it together.

I could hear the blood pounding in my ears, a deafening roar that drowned out everything but the weight of the choice that loomed between us. Every breath was an act of defiance. Every move was a fragile gamble. The world around us had collapsed into an endless loop of chaos and decision, with Vance and me standing at its center, poised on the edge of something bigger than both of us.

The pressure mounted as I stood shoulder to shoulder with him, my eyes never leaving the circle of men who surrounded us. The fog was thick, suffocating, and I couldn't shake the feeling that there was something else out there, something watching us from the darkness just beyond our reach.

Vance's gaze flicked to mine, those dark eyes of his glinting with determination, but something else there too. Something more—something I couldn't quite name. I wanted to ask him what it was, why it felt as though the air between us had shifted, but there was no time for questions. No time for answers.

He moved first, like a wolf springing into a hunt, and I followed instinctively, every muscle in my body attuned to his. It was a strange, almost surreal feeling—this unspoken understanding, this pull toward each other that seemed stronger than any sword or shield. He was a part of me now, in a way that both terrified and exhilarated me.

One of the attackers lunged at me, and for a moment, I saw nothing but his gleaming blade, the sharp curve of metal catching the dim light as it came down toward me. Instinct took over. I stepped sideways, ducking low, and with a swift motion, my dagger was out and slicing toward his unguarded side. The man staggered, gasping as the steel bit into his ribs, but he didn't go down.

Vance was there in an instant, his sword flashing in a deadly arc, cutting through the air with a precision that left no room for mercy. The attacker crumpled, his body folding in on itself like a house of cards.

"Keep your head," Vance muttered, his voice tight with tension as he swept his blade through another assailant. He moved with grace, but there was a coldness to his movements—efficiency, purpose, and something else I couldn't quite grasp.

I nodded, even though my heart was still racing. I wasn't sure if the adrenaline made me numb or if I was simply trying to hold onto the fragments of myself that were slipping away in the chaos. Either way, I couldn't afford to dwell on it.

Another man came charging at us, his battle cry cutting through the fog like a knife. He swung a large club in wide, reckless arcs, aiming for Vance's head, but Vance parried the blow with effortless skill, deflecting it with a flick of his wrist. There was no hesitation in him, no sign of faltering.

I didn't think. I just reacted. With a quick sidestep, I took advantage of the opening Vance had created, lunging forward with my dagger, striking the man in the stomach before he even had time to register the attack. He gasped, his body jerking back, but I didn't stop. I pushed harder, twisting the blade deeper until he fell to the ground with a final, sickening thud.

The blood roared in my ears again, the sound of my breath filling the space between us as the last of the attackers circled. But I could feel the shift now—the balance was tipping. We had won this round, but the fight wasn't over.

One man remained, his face twisted in a scowl, his sword at the ready, and the tension between us stretched tighter than a wire pulled too far. His eyes darted to Vance, then to me, calculating, weighing. He knew he was outmatched, but there was a stubborn glint in his eyes—a defiance that spoke of something deeper than just a fight.

"You think you've won?" he spat, his voice thick with venom. "You think you've got what it takes to stop this? You don't know what's coming next."

I glanced at Vance, but his expression was unreadable. Was this man just trying to intimidate us, or was there more to it than that?

Without a word, Vance stepped forward, his sword raised, his gaze never wavering. "You've had your chance," he said, his voice low and steady. The words hung in the air, heavy with the weight of finality.

The man hesitated, as if weighing his options, but in that split second of indecision, Vance was on him. The fight was quick, brutal, but over before I had a chance to fully register the sequence of events. The man crumpled to the ground, his body lifeless before it even hit the wet pavement.

We stood there, panting, the only sounds the harsh breaths we took and the distant hum of the city behind us. I wiped the blood from my blade, my hands trembling slightly as the adrenaline began to fade, leaving behind a dull, gnawing exhaustion.

But even as we stood victorious, I couldn't shake the feeling that something was wrong. That something deeper was at play. There had been no time to ask what had just happened, no time to question Vance's decisions or his sudden shift in behavior. But the unease lingered, pressing against my chest like a heavy weight.

Vance looked at me then, his gaze sharper than I had ever seen it before, his eyes narrowed as if assessing something—something just beyond my reach. For a moment, neither of us moved. The world around us seemed to hold its breath, as though waiting for the next move.

And then, without warning, the air shifted again.

A crackle, low and almost imperceptible at first, then a rumble that shook the ground beneath our feet. The fog swirled violently, and I barely had time to react before a sudden, blinding light exploded in front of us. My vision blurred, and my ears rang, the sound deafening as I stumbled backward.

I didn't know where Vance had gone. I didn't know where anything had gone.

But I knew one thing for sure.

The real battle had only just begun.

Chapter 14: Echoes of the Heart

The night had settled thickly over the camp, draping the world in heavy silence. It was the kind of silence that made your thoughts too loud, the kind that reminded you that nothing good could last forever. I didn't want to think about it, but I could feel the weight of the past pressing down, heavier than the wet blankets thrown over our shoulders to ward off the cold. The fire flickered weakly in front of me, sending bursts of warmth into the otherwise frigid air, but it could do nothing to chase away the chill in my bones.

I shifted uncomfortably on the rough wooden bench, the scent of wood smoke mixing with the tang of blood and sweat that clung to my skin. The battle was over, but it didn't feel like it. My hands were still slick with the remnants of a life I'd taken, and no amount of scrubbing would make that feeling go away. The distant thud of hooves in the dark was a reminder that our enemies never rested, that they were always lurking, waiting for a crack to form in our fragile armor.

Vance had been quiet since the ambush—too quiet. His normally boisterous laugh was absent, replaced with a somber look in his eyes that only deepened with each passing hour. He sat beside me now, his fingers twitching slightly as if he didn't know what to do with them. I could feel the weight of his gaze, the burden of whatever thoughts were pressing in on him. He wanted to say something, I could tell. He always did, always ready with some sharp remark or sarcastic comment that could break the tension. But not now. Not tonight.

"I'm not sure if I'm glad it's over or if I'm just exhausted," I finally said, the words slipping out before I could stop them.

Vance turned to look at me, his face softened by the flickering light, but there was something unsettling in his eyes—something

I couldn't name, not yet. "Both, probably," he said, his voice low, rough.

I let out a soft laugh, half-hearted and more bitter than I intended. "Yeah, probably."

His hand moved toward mine, hesitated for a moment, and then found its way into my palm. It was a simple gesture, the kind that shouldn't have meant much, but in that moment, it felt like a lifeline. We hadn't spoken about it, hadn't even acknowledged the way we had fallen together in the midst of chaos, our bodies pressing close in desperate need for solace. It was something we both knew but didn't want to examine too closely—especially now. Now, with the weight of everything pressing in around us, it felt too fragile, too fleeting.

"You're different," he said after a long pause, his thumb brushing gently across the back of my hand.

I swallowed. "Different how?"

He tilted his head, his gaze not leaving me. "Like... you're quieter. More... closed off."

I shrugged, my fingers tightening around his. "Guess I've just had a lot on my mind." It wasn't a lie, not entirely. But I knew it wasn't the whole truth either. There were things I couldn't say—things I didn't even know how to articulate. I had always been good at shutting things out, at compartmentalizing my feelings. But Vance had a way of seeing through me, peeling away the layers I'd carefully constructed. It made me feel vulnerable in a way that both terrified and thrilled me.

He studied me for a moment, the weight of his gaze making me shift uncomfortably. "You're not the only one carrying something, you know."

His words cut deeper than I expected. I turned to face him, trying to hide the way my heart seemed to stutter in my chest. "What do you mean?"

He sighed, his fingers threading through mine more tightly. "I mean... we're in this together, right? You don't have to carry it all by yourself."

I didn't answer at first. How could I? It wasn't that I didn't want to share with him, to tell him what had been gnawing at me for days. But the more I thought about it, the harder it became to put into words. The lives lost in that ambush—my fault, or maybe not. The choices we made to get here, to this point. What if I told him the truth? That I was afraid. Afraid that the more I allowed myself to care for him, the harder it would be to walk away when it all came crashing down.

"What if this isn't enough?" I heard myself say, the words spilling out before I could stop them. "What if it's not enough to get us through?"

Vance's face hardened for a moment, his jaw tightening as if my words had physically struck him. But then, just as quickly, he softened, his hand cupping my cheek, his thumb tracing the line of my jaw. "We'll make it enough," he said firmly. "We'll make it through. Together."

The certainty in his voice made my breath catch. It was the kind of certainty that I wanted to believe in, the kind that would be easy to hold onto if only the world outside didn't feel so ready to tear everything apart. I wanted to trust him, I wanted to believe in the promise of his words. But there were too many shadows lurking, too many uncertainties that clouded my mind. Love, I knew, was a dangerous game to play. One wrong move, one misplaced word, and everything could shatter into pieces.

I leaned into his touch, closing my eyes for a moment, trying to block out the growing sense of dread that twisted in my stomach. "What if love isn't enough?" I whispered, the words barely audible in the quiet of the night.

Vance didn't answer right away. Instead, he kissed me, a slow, lingering kiss that spoke of everything we hadn't said. It wasn't a promise, not exactly. But it was a shared understanding. We both knew that whatever came next, whatever the world threw at us, we'd have to face it together.

And maybe, just maybe, that was enough.

The morning light was a cruel thing. It washed over the camp with no regard for the quiet devastation still hanging in the air, a soft golden glow that was far too pure for the place it touched. It was as if the world had conspired to mock our suffering, to pretend that everything was fine when it clearly wasn't. I stood there, staring out at the horizon, the soft wind stirring the strands of hair that had escaped from my messy braid. The smell of damp earth mixed with something sharper—blood, sweat, and fear. That was the scent of this place now. It was the scent of all that we had become.

I tried not to think about the bodies, not to remember the sound of steel on flesh, the sickening thud that followed. I had been trained for this, and yet, no amount of training could have prepared me for the way it had felt, the way it had torn through me. Vance had been there, as always, watching my back, keeping me steady. And yet, I had sensed the distance between us the moment the dust had settled. We had fought side by side, but now, it seemed as if the space between us had grown wider than the battlefield itself.

I didn't want to admit it, not even to myself, but I couldn't shake the feeling that something was slipping away. Something I couldn't grasp, couldn't keep close. I wanted to turn and find him, to seek the solace of his presence, but I was afraid of what I might find. Was it the same hunger, the same desire to push past the pain? Or was it something else? Something quieter, more dangerous.

The camp was still waking up, the sounds of boots on gravel and murmured conversations filling the air. I could hear Vance's voice in the distance, sharp, quick, a contrast to the heaviness of my thoughts.

His laugh echoed through the camp, and for a moment, I thought perhaps everything would return to normal. Perhaps I was overthinking it, like I often did. But then I saw him, standing in the middle of a group of soldiers, his hands gesturing animatedly as he spoke. His usual bravado was back, but there was something about the way he looked at me from across the fire that made my chest tighten. It was as if he were seeing me for the first time—and the weight of that glance was almost too much to bear.

When he finally made his way over to me, the air between us felt charged, as if something was brewing just beneath the surface. He flashed me a grin, a flicker of the man I had come to know, but it didn't reach his eyes. The smile was more a mask than anything else.

"You look like you're about to start a war with the sun," he said, his voice light, teasing, but there was an edge to it. A sharpness that didn't belong.

I couldn't help but laugh, though it came out strained. "You always know how to make me feel better," I said, trying to force the tension out of my body, but it lingered, thick and suffocating.

He studied me for a moment, his brow furrowing slightly. "What's going on in that head of yours?"

I hesitated. It wasn't that I didn't trust him, or that I didn't want to be honest, but the truth felt too raw, too fragile. "Nothing," I said, almost too quickly. "Just... thinking."

Vance nodded, but I could see the way his lips pressed together, the way he shifted slightly, as if trying to decide whether to push me further. But then, as if he realized it was a battle he wouldn't win, he dropped the subject, his grin returning, albeit a little forced.

"We leave at dawn," he said, his voice suddenly serious. "Get some rest."

I nodded, not trusting myself to speak. What did I even say to that? Rest was something that had been eluding me for days now, and it wasn't just the lack of sleep. It was the weight of everything—everything we'd seen, everything we'd done. The fear that it was all falling apart, bit by bit.

As the evening wore on, I found myself retreating into the shadows, away from the campfire, away from the prying eyes of those around me. I couldn't bear the thought of being close to Vance, not when everything between us felt so uncertain. We had shared something, something fragile and fleeting, but now it seemed like a distant memory, fading with each passing hour. And yet, I couldn't let go. I couldn't let him go.

The night grew colder, and the fire flickered low, its warmth barely enough to ward off the chill. I wrapped my cloak tighter around my shoulders, the fabric rough against my skin, and leaned back against the stone wall. The camp had quieted, the only sounds now the occasional rustle of leaves in the wind and the distant calls of night creatures. But even in the quiet, the tension was palpable. It buzzed in the air, thick and oppressive, a reminder of all the unsaid things between us.

A figure approached from the shadows, and my heart skipped a beat. I didn't need to turn to know who it was. The familiar, heavy tread of boots on the ground, the scent of leather and smoke—it was him.

"You're avoiding me," Vance said, his voice low, laced with something I couldn't quite decipher.

I didn't answer right away. How could I? The truth was, I was avoiding him because I didn't know what to say, because the words I wanted to speak felt too heavy for this moment. And yet, he stood there, waiting, as if he had a right to them, as if he knew I would eventually have to admit the things I was too afraid to say.

"Why?" he pressed, stepping closer.

The air between us crackled, and for a moment, I was sure the world would come to a stop, as if it were waiting for me to make the choice—whether to open up, whether to let him in, or to keep everything locked inside, where it would slowly consume me.

I finally turned to face him, my voice barely a whisper. "Because I don't know what comes next."

The silence between us stretched longer than I cared to admit. Vance stood there, his eyes searching mine, but I couldn't find the words to break the tension. His question hung in the air, pressing in on me, heavier than the starlit sky above. He was waiting for an answer, but how could I give him one? How could I tell him the truth when I didn't even understand it myself?

"I don't know what comes next," I repeated, my voice sounding distant, even to my own ears. "And that scares me more than anything."

His expression softened, just a fraction, but the edge of concern didn't leave his face. He stepped closer, his presence filling the space between us with a warmth that should have comforted me but instead made my chest tighten further. The flickering light from the dying fire caught in his eyes, making them seem impossibly deep, like there was a storm raging just beneath the surface, one I couldn't quite see but could certainly feel.

"You're not the only one," he said, his voice barely above a whisper. "I don't have the answers either."

I looked up at him, surprised by the honesty in his tone. "Then why—"

"Because," he cut in, "I can't walk away. Not from you."

The words hit me like a sudden gust of wind, throwing my thoughts into chaos. "You're not walking away," I managed to say, my voice thick. "But I think you should. You should walk away before it gets worse."

He stared at me, confusion flickering across his features. "Worse? It's already worse."

I could feel the tremor in my hands, and I clenched them into fists, desperate to hold onto something stable. "No," I said, my voice harder now. "I mean... whatever happens next, whatever's coming, I don't want to drag you into it."

"You're not dragging me into anything," Vance shot back, his words sharp but his eyes soft. "We're already in it. Whether you want it or not."

I swallowed, a bitter taste creeping up my throat. He was right. We were already so deep in this mess that I couldn't see the way out. I had thought, back when the first shot had been fired, that we could make it through the battles together. I thought that the nights of laughter, the quiet moments, the simple touch of his hand on mine—those things would be enough to carry us through. But now I wasn't so sure.

The distant sound of hooves broke the spell between us, a reminder that the world outside our conversation wasn't waiting. The war wasn't waiting. The fight, the threats, the betrayal—none of it had stopped, and none of it cared about how we were feeling. It was relentless, a force that didn't allow for distractions, for feelings, for love.

"They're coming," Vance said suddenly, his eyes narrowing toward the shadows. "They'll be here by dawn."

I felt a shiver run down my spine at the mention of dawn. It wasn't just the time of day that scared me. It was everything that came with it. The idea that, with the first light, everything could change again. That the fragile moment of peace we'd found together—however fleeting it was—would be ripped away, leaving us exposed and alone.

"We don't have time for this," I said, my voice steady now, the weight of responsibility settling on my shoulders like a familiar coat. "We need to make decisions. We need to decide if we fight or if we run."

Vance's jaw clenched, his stance stiffening, the air around him shifting. "And you think running is an option?"

I shook my head. "It's always an option, Vance. It's always been an option."

"But not one you'll take," he countered, his gaze unwavering.

I didn't answer him right away, didn't know how to. Because the truth was, I didn't know what I would do. I had made so many choices that had led me here—so many moments that could have been different, should have been different. But I wasn't sure anymore if there was a right answer. I wasn't sure there ever had been.

The sound of the hooves grew louder, and I could see the flickering of torches in the distance, casting long shadows against the tree line. It was them. The enemy. They were coming, and they weren't the type to ask questions or offer mercy.

"We have to go," I said, grabbing his arm and pulling him toward the edge of the camp. "We can't wait for them to find us."

Vance didn't fight me. He followed, his footsteps heavy behind mine, but I could feel his hesitation—feel the tension building between us once more. It wasn't just the threat of what was to come. It was something deeper, something unspoken. We were running, but running from what? The battle? Or from each other?

"Do you trust me?" he asked suddenly, his voice quiet but urgent.

I didn't look back at him. "Of course, I trust you."

"Then trust me now," he said. "We'll make it through. Together."

I almost laughed, the sound hollow in the tense air. Together. We had been together once, but was it enough? Would it ever be enough? I didn't have the answers, but I knew one thing for certain—there was no turning back now.

The enemy was close, too close. We could hear the clash of metal as they set up their camp on the outskirts, their voices low and angry.

We had minutes, maybe seconds, to decide what to do. My heart pounded in my chest, my breath coming in shallow bursts.

"Vance," I whispered, but before I could say another word, the unmistakable sound of a blade scraping against metal echoed through the night.

We weren't alone anymore.

Chapter 15: Threads of Fate

The air in Crescent City felt thick, as if the very sky was holding its breath, waiting for something to happen. The usual hustle of people on the streets had faded into a strange kind of stillness, like the city itself had sensed the approaching storm. It was late—so late that the moon, full and luminous, seemed like a foreign object hanging above us, casting sharp shadows in the alleys. I could hear the soft shuffle of footsteps behind me, the faintest scrape of metal against stone, but when I glanced back, no one was there.

Vance walked beside me, his stride long and steady, his presence a quiet force that grounded me even when the world felt like it was slipping through my fingers. The whispers had led us to a narrow street that seemed too old to belong to Crescent City, a forgotten place where the cracks in the pavement were like scars on a weary face. There was something about it that made the hairs on the back of my neck stand up—an eerie familiarity, like I'd been here before, but that couldn't be right.

"Are you sure this is it?" I asked, my voice low, almost swallowed by the night. The last thing I wanted was to seem uncertain, especially now. Every instinct told me that we were getting close, closer than I wanted to be.

Vance glanced at me, the corner of his mouth curving just slightly, like he was sharing a joke only he understood. It was a look I'd gotten used to, the silent reminder that, while I was just learning to navigate this world, he'd been in it far too long.

"Trust me," he said, but it wasn't the usual confident assurance. There was something deeper in his tone, something buried underneath layers of guarded experience, something that made my chest tighten. "You'll know when we get there."

His words lingered in the air, and I tried to shake off the discomfort swirling inside me. Vance was the kind of person who rarely spoke unless it was necessary, and even then, it was like each word had been carefully considered, weighed against some invisible scale. He wasn't one for small talk, and he didn't believe in pleasantries. But there was something about the way he said that—something that almost sounded like a warning.

I followed him through the crooked street, the sound of our footsteps muted against the uneven stones. The farther we walked, the quieter the city seemed to get. Not the kind of quiet that comes with peace, but the kind that drapes over everything like a shroud. The air was thick, heavy with the scent of damp earth and something I couldn't quite place—like old books mixed with the faintest trace of burnt metal.

Eventually, we came to a stop in front of an unmarked door, barely visible beneath a twisted iron awning that had long since lost its luster. I could barely make out the outline of the wood, old and weathered, but sturdy enough to have stood for centuries. A small brass plaque beside the door bore a symbol I didn't recognize, a sharp, angular shape that seemed almost like a warning in itself.

"This is it," Vance said, his voice a little softer now, almost reverent.

I raised an eyebrow. "This is your secret network of allies? Seems... unassuming."

He gave me a small, tight smile. "It's not about appearances, Ivy. It's about trust. And this is where we need to be."

I nodded, though I wasn't entirely convinced. Trust. That word had become a slippery thing over the past few months, something that could easily slide through my fingers no matter how tightly I gripped it. It was hard to trust anyone when every corner of my life had been upended, when everyone seemed to have their own motives, their own hidden agendas. But if I was being honest with myself, the only reason I was still standing here was because of Vance.

There was something about him, something deep and unspoken, that kept me tethered to this strange, dangerous path.

With a resigned sigh, I stepped forward, pushing open the door. The creak of the hinges echoed in the silence, and as soon as the door fully opened, I was hit with a rush of warmth and the smell of something familiar—something comforting. The air inside was thick with the scent of tobacco and wood, and the low hum of murmured conversations filled the space.

The room was dim, lit by soft, flickering lanterns hanging from the rafters. The walls were lined with shelves full of dusty tomes, their spines cracked and worn, as if they'd been read more times than anyone could count. A fire crackled in the hearth, casting a warm glow across the faces of the people gathered around the room.

They all stopped talking the moment we entered, their eyes turning toward us, assessing, calculating. There were no greetings, no introductions—just that same silent understanding that passed between us all. Vance didn't flinch under the scrutiny. Instead, he stepped forward, his gaze sweeping over the room with a kind of quiet authority that was as effortless as it was unnerving.

"These are the people who are going to help us," he said, his voice carrying across the room. "We're not just fighting for our lives anymore. We're fighting for the future."

The words felt heavy, like they'd been burdened with years of hidden meanings and untold stories. But it wasn't the weight of the declaration that made the air feel even thicker—it was the sudden realization that we were no longer just pawns in a game. We were part of something much bigger than ourselves.

As I glanced around the room, my eyes caught the gaze of a woman sitting in the far corner, her face hidden by a cloak of shadow. There was something about her, something that tugged at my memory. But before I could piece it together, she stood, her movement fluid and graceful, as though she were part of the very air around her.

"I hope you've come prepared," she said, her voice like silk, but sharp enough to cut through the tension in the room. "Because this is where we find out if we're truly ready for what's coming."

And in that moment, I knew. The threads of fate had already begun to weave themselves around us.

The woman's eyes were the color of storm clouds, swirling with layers of secrets I knew I had no business uncovering. Her presence seemed to fill the room, like the air was thickening with every word she spoke, wrapping itself around us in invisible threads. She wore no adornment, no jewelry that might have suggested wealth or power—only a cloak so dark it absorbed light, the kind of black that was almost unnatural, as though it belonged to the night itself.

"I'm Elyse," she said, her voice soft, almost melodic, but carrying an undeniable weight. Her gaze flicked briefly to me, and I felt something shift in the room, like a tightening of the atmosphere. "And you've come just in time to help unravel a very old problem."

A flash of heat rushed through my chest, settling somewhere just beneath my ribs. I couldn't tell if it was anger or fear, but it didn't matter. The words hung in the air like smoke, thin and fragile, but threatening to choke anyone who dared to breathe them in too deeply. I met her gaze and felt the unmistakable shiver of recognition. I didn't know her, but in some odd way, I felt like I did. The question of how hovered on the edge of my tongue, but I kept it there. Questions could wait.

Vance, ever the picture of composure, stepped forward and addressed her with a small nod. "I trust you've gathered everything we need?"

Elyse's lips quirked, though the expression was more akin to a smirk than anything friendly. She didn't answer immediately, instead letting her gaze linger on Vance for a long beat. Then, as if the weight of that shared moment passed between them like a coded message, she nodded.

"You're both here because you're no longer just outsiders. You've crossed into the heart of this war." Elyse's voice dropped low, almost conspiratorial, but there was no mistaking the gravity behind her words. "And the war is no longer just about survival."

I bristled, half-expecting a grand revelation—some sort of dramatic unfolding that would provide a sense of clarity, something to dispel the heaviness that had been pressing against my chest for days. But there was no quick fix, no silver lining. Just the hollow truth that stretched between the cracks of every conversation we'd had since I'd first set foot in Crescent City.

"Then what is it about?" I asked, the words slipping from my mouth before I could stop them. The room went still again, the kind of stillness that comes when everyone realizes someone just crossed a line they didn't know existed.

Elyse studied me for a long, uncomfortable moment before she answered, her voice soft but undeniably sharp. "It's about choice, Ivy. You've always had one, whether you knew it or not. But now, that choice isn't just yours anymore."

I stared at her, the heat creeping up my neck as a rush of questions flooded my mind. Vance's warning echoed in my thoughts, the one where he told me that there were things I wasn't ready to know. If I had any doubts about that, they were gone now. My throat tightened as the weight of her words settled in, their meaning creeping up like a vine, wrapping itself around every part of me.

"I didn't ask for any of this," I muttered, the words tasting bitter on my tongue. They were too honest, too raw for my liking, but they tumbled out anyway, propelled by a sense of frustration I couldn't quite shake.

Vance turned to me then, his expression unreadable. For a moment, I thought he was going to say something—maybe something reassuring, something to soften the hard edges of the world we were standing in—but he didn't. Instead, he placed a hand on my shoulder, a simple touch that somehow anchored me in the storm.

"You never asked for it," Elyse said, her eyes sharp as blades. "But the moment you walked into this city, you became part of it. Just like everyone else here." She gestured around the room at the other people who had begun to emerge from the shadows, some in dark coats, others in faded clothes that spoke of years of quiet endurance. "This war isn't just about us anymore. It's about you, too. And what you're willing to give up."

My heart stuttered in my chest. "What are you asking me to give up?"

The silence stretched, thick with tension. Elyse didn't answer immediately. Instead, she turned toward the far wall, where a map of the city had been pinned up. The ink on it was faded in some places, blurred by time, but the markings were clear enough. Some sections were circled in red, others crossed out in bold black lines.

"This city is more than a place," Elyse said, her voice carrying over the room like a soft breeze. "It's a battleground. And those who control it, control everything."

I took a step forward, my eyes scanning the map. "Who controls it now?"

She turned back to face me, her eyes flicking to the map briefly before settling on me once again. "That's the question, isn't it?" she said. "And the answer is complicated. There are factions within factions. Some are old, others newer, but all of them are working toward the same goal—control."

I swallowed hard, trying to push down the unease that was creeping up my spine. "So we're fighting to take control back."

Elyse nodded slowly, the flicker of something unreadable flashing in her gaze. "Yes. But it's not just about power. It's about survival. Yours. Mine. Everyone's."

I looked around the room, catching the eyes of the others who had gathered. They weren't just people who'd decided to fight. They were people who had no other choice. There was a desperation in their expressions, something raw and untamed that mirrored the growing feeling inside me. We were standing at the edge of something, something bigger than any of us could truly grasp.

Vance met my gaze then, his eyes darker than before, full of an emotion I couldn't place. Maybe it was regret. Or maybe it was just the weight of everything that had led us here. Either way, it was clear that we were no longer in control of our own fate. That, I realized, was the true cost of the war we'd stepped into.

But as I glanced around at the people in the room, the ones who were still here despite everything, I understood something else, too. We weren't alone. Not completely. And maybe that was enough—for now.

I stepped closer to the map, my eyes tracing the lines of streets and districts like a puzzle, but the pieces didn't quite fit. There was something deeply unsettling about the way the marks on the paper bled together, merging into an unsettling web that stretched across the city. If Elyse's words were to be believed, this wasn't just a map of places—it was a map of power, of secrets that had been buried too deep to stay hidden for long.

"Are you planning to explain any of this to me?" I asked, my voice a little sharper than I intended, but I couldn't help it. There was something in the air that made my skin crawl—an urgency that pulled at the corners of my thoughts, forcing them to scatter.

Vance had remained silent ever since we walked into the room, standing just behind me like a shadow, but his presence was undeniable, pressing into me in ways I couldn't fully understand.

Elyse gave me a glance that was almost pitying, her lips curling in that infuriating, knowing way she had. "You're not quite ready, Ivy. But soon, you'll see. We all have a part to play." Her eyes darted back to the map, fingers tracing the red circles with a precision that made the air seem colder. "The question is: are you ready to play yours?"

I had never been a fan of riddles, and Elyse's cryptic tone was wearing thin. But I wasn't here to ask questions—I was here to figure out how to stop whatever it was that was closing in on us. The weight of the map pressing against my chest reminded me of that unshakable feeling I'd had since the very first night I stepped foot in this city: the feeling that something far bigger than me was unfolding, and I was simply a passenger on this twisted ride.

"I don't want to be anyone's pawn," I muttered under my breath, more to myself than to Elyse, though the words weren't lost on her.

The room quieted again, the energy shifting like a charged atmosphere before a storm. I could feel the tension rising, thickening the air as though we were standing on the brink of something. Everyone in the room—each face, each set of eyes—seemed to have their own agenda, their own reasons for being there. And none of it had anything to do with me.

A voice cut through the stillness, deep and resonant, like it had been waiting to emerge from the shadows. "Maybe you won't be. But the truth is, Ivy, it doesn't matter whether you want to or not." The words seemed to hang in the air between us, heavier than the silence that had preceded them.

I turned toward the voice, narrowing my eyes at the man who had spoken. He was tall, almost too tall, with dark hair that fell across his brow and a scar that ran down the left side of his face. His presence was magnetic, like a flame that you knew would burn if you got too close. He was one of them, one of Elyse's allies, though he didn't seem to fit the mold of the others. He was too raw, too untamed.

"And who exactly are you?" I asked, feeling a touch of defiance rise in my chest.

The man didn't flinch at my tone. "Someone who's been fighting this war longer than you've been breathing, sweetheart," he replied smoothly, his lips curving into a smile that didn't reach his eyes.

Vance finally moved, his hand brushing against my arm—a small gesture, but it was enough to break the tension and send a rush of heat through my skin. "Focus," he said softly, but I could hear the underlying command in his voice. "We don't have time for this."

I nodded, forcing myself to tear my eyes away from the man who had spoken and back to Elyse, whose gaze was still fixed on the map.

"There's something else, isn't there?" I asked, my voice quieter now, but the certainty was unmistakable. "You're not just preparing us to fight. You're preparing us to sacrifice."

Elyse didn't answer right away, her fingers lingering on the map before she looked up, her expression unreadable. "Sacrifice is a part of every war, Ivy," she said, her voice low, almost a whisper, like she was sharing a secret she didn't want to, but couldn't keep in any longer. "But this isn't about just surviving. It's about making sure what comes next doesn't destroy everything."

I swallowed, the weight of her words sinking into my chest. A sharp pain throbbed in my temples, as though I could already feel the weight of what was being asked of me, of all of us.

"What happens next?" I asked, my voice barely above a whisper.

Elyse's lips twitched, but she didn't smile. Instead, she leaned closer, her eyes locking onto mine with a seriousness that almost made me step back. "The lines are already drawn, Ivy. But the battle is far from over. And when it comes down to it, you'll be the one who decides which side wins."

The words felt like a punch to the gut. I could feel my breath catch in my throat as the room seemed to shift around me. My gaze darted to Vance, who stood at my side, his face unreadable, his stance rigid.

I didn't know what to say, how to respond. There were no answers to be found here, not the kind that would bring any kind of relief. But one thing was clear: we were standing on the edge of something terrible, something that would change everything, and I wasn't sure if we were ready for it.

Before I could voice another question, the door to the room burst open with a suddenness that left me jumping in surprise. A man, breathless and wide-eyed, stepped into the space, his gaze flicking between us all before landing on Elyse.

"It's started," he said, his voice raw with panic. "They're here. The gates... they've opened."

Everything in the room went still. It was as if the very walls of the building had sucked the air out of the room, and I couldn't breathe. My heart pounded in my chest, louder than any words spoken, and I could feel the shift, feel the impending dread that coiled through the air like a tangible thing.

The gates had opened.

And I had no idea what we were about to face.

Chapter 16: The Heart's Descent

The walls of the old house groaned beneath the weight of the storm that rattled the windows. The storm outside was nothing compared to the one that raged inside, between the two of us. I could feel Vance's gaze on me, the heat of it burning through the dim light. His silence was a weapon—heavy, suffocating. There had been no words for so long, not the right ones, anyway. He didn't need to speak; I knew what he was thinking. The air between us thickened, every breath carrying an unsaid confession, one that could either save us or destroy us.

I reached for my coat, draping it over my shoulders, though it was hardly needed. The warmth of the room, the flickering fire in the hearth, seemed to mock me. My skin burned with the tension in the space, the weight of everything left unsaid. I'd never been good with silence—its suffocating grip always made me fidget. But this silence... this one was different. It felt like a bridge, stretching between us, just waiting for one of us to take the first step, to cross it into something neither of us knew how to handle.

Vance stood by the window, his back to me, staring into the blackness of the night. His broad shoulders tensed beneath the fabric of his shirt, a stark contrast to the stillness of his expression. I had spent years studying his every movement, every flicker of emotion that crossed his face. It was a skill I'd perfected, an armor I wore to protect myself from the truth. But now, standing here with him, I realized how much I had missed. How much I had been afraid to see.

His voice was low, almost a whisper, when he finally spoke. "You've been avoiding me."

I couldn't meet his eyes. Instead, I focused on the fire, the way the flames twisted and danced, throwing shadows on the walls. My pulse quickened, and I felt a knot form in my throat. "I've been avoiding myself," I muttered. The truth felt heavier than I expected, a jagged shard lodged deep in my chest.

Vance turned, finally facing me. His gaze softened, but there was something in his eyes—something I couldn't quite place. "You can't keep running, you know."

I wanted to scoff, to dismiss him with a quip, but the words stuck in my throat. What could I say to that? He was right. I'd spent my whole life running, pretending that I didn't need anyone, didn't need this—him—but now, standing here in this space with him, every instinct I had screamed otherwise. And that terrified me. The idea of needing him, of trusting him, felt like I was offering up a piece of myself I could never get back.

The fire crackled, the only sound between us as I searched for something to say that didn't feel like surrender.

"I don't trust myself," I admitted finally, my voice cracking. It wasn't what I wanted to say. The words tasted bitter in my mouth, but they were true. I couldn't trust myself, because if I did, I would have to admit that I had already fallen too far.

Vance's expression hardened, a frown tugging at the corners of his mouth. "You think I'm going to hurt you?"

I flinched at the question, because it wasn't that. It was never that. But how could I explain it to him? How could I tell him that the fear wasn't about him at all, but about me—what I was willing to risk, what I was willing to lose? "No," I said, my voice a little stronger. "It's not that. It's just... everything."

The way he looked at me then, like he was seeing me for the first time in years, broke something inside me. I had always been so careful with him, so guarded, afraid of what might slip out if I let him in. But he was here now, standing just a few feet away, and that wall I'd built around myself was starting to crumble.

"I don't want to do this alone," I whispered, more to myself than to him. The admission felt like it was scraping against the bones of who I thought I was, but it was out there now. I couldn't take it back.

Vance took a step toward me, his movements slow, deliberate. "You don't have to." His voice was steady, like a promise. His hand reached out, hesitated for a moment, before settling on my arm, the touch light but enough to send a ripple through my skin.

I swallowed hard, my heart hammering in my chest. I was afraid of this, of what might come if I gave in, but what terrified me more was the idea of walking away again. I couldn't keep running. Not this time.

The storm outside roared louder, the wind howling as though urging us to decide. And for the first time, I didn't feel like I was standing on the edge of something terrifying—I felt like I was standing at the threshold of something new, something I wasn't sure I was ready for, but something I knew I couldn't escape any longer.

"I'm not asking for you to save me," I said, my voice barely above a whisper. "I just want... I just want to be with you."

His gaze softened, the intensity of it unraveling me bit by bit. He moved closer, so close now that I could feel the heat of his body, hear the steady rhythm of his breath. "Then stay," he said, his voice a low murmur against my ear. "Stay, and I'll be here."

And in that moment, I knew. I knew that I could no longer hold myself back. Not from him, not from whatever it was that we were, not from what lay beyond the storm. For the first time, I felt something I hadn't even known I'd been searching for—a glimmer of hope.

The rain hammered against the roof, a steady, relentless thrum, as though nature itself was trying to drown out the tension thickening the air between us. His hand lingered on my arm, the warmth of his touch seeping through the fabric of my coat. I could feel his pulse, steady and strong, and my heart responded in kind—uneven, frantic, trying to catch up with the truth I'd just allowed to spill out.

Vance moved slightly, his breath a soft puff against my cheek as he leaned in closer. I could almost taste the words in the air, a confession that had been hovering between us like a shadow for far too long. It wasn't just that I'd been avoiding him—it was that I had been avoiding everything I felt for him. The thought of letting someone in, of letting myself trust, terrified me more than I was willing to admit. But I couldn't escape it anymore. Not when he was standing so close, his presence filling the room like a storm waiting to break.

"I'm not asking for perfection, you know," he said, his voice low, but warm, as though he could sense the whirlwind in my mind. "Just... a chance." He sounded almost amused, like he understood the struggle, but was too patient to call me out on it.

I let out a sharp breath, my chest tight as I searched for the right words. "I don't do chances. I don't do this," I gestured between us, though I didn't know how to explain what 'this' even was. My mind felt like it was on the edge of a precipice, teetering between everything I knew and everything I feared. I had spent so long building walls around my heart, believing I didn't need anyone. But the moment his gaze met mine, I felt them crumbling, piece by piece.

Vance didn't back away. Instead, he took a step closer, his gaze steady on mine, never flinching. "I don't need perfect either. Just you."

I stared at him, caught in the depth of those words, and for a moment, the world seemed to narrow down to just us. There was no storm outside, no danger, no looming threat. Just this quiet, intimate moment where everything I'd held back threatened to spill over. I wasn't sure I could handle it, but I knew I couldn't let it go either.

"You're not making this easy," I said, trying to deflect, trying to push away the vulnerability threatening to overtake me. I wrapped my arms tighter around myself, suddenly feeling exposed, too open.

He smiled then, that wry, charming grin of his that always seemed to both disarm and irritate me in equal measure. "I don't do easy." His hand moved from my arm to the small of my back, gentle but firm, guiding me closer. "And you know you don't want easy."

I didn't know how to respond to that. Easy had always been my escape—no complications, no risks, no heart exposed to the harshness of the world. But Vance... he made me want to take that step. He made me want to trust, to feel, and that was terrifying. Terrifying because I knew that once you opened that door, you couldn't close it again. And with the stakes as high as they were, with everything we were facing, the thought of risking it all for something as fragile as a feeling felt like a kind of madness.

I took a step back, the edge of the rug under my boots providing the tiniest bit of grounding. "You think it's easy for me to just... trust you?" The words came out sharper than I intended, but I couldn't stop them.

He didn't flinch, didn't even seem surprised. "I know it's not. But trust isn't something that's given freely, not really. It's earned, over time, with patience, with understanding." His eyes softened, his voice dropping even lower. "And I'm here. For however long it takes."

A rush of heat flooded my chest. I hated how much his words resonated, how right they felt. It was like he was reaching for something deep inside of me, something I'd buried so far beneath my walls that I hadn't even known it was there. I wanted to scream, to laugh, to run away and hide all at once. But there was no hiding anymore, not from him, not from what was happening between us.

I crossed the room, needing space, needing to think. I pressed my palm against the cold surface of the window, watching the rain cascade down, as if the world outside could offer me some clarity.

But there was none to be found. Only the reflection of my own face staring back at me, raw and exposed.

"Why me?" I asked softly, not expecting an answer, but the question had been clawing at me for days now. "Why now?"

Vance's footsteps followed behind me, quiet but purposeful. He came to stand beside me, close enough that I could feel his presence without him touching me. "Because," he said, his voice a steady anchor in the storm of my mind, "you're the one I'm here for. No one else." His words were simple, but in that simplicity, there was a weight that felt heavier than anything I had ever heard.

I turned toward him then, meeting his gaze head-on. "But I'm not ready, Vance. I don't know if I'll ever be ready for... this. For you."

His expression didn't shift, but his eyes softened in that way I'd come to recognize as his silent understanding. "You don't have to be ready. You just have to take the step. I'll be right here when you do."

A flash of doubt crossed my mind. It felt reckless, this trust, this leap into the unknown. But then I realized something—maybe it wasn't reckless at all. Maybe it was the only thing that made sense in a world so broken, so uncertain. Maybe it was the only thing that could save us both.

In that moment, amidst the storm and the quiet tension, I knew. The fear hadn't disappeared, but the weight of it had lessened. And maybe, just maybe, it wasn't as important as what lay ahead. Not with him by my side.

The fire flickered low, casting long shadows across the room, and the sudden, palpable silence felt as though it had taken up space of its own. I couldn't escape the weight of Vance's presence, his every movement so deliberate, so aware of the crackling tension that held us captive. My hands fidgeted at my sides, as if looking for something to do, anything to break the knot of nerves tightening in my stomach. The clock on the mantle ticked with unbearable slowness, each second dragging longer than the last.

Vance's voice, when it came, was quiet, but it was like a gust of wind that pushed through my defenses. "You don't need to hide from me."

My throat felt tight, and I suddenly wondered if he could hear my heart hammering in my chest. I had wanted so desperately to be in control of everything—my thoughts, my emotions, my safety—but with him, standing so close, it all seemed like an illusion. "I'm not hiding," I said, the words stiff, unwilling to betray the tremor in my voice.

Vance's lips curved into a knowing smile, a faint, almost sad acknowledgment in his eyes. He stepped closer, and the air between us seemed to crackle. "You've been running for a long time," he said, his voice soft but carrying an undeniable certainty. "But I'm not going anywhere."

I swallowed. The words, so simple, so raw, threatened to unravel me. For the first time in as long as I could remember, I was standing on the edge of something real. And as much as I wanted to leap into it, the fear was almost too much to bear. My pulse quickened, not from danger, but from the sheer unfamiliarity of it. The idea of trusting him, of letting myself fall, was both exhilarating and terrifying.

I glanced at the door, the slight panic bubbling in my chest as my feet shifted, moving toward the safety of distance. But before I could take a step, his hand shot out and caught my wrist.

"Don't," he said simply, not with demand, but with something more like a plea—one I could feel vibrating in my bones. "If you walk away now, you won't get another chance. Not with me."

I froze. My breath came in uneven bursts, and I could feel the weight of the storm outside merging with the storm inside me. It was as though the world had paused, giving me only this single moment to choose.

I yanked my wrist free from his grip, the action feeling as much like an attempt at self-preservation as an act of defiance. "I'm not asking for another chance," I said, trying to steady my voice, but it cracked anyway. "I'm not asking for any of this. Not for me, not for you."

For a long moment, Vance just stood there, watching me, his expression unreadable. His jaw tightened slightly, and I saw the flicker of something in his eyes—something soft, but painful. It was a look I wasn't sure I knew how to interpret. He exhaled slowly, and the sound, so low, was the only noise that filled the room.

"Then why are you still here?" His words hit harder than I expected. The question wasn't accusatory, but there was an undertone of frustration, of confusion. "You've been running from it all this time. Why stay now?"

I stared at him, my chest tightening, the words I needed to say caught somewhere between my ribs. It wasn't that I didn't want to be here—God, that was the problem. I did want to be here. But I wasn't sure how to do this, how to step into the vulnerability he was offering, how to trust him enough to let him see me in all the ways I was terrified of.

"I don't know how," I whispered, the honesty so raw it almost stung. "I don't know how to let someone in, not when everything I've built is... crumbling."

The room seemed to grow colder, despite the warmth from the hearth, and the weight of everything unsaid settled between us. I could hear my own breath, ragged now, as if the confession had physically drained me. I had never been one to bare my soul, not to anyone. Not like this. But the floodgates were opening, whether I was ready or not. And when Vance stepped toward me again, his eyes softer now, filled with something I couldn't place, I didn't move. I couldn't.

"I'll be here when you're ready," he said, the words like a promise, but also like an invitation. And for a moment, I wanted to collapse into it.

But just as I opened my mouth to speak, to tell him that I couldn't keep pushing him away, the sound of something—no, someone—knocking on the door shattered the moment. My heart skipped a beat. Vance's expression immediately shifted, his jaw clenching in an almost imperceptible way.

The knock came again, sharper this time, more urgent.

"Stay here," he said, his tone now dark with something I couldn't read. He moved swiftly, his posture changing from the calm, patient man who had been standing in front of me just seconds ago to someone alert, on edge. He shot me a quick glance. "Don't move."

I barely had time to process his words before he disappeared into the hallway. The sound of footsteps grew faint as he made his way to the door. I stood there, my pulse thudding in my ears, every instinct screaming at me to move, to act. But I didn't. I stayed exactly where I was, frozen, as the world outside seemed to come crashing in.

The door creaked open, and I heard Vance's low voice murmuring something to whoever was on the other side, but I couldn't make out the words. Not until the door swung open fully, revealing a figure standing in the doorway—a figure I never expected to see.

My breath caught in my throat, and my heart stopped cold. The person on the other side wasn't just a visitor. They were a threat.

Chapter 17: Secrets in the Shadows

The house had a certain stillness to it, the kind that made you feel like you were walking through the skeleton of something once full of life, now abandoned. A few worn photographs in faded frames stood on the mantle, and the scent of leather-bound books clung to the air, but there was nothing there to distract from the quiet. I had never liked quiet—too much room for things to settle in, like guilt or regret. And now, with Vance beside me, the air seemed to crackle with all the things neither of us had said yet.

He stood by the window, looking out over the sprawling grounds. His broad shoulders were rigid, his jaw set tight. I could almost see the weight of the past pressing against him, the same as it had always been—always there, always threatening to break through. It was the kind of thing you couldn't outrun, no matter how far you ran or how fast.

I leaned against the doorframe, watching him for a moment, unsure of how to breach the silence. It was the kind of silence that wrapped around you like a blanket, suffocating in its comfort. But then again, nothing had ever been easy between us, and I couldn't remember the last time I'd felt truly comfortable in his presence. We'd danced around our truths for so long, but the music was starting to fade. It was time for something real, something raw.

"Do you ever wonder if this is all some kind of... accident?" I asked, my voice quieter than I'd intended.

He turned, his eyes dark, unreadable. "What do you mean?"

"I mean..." I searched for the right words, watching his gaze flicker with the same guarded intensity he always wore. "How we ended up here. All of it. The mess, the secrets, the things we've done, the things we haven't said. Sometimes it feels like it was all set in motion long before we even knew what was happening."

He didn't respond at first. I could see him wrestling with something—anger, frustration, maybe both—but also a deep sorrow, the kind that settled in your bones when you knew you couldn't escape the past. His gaze softened for a moment, just a flicker, but it was enough. Enough to remind me that under all the walls, there was a person in there. One I had never quite figured out, but someone I couldn't stop caring about, no matter how hard I tried.

"Accidents," he muttered, his voice low, "don't always feel like accidents, you know?"

There was an edge to his words that made me shiver. Something about the way he said it, like he had seen too much to believe in the idea of chance anymore.

"I guess not," I replied, taking a step closer. "But you've been carrying this weight alone for so long. You don't have to do that anymore, you know."

He let out a short laugh, but it wasn't a happy sound. "You think I've been alone?"

"Hasn't it always felt like that?" I said, tilting my head slightly, watching his face shift with the unspoken history that hung between us. "We've both been playing this game—me pretending I'm fine, you pretending I don't matter, both of us lying to each other, lying to ourselves."

The air thickened as I spoke, each word a thread that tugged at something deep inside both of us, unraveling the lies we'd spun around ourselves. I wasn't sure what had gotten into me—maybe it was the long hours spent in the darkness of my thoughts, or maybe it was the growing realization that whatever we'd been avoiding had finally caught up to us. But I wasn't going to run anymore. I wasn't going to pretend like I could walk away from this. Not now.

"I didn't want to drag you into this mess," he said after a long pause, his voice barely a whisper, as if admitting it out loud might make it all real. "You deserve better."

I laughed softly, more to myself than to him. "Better? You think I'm looking for better? I don't even know what 'better' looks like anymore, Vance."

He took a step toward me, his eyes searching mine, as if trying to figure out whether I was telling the truth or just saying what I wanted to believe. "What does that mean? You really think you're better off in this mess with me?"

"I think..." I paused, struggling for words. "I think that no matter how twisted this all is, I'm not ready to let go of you. Not yet."

The tension between us grew, thickening the air until I could barely breathe. His lips parted, like he wanted to say something, but then he just closed them again, shaking his head slowly. "You don't know what you're saying."

But I did. I knew exactly what I was saying. I had spent too long pretending not to care, letting the bitterness fester, letting the secrets eat at me. But I was tired. Tired of pretending I could walk away from him, tired of pretending that the things we'd both done, the lies, the betrayal, were things I could just erase.

"I know more than you think," I replied, my voice steady. "I know enough to understand that the choices we've made aren't just our own anymore. They've been dragging us both down for far too long. And I'm not running anymore, Vance. Not from you. Not from whatever comes next."

For a long moment, he didn't say anything. His eyes were locked on mine, searching for something, maybe an escape route, maybe a reason to turn away. But there was nothing left to run from. Not anymore.

It wasn't until we reached the edge of the property, standing on the crumbling stone wall that overlooked the valley, that I realized just how heavy the air had become. It pressed down on us, thick and unyielding, like the weight of every decision we'd ever made was wrapped up in the silence that now hung between us. It wasn't just the world holding its breath—it was us, too. Waiting. Watching.

Vance had gone quiet, his gaze fixed somewhere far off, beyond the horizon where the last traces of sunlight were being swallowed by the encroaching night. He had that look on his face again—the one that made him seem miles away, even when he was standing right next to me. I hated that look, the one that made me feel like he was drifting, untouchable.

"You know, you don't have to do this," I said, my words soft, but sharp enough to cut through the stillness. I hadn't meant to speak, hadn't meant to break the fragile quiet that had settled around us, but it had been building in me, this need to force him to acknowledge the truth that neither of us wanted to face.

He didn't respond right away, his fingers drumming absently against the stone. He was trying to hold back, I could see it in the way his jaw tightened, the way his shoulders stiffened. But I wasn't about to let him off the hook. Not now, not when we were this close to everything crumbling.

I stepped closer, just enough to feel the heat radiating off him. "You've been running for so long, Vance. So many years of burying everything, pretending none of it matters. But I'm telling you, it does. It matters to me."

He turned to face me, his eyes dark with something unreadable. "You don't understand," he muttered, barely above a whisper, as though the words themselves were too heavy to bear aloud.

"No, I do," I insisted. "I understand more than you think." I reached out, my hand brushing his arm, the contact light but deliberate. "You're not alone in this, Vance. Not anymore."

For a moment, he stood there, silent, his expression a mixture of disbelief and something like desperation. He was fighting it, I could tell. Fighting the pull between us, the truth of what we'd become to each other, the thing neither of us could name but both of us felt.

"You've always been so sure of everything," he said suddenly, his voice low and strained. "But I'm not sure about anything anymore. About us. About what happens next."

I laughed, but it wasn't an amused sound. It was more like a bitter thing, one born of frustration and confusion. "You think I'm sure about any of this?" I shook my head, looking away, because I couldn't bear to meet his eyes while I said this next part. "I've been pretending, too, you know. Pretending like I know exactly what I'm doing, like I have some sort of plan, like I can handle whatever happens. But I don't. I'm just... trying to figure it out. One mess at a time."

There was a long pause, and I could hear the night settling in around us. The distant chirp of crickets, the soft rustle of leaves in the trees, all of it felt so far away, like it belonged to a different world altogether.

Finally, he spoke again, and when he did, his voice was softer, almost hesitant. "I'm not the man you think I am, Olivia. You don't know what I've done, what I've been a part of."

I swallowed hard, my throat dry as the words lodged in my chest. "What is it with you and secrets, Vance? Why do you think I'm going to run if you tell me the truth? That I'll walk away, like all the others?"

His gaze dropped to the ground, and for a moment, I thought he might pull away, might give me that same look he always did—the one that made me feel like I was asking for something I didn't deserve. But instead, he exhaled, a slow, heavy breath, as though he was finally giving in to something he'd been holding back for too long.

"You think you can handle it?" he asked, his voice quiet but laced with a challenge. "You think you can handle the fact that I've done things... things that I can't take back?"

I stepped closer, my voice steady, but my heart pounding in my chest. "You think I'm afraid of your past? Because I'm not. I'm not afraid of you, Vance. Not anymore."

There was a flicker in his eyes, like a storm about to break. He opened his mouth to speak, but before he could, the distant rumble of thunder interrupted us, and a cool wind swept across the valley, carrying with it the scent of rain. The sky above was heavy, pregnant with the promise of a downpour.

"We don't have time for this," he said abruptly, his tone shifting, almost dismissive. "We need to focus on what comes next."

And just like that, the vulnerability between us was gone, replaced by the sharp, brittle edge of necessity. There was no more room for feelings, no more time for honesty. The storm was coming, and whether we were ready or not, we would have to face it.

I nodded, my stomach knotting with a mix of anticipation and dread. I didn't know if we were ready. But somehow, I knew that whatever happened, we couldn't back down now.

The rain began to fall in a steady, relentless rhythm, the kind of downpour that makes you feel like the sky's forgotten how to do anything in moderation. The droplets splattered against the ground, the earth beneath our feet softening with every passing second. I glanced over at Vance, his silhouette cut out against the flashing sky, and for a moment, it was like we were standing in a world that didn't belong to either of us. The distance between us had stretched so far that it was almost unbearable.

"You're right," I said, wiping the raindrops off my face, forcing my thoughts into the present. "We don't have time for this. Not anymore."

Vance didn't respond, his gaze fixed ahead, his expression unreadable. I couldn't tell if it was the storm or something else that had made him retreat behind that familiar mask of indifference.

He was good at that, the wall-building, the pretending like nothing phased him. But I could see through it, just like I always could.

We stood there for a moment longer, listening to the storm roar around us, before he finally turned to me. His face was now wet with rain, his dark hair plastered to his forehead, but his eyes still held that same dangerous intensity. "You should get inside," he said, his voice low, an edge of finality in it. "It's not safe here."

I frowned, crossing my arms over my chest, feeling the cold from the rain seep into my skin. "Not safe? What are you talking about?"

But before he could answer, there was a sharp crack of thunder, so close that it shook the ground beneath us. The next moment, I heard the unmistakable sound of footsteps approaching from behind us, and my stomach lurched in response. I spun around, my heart hammering in my chest, but there was nothing there—just the dark, rain-soaked woods stretching endlessly in every direction.

Vance didn't flinch, didn't move, his stance still like a rock. But his eyes, those dark, unreadable eyes, flickered toward the trees, then to me.

"We need to go," he said again, more insistent this time. "Now."

I opened my mouth to argue, to demand answers, but something in his voice stopped me. It wasn't the usual dismissive tone he used when he didn't want to talk about something—it was... urgency. Raw, unfiltered urgency that made my blood run cold.

Before I could ask what he meant, I heard it—a low, guttural growl, the kind of sound that shouldn't be possible from anything human. My skin prickled with the sudden knowledge that something was very wrong. My pulse quickened as the shadows of the trees seemed to grow darker, the wind picking up in a howl that sent the hairs on the back of my neck standing on end.

"What the hell is that?" I asked, my voice barely above a whisper, but it felt too loud in the thickening silence.

Vance didn't answer immediately. Instead, his eyes swept over the dark woods as if calculating something. "You don't want to know."

That was the last thing I wanted to hear from him, especially when he looked so damn serious. It wasn't just the words he said—it was the way his jaw clenched, the way he took a step closer to me, his hand brushing against my arm in a gesture that felt far too deliberate, as if he were trying to hold me together.

"Vance, what is going on?" I demanded, my voice shaking, despite my best effort to sound steady. The growl was getting louder, closer, and the fear was beginning to crawl up my spine, coiling tighter with each passing second.

He looked over at me, his eyes dark, and for the first time since I'd met him, I saw something raw, something vulnerable flicker in his gaze. It only lasted for a fraction of a second, but it was enough to make my heart skip.

"Whatever you think you know," he said, his voice low, "you don't. This isn't just some game, Olivia. It never was."

The words hung in the air between us like a promise or a curse, I wasn't sure which. The growl got louder again, and this time, I could hear the unmistakable crunch of leaves underfoot. Something was coming, and it was not going to be something we could outrun.

Vance didn't wait any longer. Without warning, he grabbed my wrist and started pulling me toward the house, his grip tight and insistent. I stumbled along behind him, the rain pouring down, soaking through my clothes, but I barely noticed. My thoughts were consumed with what I had just heard and what it meant. What game was he talking about? What was coming for us in the woods?

"I need you to trust me," Vance said, his voice rough, as though the words were too difficult to say. "No matter what happens, don't look back."

I wanted to protest, wanted to ask why, wanted to scream at him to just tell me what was going on, but the look in his eyes—the fear, the desperation—shut me up. He wasn't the kind of man who showed fear. Not unless it was something serious.

We reached the door, and he shoved it open, dragging me inside. I barely had time to register the warmth of the interior before he slammed it shut behind us, locking it with a speed and efficiency that made it clear this wasn't the first time he'd done this.

I turned to face him, my breath coming in quick gasps. "What's happening, Vance? What is it? What's in those woods?"

His jaw tightened, but before he could answer, the sound of something heavy crashing against the door made both of us jump. The entire house shook, the walls groaning with the impact. My heart skipped a beat as I realized whatever was out there was no longer hiding.

Vance didn't hesitate. He turned to me, his face pale in the dim light, and whispered one word.

"Run."

Chapter 18: The Gathering Storm

The city hummed beneath my feet, a strange and uneasy vibration that seemed to echo in the marrow of my bones. The streets of Crescent City, usually alive with a pulse of purpose and possibility, now thrummed with the heavy weight of inevitability. The windows of the buildings shimmered with an eerie glow, their faces reflected like forgotten ghosts in the waning light. I could almost taste the electricity in the air—sharp, tangy, and thick with the promise of chaos.

Beside me, Vance stood like a monolith, his silhouette etched against the gathering twilight. I could feel the tension radiating off him in waves, and it settled in the pit of my stomach, making my heart flutter with something that was neither fear nor excitement. It was a blend of both, a heady mixture that made it difficult to focus, but I knew one thing for certain: I wasn't afraid.

I'd long since given up on the idea of being safe. The world we lived in, the one we fought for, was never built on security—it was built on resilience. The cracks we filled, the fights we won, they all led to this moment, and now it was too late to back away from it.

"Are you sure about this?" Vance's voice broke through the tension, low and gravelly, yet edged with something I couldn't quite place—concern, perhaps. Or maybe it was that familiar edge of protectiveness that had kept us tethered to each other since the first time we'd crossed paths.

I looked up at him, his sharp jawline cast in shadows, his eyes dark pools of stormy resolve. The corners of his mouth twitched, but there was nothing soft in his expression, nothing that resembled the easy humor he was capable of. We were both too far gone for that now. The enemy was coming, and we could either face them with our hearts beating as one or let fear tear us apart.

"I'm sure," I said, my voice steady, despite the tremor I felt in my chest. My fingers brushed the hilt of the dagger strapped to my side, the cool metal grounding me. It was a weapon that had seen too much bloodshed, but I had made it my own. "We don't have a choice."

He gave me a long look, searching for the cracks in my facade, the signs of doubt that I knew he'd find if I let him look long enough. But I had learned, over the years, how to guard those weaknesses, how to protect the fragile spaces inside me that he could so easily destroy with just a word. Still, I felt a pang of something—guilt, maybe—that I didn't want to share this burden with him. It was my fight, after all. But as he stepped closer, I knew he wouldn't let me go it alone.

"I never said we didn't," Vance muttered. He exhaled sharply, his breath clouding in the cool air. "But there's something in the air tonight, something that feels like the calm before the storm."

The wind picked up, carrying the scent of rain with it, but the sky remained stubbornly clear, as if holding its breath. The city had always been a place of contrasts—raw energy paired with ancient elegance, beauty twisted by the grind of constant survival—but tonight it felt different. The familiar hum of life was gone, replaced by the grinding gears of something darker, something that knew how to tear things apart.

And I wasn't sure I was ready for it. But there was no turning back.

"We'll handle it," I said firmly, more to myself than to him, though I felt his eyes on me, always watching, always waiting for me to slip. "We have to."

Behind us, the others were gathering, forming the ragged, bruised line of our resistance. My gaze flickered over them—some of the faces I knew well, others mere shadows of strangers who had been pulled into this war whether they'd asked for it or not. They stood tall, but there was no denying the weight in their eyes, the exhaustion that hung from their shoulders like invisible chains. We were all tired, but we weren't done yet.

"I'll hold the east side," said Kael, his voice cutting through the murmurs. He was tall and lean, the kind of man who always had a quiet smile ready for anyone who needed it. Except tonight, there was no smile. Only determination.

"I've got the west," said Mara, her dark hair whipping around her face as she surveyed the skyline. "We keep them from getting too close."

"We'll meet in the middle," Vance said, his tone commanding, the leader he was without even trying. I hadn't expected anything less.

I nodded. "And I'll take the front."

A collective shiver ran through the group at my words, though I could tell no one doubted the finality in them. We'd all chosen our positions, our roles in this battle. I wasn't the strategist or the diplomat—I was the one who went in first, the one who carried the weight of all their hopes on my shoulders. No pressure, right?

The wind kicked up again, a gust so strong that it nearly sent me stumbling. But I caught myself, tightening my grip on the dagger. The tension in the air thickened, and the first distant rumble of thunder reached our ears, a harbinger of the storm that was to come.

I turned to Vance, feeling his presence beside me like a steady flame against the storm. "Are we ready?"

He didn't answer right away. Instead, he reached over and touched my arm—just a brush of his fingers, but enough to send a jolt of warmth through me. His gaze softened, just for a moment, as if reminding me of everything we had already fought for.

"I don't know if anyone can ever be ready for something like this," he said, voice barely above a whisper. "But I'll be right behind you."

I took a deep breath and squared my shoulders. The night was about to break, and I would face it head-on, with nothing but my wits and my resolve. And the unwavering presence of those I called my family. Together, we would face the storm.

The streetlights flickered, casting sharp shadows that sliced through the quiet tension in the air. We were ready, or at least we thought we were. The city around us pulsed with life, a heartbeat steady but quickening, echoing in time with our own nervous anticipation. Even the stars seemed to hold their breath, their soft light barely enough to cast away the growing darkness as the horizon stretched out before us, endless and unyielding.

I turned to face the gathering at my side, the familiar faces of those who had walked this path with me. They stood close, yet there was a careful distance between us, an invisible line none of us dared to cross, not yet. It was a strange thing, this camaraderie built from years of survival—this bond that wove itself between us, silent and unspoken, like the pull of gravity.

"We don't have much time," Kael's voice broke through the heavy silence, rough and direct. "They'll be here soon."

I could see it in his eyes—the same fire that had burned in me the first time I had stepped into this fight. Determination was no longer enough; it had to be more. We had to be more. Each person here carried their own weight, their own personal demons that they had been dragging through this war. And still, they stood, their backs straight and their heads held high. It was a silent testament to everything we had already sacrificed, and everything we were about to lose.

"I know," I said, my voice surprisingly calm, as though the world hadn't just tilted on its axis, about to crash down upon us. "But we'll hold them off."

Mara gave a single nod, though I could see the uncertainty flickering in her eyes. She always wore her emotions like a heavy cloak, her every feeling as vivid as a painting splashed across a canvas. But tonight, even the bravest among us had their cracks. Even the fierce warriors in our ranks were unsure of what we were walking into.

Vance remained by my side, a quiet strength, as steady as the earth beneath our feet. His fingers brushed the side of my arm once more, as though reminding me that we were a unit, a single force tethered together by necessity, by choice, by fate. His silence spoke volumes, but even more was said in the way his eyes met mine—dark, intense, and yet warm, as though the world could end and he would still be standing beside me, his presence the only thing that anchored me to reality.

I couldn't help but smile despite the heaviness in the air. "Don't look so grim, Vance. We've been through worse."

His lips twitched into something close to a grin, but it didn't quite reach his eyes. "You've got a funny way of defining worse."

"You say that like I'm the one who likes to get into trouble."

A low chuckle rumbled in his chest. "I don't have to say it. You're a walking disaster zone."

"Hey," I shot back, half-serious, "I prefer to think of myself as a high-risk investment."

"High-risk," he repeated, shaking his head. "That's one way to look at it."

We both paused, our banter falling away as a fresh wave of tension surged between us. The laughter had faded quickly, but the warmth of the moment lingered, a brief reprieve from the anxiety clawing at my chest. As always, the world seemed more bearable when we could joke about it, even if that joke was a thin veil over everything else.

"They're close," Mara called out, her eyes narrowed as she scanned the horizon. "We need to move."

The finality in her tone cut through the air, and the momentary sense of comfort I had allowed myself vanished like smoke on the wind. We were here now, standing on the edge of something that had been years in the making, and it was impossible to ignore the reality of what was coming for us. The wind had picked up, and the sky above us darkened, casting long, grim shadows over the landscape. A low rumble of thunder rolled in the distance, but this time it didn't feel like nature's benign warning. It felt like the beginning of something far more dangerous.

I stood taller, my fingers tightening around the hilt of my dagger, and made my way toward the front of the line, the cold steel of it familiar beneath my touch. The weight of it was reassuring in its own way—nothing could change what was coming, but the blade in my hand was a constant, a promise that I would not go quietly into whatever storm was coming.

Vance followed close behind, his steady presence a constant reminder that I wasn't alone. I felt the eyes of our people on me—hopeful eyes, expectant eyes, the ones that had been with me from the start. They believed in me, and in some strange way, that made this moment even heavier. I couldn't afford to disappoint them. I couldn't afford to fail.

"We do this together," I said, turning to face them, my voice steady, my gaze unwavering. "We hold the line. No matter what."

The faces around me hardened, and I could see the fire rekindled in their eyes. It was a shared resolve, an unspoken understanding that, for all the fear and doubt that lingered in our minds, there was something stronger between us—a bond forged in the fire of battle, stronger than steel, stronger than any of us alone.

We formed our positions quickly, our movements sharp and efficient. I took my place at the forefront, where I could see the approaching storm—the distant shadows that were the enemy, growing closer with each passing second. I could feel it then, the unmistakable weight of the moment pressing down on me, thick and suffocating. My heart beat a little faster, the drum of it steady beneath the mounting tension. The air felt thick now, heavy with the scent of ozone, as if the storm had already begun to churn its fury.

A distant shout echoed across the city streets, and in that instant, I knew that there was no turning back. Whatever happened next, we were going to face it head-on, together. We would fight, or we would fall. But either way, we would go down with the city's heartbeat pulsing in our veins.

The first wave hit us with a ferocity I had not anticipated. It wasn't the thunderous clash I had expected—no dramatic clash of steel and flesh—but something quieter, more insidious. It was the whisper of motion in the dark, the sudden feeling that the ground beneath us had shifted, just enough to make everything feel wrong.

Vance was beside me instantly, his presence like a shield that steadied my nerves even as the hairs on the back of my neck stood on end. He didn't need to speak—his hand on my arm was enough, his fingers warm against my skin as he surveyed the line, scanning for threats with the deadly precision I had come to trust without question.

I wanted to look away, to pretend it wasn't happening, but I couldn't. The enemy was closing in, weaving through the narrow streets, their figures moving like shadows that blurred with the city itself. They were quick, too quick, and the darkness seemed to swallow them up, making it impossible to keep track of where they were, what they were doing.

"Stay sharp," Vance muttered, his breath a low hiss in my ear. "Don't let them get close."

I nodded, already reaching for my dagger as I scanned the perimeter. The air was thick, oppressive, as though the very atmosphere was holding its breath in anticipation. Every footfall sounded too loud, the distance between us and them closing with every passing second. My pulse quickened, matching the rhythm of my thoughts, which seemed to be racing ahead of me, wondering if we would survive this, wondering if any of us would make it out.

Suddenly, there was a blur of motion to my right. I barely had time to react before the figure lunged forward, a twisted mask of desperation in their eyes, hands outstretched, and teeth bared in a snarl. I didn't hesitate. I stepped forward, my blade a blur of silver in the moonlight, and the figure collapsed to the ground with a sickening thud, my heart hammering as I stood over them, chest heaving.

"We're not alone." The words tumbled from my mouth before I could stop them, and I could feel the weight of them settle on the air around us, thickening the silence.

Vance's gaze flicked over me, checking for injury, though his hands remained steady as he scanned the horizon. "I know," he said. There was no bravado in his voice, no false bravado. Only the grim understanding that we were surrounded, and that we needed to be more than we had ever been to survive.

"We have to move," Mara called from the left, her voice sharp, adrenaline tinging her words. "They're coming in from all sides."

Her warning was unnecessary. We were all aware now, each of us feeling the creeping inevitability that the fight was no longer just about defense—it was about survival. The streets were no longer a safe haven. They were a battleground, and the very ground beneath us seemed to shift with every passing moment, as though the city itself was turning against us.

Without a word, I motioned for Vance to follow me, my feet carrying me forward with purpose. My senses were on high alert now, every nerve firing at once, every muscle coiled tight, ready to spring into action. The sharp scent of sweat and steel filled my nostrils, and I could feel the weight of the city pressing down on me, a reminder that this was where it would all end—whether in victory or defeat.

We moved quickly, weaving through the alleys, staying low, staying quiet, like ghosts among the shadows. The city was a maze of its own making, its streets twisted and narrow, and for the first time, I cursed the familiarity I had once cherished. The enemy knew these streets as well as we did, if not better. And they knew how to use that knowledge to their advantage.

A shout rang out in the distance, sharp and high-pitched. The battle had already begun in earnest, but the sound was far too close for comfort. I turned to Vance, whose face had hardened into something like stone, his eyes unreadable in the dim light.

"I'm going in," I said, though it felt more like a declaration than a suggestion. The time for hesitating was long past.

Vance's jaw tightened, but he didn't argue. Instead, he grabbed my arm, his grip firm but not forceful, a reminder of how easily he could keep me in place. "I'm going with you," he said, his tone low, but there was no doubt in his voice.

"I work better alone," I shot back, not because I thought he couldn't handle himself, but because I couldn't afford to let anyone else's fate weigh on me tonight. It had always been this way with him—him, always there, always protective, always too much of everything I didn't know how to handle. But now, with the battle raging around us, I had to be ruthless. There was no room for distraction, no room for hesitation.

Vance didn't say a word, only nodded once, as though he understood. But I could feel the unease in his silence, the tension that was building between us. I knew him well enough to read the signs. He was holding back, not out of fear, but out of a deep, consuming need to protect me from whatever came next.

I took a deep breath, trying to focus. The air tasted like smoke, sharp and bitter, and the sky above us seemed to throb with the promise of more to come. It was no longer about the enemy we could see; it was about the one we couldn't. The one who was lurking just out of reach, waiting for the perfect moment to strike.

And strike they did.

A figure appeared in the alleyway ahead, so suddenly, so impossibly fast, I barely had time to react. Before I could even draw my blade, there was a flash of movement, and the world around me tilted violently. My body slammed against the cold stone of the wall, and I tasted blood before I even realized I had been hit.

I tried to push through the dizziness, tried to clear my mind, but before I could get my bearings, I heard Vance's voice—urgent, sharp, and filled with something raw.

"Watch out!"

And then, everything went dark.

Chapter 19: The Battle Within

The weight of the city's silence pressed against me like a thick fog. Every step I took along the cracked streets felt heavy, as though I was walking through water, the weight of the impending night sinking deeper into my bones. The city, once full of life and chatter, now seemed like a ghost of its former self. Shadows clung to every corner, every broken window, every alleyway that I passed, and the whispers of danger slipped through the cracks, curling around me like a noose.

I didn't know how we had arrived at this moment. The path had been so simple once, or so I had believed. Survival had been our goal—Vance and I, pushing through our grief and anger, surviving together. But now, I was standing on the precipice of something far more complicated. My heart had been torn open, shredded into pieces, each one pulling in a different direction. There was love, yes, that deep, familiar ache that connected me to him in ways I couldn't explain. But then there were the shadows—the ones that had always been there, growing ever darker and more threatening, tainting everything I thought I knew.

Vance's face, etched in my memory, had become both a comfort and a question mark. He was the fire, burning brightly in the darkness, yet sometimes I wondered if he would consume me whole. There was always something underneath that smile of his—something hard and cold, like ice running through his veins. His words, so carefully chosen, sometimes felt like knives disguised as promises.

"You're still thinking about it," Vance's voice broke through my thoughts, smooth and calm, but there was an edge to it, a crack of something deeper, something darker. I hadn't even heard him approach, but he was there now, leaning against the doorway like he owned the very air I breathed.

"I have no choice," I replied, not looking at him. The words hung in the air between us, thick with unsaid things.

"You're afraid, aren't you?" Vance's voice softened, a trace of something—sympathy?—lurking behind the sharpness. I couldn't tell if he was mocking me or if he genuinely cared. That was the trouble with Vance. You could never tell.

"I'm afraid of losing everything," I said finally, the truth slipping out before I could stop it. "Of losing you, of losing the city, of—"

He cut me off, his finger tracing the edge of my jawline in a motion that felt far too intimate for the gravity of the moment. "You don't have to lose anything. Not if you trust me."

Trust. It was such a fragile thing, and I wasn't sure I had it left to give. I had trusted him once, but everything had changed. People changed, and in this city, nothing ever stayed the same for long.

I pulled away, stepping back from him, needing space to breathe. The room felt smaller now, suffocating, the walls closing in with the weight of his proximity. "I don't know if I can do this anymore, Vance. The darkness—it's too much."

He didn't reply at first, just stared at me, those dark eyes of his calculating, unreadable. The silence between us stretched out like a chasm. The tension in the room crackled like static, a storm about to break.

"I know what you're thinking," he said finally, his voice low, almost a growl. "You're afraid of the future. You're afraid of what's coming. But we have to face it together. You can't walk away from this. From me."

There it was again—the weight of his words, the way he framed the situation like there was no other choice. And maybe there wasn't. My gut twisted with the knowledge that he was right. The city was about to burn, and I was tied to him in ways I couldn't escape, even if I wanted to.

"I don't have a choice," I murmured, more to myself than to him.

"You do," he replied, stepping closer again, his presence overwhelming. "You have a choice to fight. To stay by my side."

But I was so tired. The constant battles, the secrets we were both keeping, the way my own heart seemed to be splitting in two. How could I fight for a future when I wasn't even sure what that future looked like? What if the cost was too high? What if it was all a lie?

"Maybe I don't want to fight anymore," I whispered, the words trembling in the space between us.

Vance's face hardened, his jaw clenching. "You think you're the only one who's tired? You think this has been easy for me?" He reached out then, grabbing my wrist with a force that surprised me, pulling me toward him. "You think I'm not scared too? Every day, every hour, I wonder if this will be the day I lose you. But I'm still here. I'm still fighting, and I need you to do the same."

His grip on my wrist tightened, and I knew in that moment that he wasn't just holding me physically—he was holding me in every way possible. I could feel the weight of his need, the weight of his fears, and something inside me shifted. Maybe I was afraid. Maybe I wasn't ready. But I couldn't walk away from him, not now. Not when the city, and everything we cared about, was teetering on the edge of ruin.

I lifted my chin, meeting his gaze, the fire inside me burning once more. "I'm not walking away. I'm just... figuring out how to fight."

Vance's lips curled into a smile, that dangerous, knowing smile that made my heart stutter. "That's all I need to hear."

The storm was coming, and I knew, deep down, that this battle—this war for the city, for our lives—wasn't just about survival anymore. It was about something much deeper. Something we couldn't walk away from.

I had always imagined moments like this—those rare, apocalyptic moments where the fate of everything seemed to hang by the thinnest of threads. In the past, I'd always been a spectator of such stories, watching from the comfort of a safe distance, as heroes wrestled with their choices and saved the day. But here I was, no longer an observer. I was in the thick of it, tangled in the contradictions of love and duty, longing and fear, each of them pulling me in a hundred different directions. I wasn't just a pawn anymore. I was a player in a game I wasn't sure I knew how to win.

The streets outside were quiet, eerily so, considering the storm that was about to break over Crescent City. Everything felt brittle. The air, the buildings, even the ground beneath my feet. It was as if the city was holding its breath, waiting for the inevitable clash between what we'd tried to build and the darkness that had always loomed just beyond our borders.

I met Vance's gaze again, the flicker of something—fear?—passing between us like an electric current. It made me wonder if he felt the same weight, the same fear that I had buried deep down. The fear that we were about to lose everything, and that there would be no one left to pick up the pieces when the dust settled.

"You should go," I said, my voice barely above a whisper. It felt like a betrayal to say it out loud, but it was the truth. The thought of him out there, in the heart of the coming storm, made me sick. The selfish part of me wanted to pull him close, lock him away somewhere safe, and pretend that the world wasn't about to crumble at our feet.

Vance's expression softened, though the tension still clung to his every movement. He had that air about him, like a man who always knew more than he let on. "You think I don't want to protect you?" he asked, his voice low and intimate, just for me. "You think I haven't been running the same thoughts through my head for the last twenty-four hours?"

I shook my head, feeling that familiar knot tighten in my chest. "It's not just you. It's all of us." My voice cracked, and for a split second, I hated myself for showing weakness in front of him. "We're standing on the edge of something we can't control anymore. And I don't know if I can keep fighting, Vance. Not like this."

He stepped closer, his hand brushing the side of my arm. "You think I know how to fight? You think I have all the answers? Hell, I barely know what's coming next. But I know this much: we fight together, or we don't fight at all."

His words were like a lifeline, pulling me back from the edge I'd been teetering on. He was right. I wasn't alone in this, even if it often felt that way. We'd both been born from chaos, raised by a world that had always demanded more than we had to give. But there was something in Vance's eyes that made me believe, just for a moment, that we could weather this storm together.

And yet, there was the ever-looming question that gnawed at me like a hungry wolf: What if he was lying to me? What if this wasn't about us, about love, about survival? What if the storm was just the beginning of something darker, something neither of us could escape?

I didn't have an answer. And maybe that was the point.

Vance reached out then, his fingers brushing against my cheek in a touch so soft it almost felt like a dream. "I can't promise you we'll win this, love. But I can promise you this: I'm not letting you go. Not now, not ever."

I closed my eyes, feeling the weight of his words sink into me like they were a part of my very skin. I didn't know if I could believe him. But I wanted to. I wanted to believe in him, in us, in the possibility of a future where we were more than just two broken souls clinging to each other for survival.

The sound of footsteps echoed down the hallway, and I knew it was time. Time to stop pretending we had any control over the path we were about to walk. Time to face whatever horrors the night had in store.

"We should go," I said, my voice steadier now, despite the tremble in my hands. "We can't keep waiting."

Vance gave me a small, rueful smile, as if to acknowledge the truth in my words, but he didn't argue. He didn't need to. His hand found mine, pulling me along behind him as we moved toward the door.

The air outside felt different—colder, sharper, as if the world had somehow braced itself for the collision that was coming. I could feel the tension in the city, a subtle hum of fear and anticipation that threaded through every corner, every crevice, every heart. We weren't the only ones who could sense it. Everyone was bracing for impact, unsure of what would be left when it finally came.

As we walked side by side through the desolate streets, I could hear the distant sounds of movement—the city's last efforts to prepare for the fight ahead. The flicker of lights in the distance, the hum of engines, the soft murmur of voices, all drowned beneath the weight of the approaching battle. It was as though the city was holding its breath with us, unsure of whether it could survive what was coming.

"Are you ready?" Vance asked, his voice low, his breath visible in the frigid air.

I didn't answer immediately. What was there to say? Was anyone truly ready for this?

"Do I have a choice?" I finally muttered, my voice sharp, but with a trace of humor—because if I didn't laugh, I might cry.

Vance chuckled softly, squeezing my hand. "Guess not."

And so, together, we stepped into the unknown, the tension in the air thick enough to choke on, the weight of our decisions pulling us forward, toward a future we couldn't predict, but couldn't avoid.

The city had never looked more alive—and yet more dead—than it did that night. As I walked beside Vance, our feet barely making a sound on the cracked pavement, the weight of the world settled on my shoulders like a cloak I didn't want to wear, but had no choice but to. The air was thick with tension, and not just from the battle that loomed on the horizon. The whole city seemed to be on the edge, held together by nothing more than the collective hope that we could somehow, against all odds, survive. But survival was never guaranteed, not for any of us.

The glow of the distant streetlights was dim, flickering as though they, too, knew something was wrong. The wind had picked up, carrying the scent of rain and something else, something metallic, that made the hairs on the back of my neck stand at attention. In the distance, the sound of an engine roared, too loud and too urgent to be anything but a warning.

Vance's hand brushed against mine, a fleeting touch, but the weight of it was undeniable. His presence, both comforting and unsettling, hovered beside me like a shadow. I didn't know how to feel about him anymore. Each time I thought I understood him, another layer of mystery peeled away, leaving me more unsure of what was real and what was illusion. Was he truly fighting for me, for us, or was this all just part of the game?

I glanced at him, trying to read his expression, but it was as unreadable as ever. His jaw was clenched, eyes scanning the surroundings with a sharp intensity. He'd always been the one to take charge, to plan, to dictate the moves. But tonight, I wasn't sure what we were up against—or who was in control anymore.

"You're thinking too much," Vance said, his voice low but sharp enough to pull me from my spiraling thoughts. "Stop it."

I huffed, incredulous. "What, you think I can just switch it off? That's not how my brain works, Vance."

He shot me a side glance, a trace of a smirk curling the corner of his lips. "I know. But it's exhausting, watching you twist yourself into knots over something that's already decided."

The words stung more than I wanted to admit. "What's decided?" I asked, my voice tight, betraying the unease gnawing at me. "That we're doomed to repeat every mistake we've ever made?"

Vance stopped in his tracks, turning to face me fully. "You're not the only one who's scared, you know. I'm not exactly skipping through fields of daisies here." His hand reached out, cupping my face gently, the warmth of his skin seeping through the layers of my doubt. "But if we keep fighting—if we keep choosing each other—then maybe, just maybe, we'll make it through this. Alive."

I swallowed hard, the words he spoke both a comfort and a curse. Alive. The barest possibility that we might survive this was enough to make my chest ache, but it also felt like a lie. Survival didn't come without a price, and I was beginning to wonder just how much we were willing to pay.

The silence between us was thick, heavy with the weight of everything we weren't saying. The city stretched out before us, its darkened streets yawning wide, as though it, too, was holding its breath. And then, like a crack of thunder, the first blast of gunfire rang out in the distance.

The sound sent a shock through my veins, snapping me to attention. Vance's eyes were locked on mine, his grip tightening just enough to anchor me to him. "It's starting," he muttered, and for the first time tonight, there was something in his voice that wasn't just confidence—it was fear. "Get ready."

The sound of boots pounding the pavement filled the air, and we were off, running through the streets in a blur of motion and adrenaline. The world around us seemed to melt into a haze of shapes and shadows, the sounds of battle ringing louder with every step we took. The distant explosions rumbled beneath our feet, shaking the ground with each blast. My heart pounded in my chest, each beat a reminder that there was no turning back now. No escape from the chaos that was descending on the city.

We reached the main square, the heart of Crescent City, where the fighting had already begun in full force. Shadows moved with deadly precision, flashes of steel and fire lighting up the night. I could barely make out the figures ahead of us, but I knew enough to recognize the bloodshed, the violence, the raw, unchecked desperation. This was no longer just about us—it was about survival for everyone who had dared to remain.

Vance pulled me close, his hand around my wrist like a vice. "Stay close," he ordered, his voice low and urgent.

I nodded, though the panic clawing at me threatened to swallow me whole. There was no plan. Not anymore. Just fight, just survive, just make it through. That was all we had left.

The first clash was brutal. The impact of bodies crashing into each other, the scream of metal against metal, the snap of bone as the world around us turned into a war zone. I swung my knife in a wide arc, the blade biting into flesh, but my mind was miles away, lost in the chaos, in the whirling noise, in the fight that had somehow become more than just about the city. It was about us now—me, Vance, the twisted tangle of feelings and fear that bound us together.

And then, in the middle of it all, I saw him. A figure moving in the shadows, too tall to be anyone I recognized. The flicker of his coat was too familiar, his posture too deliberate. My heart skipped a beat.

No.

Not now. Not here.

Vance must have seen the shift in my expression, the way my body stiffened, because he pulled me tighter to his side, his voice harsh in my ear. "What is it?"

I couldn't speak. I couldn't move. All I could do was stare at the figure who had no business being here. The one who was supposed to be dead. The one who knew too much.

And then, like a phantom out of the darkness, the figure stepped forward—and smiled.

Chapter 20: The Climax of Chaos

The sky hung low over Crescent City, thick and bruised, the air heavy with the promise of a storm that didn't just threaten the weather. The streets buzzed beneath my feet, the hum of life and fear intertwined like a tangled knot. I hadn't slept in days—not that I could've managed it even if I'd tried. Every corner I turned seemed to pulse with an invisible current, the weight of what was coming pressing in on me from all sides. I could feel Vance beside me, his silence a kind of comforting presence, but there was a sharp edge to him tonight, something tight in the way his hand brushed mine as we walked through the darkened streets. We didn't speak much. Words felt like they might shatter the fragile armor of resolve I had been carefully building all day.

The shadows stretched long across the alleyways, but the flickering lamps lining the streets seemed to offer no real warmth, only a dim suggestion of security that made the hairs on the back of my neck stand on end. The closer we got to the center of town, the more the city felt like it was holding its breath, waiting for something terrible to happen. It wasn't a coincidence that tonight had become the night. The pieces had been falling into place for weeks, each step a calculated move in a game that none of us wanted to play.

Vance's voice, low and strained, broke through the tension. "You're sure you want to do this? We don't have to go in right away." He didn't meet my eyes. I could tell he was waiting for me to say something—anything that would justify pulling back, delaying it just a little longer. But I knew what needed to be done. There was no more time for hesitation.

I turned to him, my breath a mist in the chilly air. "I don't think we have the luxury of time anymore. If we wait any longer, we lose everything." The words tasted like iron, bitter and unyielding, but I meant them. We had no choice but to go forward. There was a strange sense of inevitability in the air, like the city itself had been waiting for us to take that final step. "Besides, it's not just about us anymore. It's about everyone who's been hurt because of this—everyone who's lost something they'll never get back."

He was quiet for a moment, his jaw tight as he stared ahead, eyes scanning the streets, always on guard. I could see it in the way he moved—every step a calculation, every glance a warning. But the truth was, he'd never wanted this for me. He didn't want me tangled in the mess we were walking into. And I wasn't sure if that made me more determined or more terrified.

"We're going to make it through this," I said, almost to myself. The words felt like a promise I couldn't break, even though a part of me wondered if I was lying to myself just to keep moving forward.

He glanced at me then, a small, almost imperceptible shift in his expression, something between understanding and caution. "You say that like it's a guarantee." His voice was soft, but the weight behind it pressed down on me, like the entire city was holding its breath alongside us.

"I don't know if it is," I admitted. "But we don't get to choose the outcome. We just get to decide how we face it."

A low rumble of thunder rolled across the sky, echoing through the narrow streets. The storm had arrived, though not the kind of storm that had clouds and rain. This one was much darker. The kind of storm that settled in your chest and stayed there, gnawing at your insides until you couldn't tell where it began and you ended.

We rounded a corner and there it was—the heart of the city, where it all began. The building loomed ahead, its stark silhouette against the backdrop of the storm like a dagger poised to strike. My stomach tightened. I could feel the pulse of power thrumming in the air around it, thick with danger and history. This was it. The place that had birthed every nightmare we'd been running from. The place where it would all end.

I stopped just outside the entrance, my heart thudding in my chest, the weight of every decision pressing down on me. Vance stopped beside me, his hand brushing mine again, but this time there was no hesitation. He was with me, for better or worse. And whatever happened in that building, whatever unfolded in the next few hours, I knew it would change us. I could only hope we'd be strong enough to survive it.

"You ready?" Vance asked, his voice tight, but there was something else in it too—something like an unspoken promise. No matter what happened, we would face it together.

I nodded, swallowing the lump in my throat. "Let's end this."

The doors creaked open as we stepped inside. The air inside was thick, stifling—like the building itself had been holding its breath, waiting for us to arrive. Shadows moved in the corners, shapes that didn't belong, whispers that felt far too close.

Every sense in me screamed to turn back, but I didn't. Because this was the only way forward. And this time, I wasn't running anymore.

The moment we crossed the threshold, the air changed. The building's interior smelled like age—dust mingled with a bitter scent that lingered like forgotten secrets. I could almost taste it on my tongue, a tang of something metallic, as if the past had left its mark on the very walls. The corridors ahead stretched long and narrow, a labyrinth of shadows that beckoned with eerie silence. No creak of wood, no footstep echoing off the stone—just the press of the air against my skin, the kind that made your heartbeat sound too loud, too desperate.

Vance's hand brushed against my arm, and I startled, though I tried to hide it. I hadn't realized how much of me had been coiled tight, waiting for something to jump out at us. He raised an eyebrow, the corner of his mouth curling slightly, the look in his eyes a mix of affection and irritation.

"You alright?" His voice was low, the edges rough from hours of tension. He had that look—the one he always wore when he thought I was about to crack. It was maddening, but endearing.

I forced a smirk, stepping further into the darkness. "What, you think I'm going to fall apart at the first sign of trouble?"

His lips quirked upward in a way that made my heart stutter. "I know better than that," he said, then glanced around. "Just... be careful. We both know who's waiting for us."

I couldn't argue with that. Not when the very building seemed to pulse with a cold, invisible presence. There was no one here—not yet, anyway—but the silence screamed. I didn't need to hear footsteps or voices to know that we weren't alone. It was the kind of stillness that spoke louder than any words could. It whispered of things watching, waiting, ready to pounce when we least expected it.

We moved through the halls in tandem, every step deliberate, every breath a slow exhale that sounded far too loud in the quiet. I tried not to think about the doors we passed, each one a potential trap, each room an unspoken promise of what was to come. My hands were clammy, heart pounding against my ribs. But I kept my eyes forward. No looking back. No hesitation.

There was a sharp turn ahead, and I could see the faintest flicker of light from beneath a door at the end of the hall. The room beyond wasn't a surprise. I knew what was waiting for us. It was the very heart of everything we'd been running from—the control room, the nerve center. The place where all the strings had been pulled. The place where our fate had been sealed before we even realized it.

Vance stopped just before the door, raising a hand. I halted beside him, the tension between us thick enough to choke on. "This is it," he muttered, eyes scanning the door's edges. "Stay sharp."

I nodded, though my throat had gone dry. "Always."

He reached for the handle, but before he could turn it, the door swung open on its own, the hinges protesting with a loud, grating screech that cut through the stillness like a knife. I felt the weight of the moment settle on my shoulders, the space between anticipation and action narrowing to a sliver of nothing.

Inside, it was dim, lit by the soft glow of monitors and old-fashioned lamps. The space was an odd mix of chaos and control, as if it had once been meticulously organized but now was falling apart at the seams. Papers were strewn across the floor, chairs overturned, and the once-pristine desk sat at an angle, as if someone had been in a hurry to leave—or to destroy everything. But what stood out the most was the figure standing by the far wall, silhouetted in the gloom.

He was waiting for us, as expected. And when he turned, I felt a chill crawl down my spine. Not because of his appearance, though he was striking in a way that unsettled me, but because of the sheer weight of recognition that settled in my gut. The person standing before us wasn't just an enemy. He was someone I knew—someone I thought I could trust.

"Vance. Kiera," he said, his voice smooth, cold. "I was wondering when you'd come."

I couldn't move, couldn't breathe, as the truth settled like stone in my stomach. "You?" My voice cracked, the shock of seeing him here, now, in this place, was almost too much to process. "How? Why?"

He smiled, but it was the kind of smile that didn't reach his eyes. "You really didn't think it would be that simple, did you?" The words dripped with disdain, but there was something more—something beneath them, something darker. "You should've known. You've been a pawn in this game since the beginning."

I blinked, trying to steady myself, trying to think clearly. "You've been playing us this whole time?" My voice was barely above a whisper, the disbelief knotting itself tighter in my chest.

The man before us chuckled, taking a slow step forward. "Not just you. Everyone. The city, the factions... they were never meant to be allies. They were always meant to fall apart, just like everything else."

Vance's hand twitched beside me, but he didn't make a move. Instead, he stood still, eyes narrowing, lips pressed tight. I could see the muscle in his jaw working, the controlled anger boiling just beneath the surface. "You're the one behind all of it," he muttered, almost as if to himself. "You were the architect."

He didn't deny it. In fact, he seemed almost amused by the revelation, like he'd been waiting for us to piece it together. "It was never about who wins or loses," he said softly. "It was always about watching it all burn."

And then, without warning, the floor beneath us seemed to shift, the room around us beginning to hum with a low vibration that I could feel in my bones. Something was happening, something I couldn't see but could feel tightening around us. And in that moment, I realized something worse than the betrayal we were facing—it was that we hadn't even begun to understand the full scope of what we were dealing with.

The hum that had started as a soft vibration beneath our feet was now a throbbing pulse, resonating through the walls, the floor, even the air around us. It felt like the very building was alive, a monstrous beast slowly waking from a long slumber. I could feel the ground shifting, the faintest tremors, but they were enough to make my skin crawl. My heart was racing, but it wasn't just fear—it was the kind of adrenaline that comes with knowing you've crossed a line and there's no going back. The man standing before us, the one I had trusted, now stood as the architect of everything we'd been fighting. His smirk widened, his eyes gleaming with a satisfaction that was both chilling and utterly disorienting.

"I knew you'd be surprised," he said, his voice sliding through the air like a snake. "But you've always been a little slow to catch on. Too trusting. It's why this plan has worked for so long."

Vance's jaw tightened, the muscles working beneath his skin, but his expression remained unchanged—stone, cold, impenetrable. I could feel the weight of his anger, his disbelief, the years of careful restraint unraveling in tiny threads. I knew what he wanted to do. The same thing I wanted to do: rush forward, tear the smug look off his face, and demand how it all came to this. But something told me that wasn't the answer. Not this time. I could sense the danger hanging in the air like smoke—thick and suffocating—and I didn't want to make a move until I knew exactly what was happening.

"What's the endgame?" I asked, forcing my voice to stay steady. "You've got us here, you've got the city under your thumb. What do you want from this?"

He chuckled, a sound that grated on my nerves, like fingernails against glass. "Endgame? Oh, Kiera. There is no endgame. There's just the game. The destruction. The chaos. It's all part of the plan. It always has been."

"You're insane," I muttered, the words slipping out before I could stop them. It felt too easy to say it, too easy to dismiss him as nothing more than a delusional lunatic. But the problem was, he didn't seem insane at all. He seemed perfectly in control, every word, every movement calculated.

The room shifted again, the humming sound now growing louder, vibrating through my chest. I pressed a hand to the wall, steadying myself, trying to think. Trying to piece together the puzzle that had felt so right in its simplicity before, but now seemed shattered into a thousand jagged fragments.

"You really thought you had it all figured out, didn't you?" he continued, his voice like a slow drizzle of poison. "All of you—so certain you were making the right decisions. So certain you had the moral high ground. But the truth, Kiera, is much more complicated than you realize. You're just as trapped as the rest of them."

His words hung in the air, thick and suffocating, like smoke from a fire you couldn't see. I felt it in my bones, that familiar sensation—the realization that everything I thought I knew had been a lie. I wanted to push it away, wanted to fight the suffocating weight of his words, but the truth was gnawing at me, gnawing at my insides like a bitter taste I couldn't wash away. He was right in one thing: we had always been just one step behind him. We had been moving forward, but not because we were winning, only because he had allowed us to.

"You really think the destruction of the city is the goal?" Vance finally spoke, his voice cutting through the silence. "You think all this suffering is worth it for some grand design?"

The man's smile faded slightly, as if he was growing tired of the conversation. "Not all of us want to live in a world of rules, Vance. Some of us are more than willing to watch it all burn to the ground if it means we get to create something new from the ashes." He stepped closer, the confidence in his movements unsettling. "The thing is, you two never understood what I wanted. You thought you could save this place, keep it whole. But people like me? We're born for chaos. And chaos is coming. Whether you're ready or not."

I took a step back, my head spinning as his words echoed in my mind. "You're telling me this is all just a game for you? That you've been playing with people's lives for nothing more than a sense of control?"

He tilted his head slightly, eyes narrowing as though he were studying me, assessing my reaction. "You still don't get it, do you? Control isn't the end. It's just the beginning. I've watched every move you've made, Kiera. I've known what you'd do before you did it." He looked at Vance then, his smile returning, sharp and cold. "I knew how you'd react. I knew how she'd react. Everything is going exactly as planned."

The world around us seemed to shift again, the vibrations in the floor stronger now, more insistent. I glanced at Vance, but he was staring at the man with that same calculating expression he always wore before he made a move. But this time, something was different. This time, I could feel the weight of the moment. Something was coming, something that we weren't prepared for. And I couldn't help but wonder if we had already lost.

The hum of the building grew louder, and suddenly the air was thick, dense with an energy I couldn't explain. The walls seemed to pulse, the light flickering as if the building itself was alive, aware of our presence. I felt my pulse quicken, a knot of dread tightening in my stomach. I wasn't sure if it was the storm outside or the chaos inside that was driving me mad, but I had a terrible feeling that we were standing on the edge of something far worse than we had anticipated.

And just as the ground beneath us seemed to shift again, a voice rang out, echoing through the room. But this time, it wasn't the man in front of us who spoke.

It was something else entirely.

Chapter 21: Unmasking the Villain

I never imagined that the truth could taste like ash in the mouth. There we were, in the midst of it all—the scattered pieces of the puzzle finally aligning, clicking into place with an eerie precision. But as I looked at Vance, standing next to me with his jaw clenched and his eyes narrowed, I realized something. The weight of the revelation wasn't just heavy—it was suffocating. The truth had a face, and it belonged to someone I once trusted.

"You've got to be kidding me," I said, my voice barely above a whisper. "No way."

Vance's gaze met mine, and for a moment, the air between us grew thick with the unsaid. The kind of silence that made the walls feel like they were closing in. "It's true," he replied, his tone rough, raw. "It's all true."

We were standing in the very room where it all began—where the first whispers of betrayal had crept into our lives, staining everything they touched. The cold, sterile lighting above us flickered, casting long shadows against the walls, and for the briefest of moments, I wondered if I had imagined all of this. If this tangled mess of lies, deceit, and manipulation had been a product of my overactive mind.

But then I saw the papers scattered across the desk, the files with names, dates, and sinister plans carefully documented. Every line, every detail, was an unholy testament to the damage one person could inflict from the shadows. The person we'd never suspected, the one we'd never thought capable of such cold, calculated evil.

"It's not possible," I muttered again, the words tasting foreign as they slipped from my lips. My head spun with the implications. This was the last person I would have ever pegged for being involved in something like this.

Vance stepped forward, his boots clicking softly against the polished floor, the sound impossibly loud in the silence. "It makes sense," he said, though his voice was rough as though he were still digesting it himself. "All those little things that didn't add up—the way they always seemed one step ahead of us, the way they were always in the right place at the right time."

I nodded slowly, my eyes tracing the papers again, the truth slithering beneath the surface of my thoughts. The pieces fit too well. It was all too perfect a picture—everything falling into place like dominoes that had been set up over months, if not years. "But why?" The question tumbled out before I could stop it, my frustration finally breaking through. "Why would they do this? To us, of all people?"

Vance ran a hand through his hair, a gesture that was as close to defeat as I'd ever seen him. "I don't know," he said, his voice losing some of its usual edge. "But whatever the reason, it's big. Bigger than we could've imagined."

I let the silence stretch between us, feeling the weight of the moment press down. The idea of the betrayal was dizzying. I wanted to scream, to rage, to do anything but stand there like a helpless spectator in my own life. It was too much, too overwhelming. But I couldn't look away. I had to face it, even if it felt like it might swallow me whole.

The sharp sound of a phone ringing broke through the tension, the noise cutting through the air like a blade. I glanced at the screen, my heart skipping a beat when I saw the name flashing across it. "It's them," I said, my voice tight with dread.

Vance didn't need to ask who I meant. "Take it," he ordered, his hand already reaching into his jacket pocket for his own phone. We had no idea what to expect now—what other secrets were waiting to be dragged into the light.

I answered on the second ring, the connection crackling in my ear. "Hello?" My voice was shaky, but I steadied it quickly. No room for weakness now. Not with the world crumbling around me.

The voice on the other end was smooth, too smooth. "Well, well, well," the voice purred, a note of amusement in the tone. "I see you've figured it out. I was hoping it wouldn't be this messy, but here we are."

I felt my stomach churn. "You," I said, the word feeling like poison on my tongue. "How long? How long have you been behind all of this?"

There was a long pause, followed by the softest chuckle. "You're a bit slow on the uptake, aren't you? But I suppose that's to be expected. Let's just say I've been watching you... both of you... for a very long time."

My fingers clenched around the phone, my knuckles going white. "Why? What do you want from us?"

"Oh, I don't want anything from you," the voice replied, as though I were asking the most trivial of questions. "I simply wanted to make sure you understood your place. That's all. You see, in the end, everything is a game. And I'm very good at playing it."

The connection cut abruptly, leaving only a hollow silence in its wake. My breath came in shallow gasps, my mind racing. "They were playing us," I whispered, the words coming out more like a prayer than a statement. "This whole time, it was all just a game to them."

Vance's jaw tightened. "And we were the pawns," he said, his voice a low growl. "But not anymore. We're done being played."

I nodded, feeling the fire start to rise inside me, a slow burn that was both terrifying and exhilarating. "No more games. No more secrets. It's time we ended this."

Vance's eyes met mine, the promise of vengeance in them. It was a fire I'd never seen before, but it mirrored the one growing in my own chest. The truth was out. The enemy had been revealed. And there was nothing left to do now but fight back.

The walls of the room seemed to close in around me as I sank into the nearest chair, the overwhelming weight of it all pressing down, suffocating. The glow from the desk lamp illuminated the papers scattered like confetti—each one a sliver of the truth, each one a reminder of how badly we had been outmaneuvered. The phone call had shattered the last of my illusions. The game had never been about us. We were just the means to an end, pawns in a carefully calculated maneuver that stretched back further than I could comprehend.

Vance stood across from me, still seething, but his anger had taken on a quiet edge, like a blade held in check. His hands were clenched at his sides, his entire posture tight with the kind of restraint that could snap at any second. He was always the composed one, the one who kept his cool in the face of a storm. But this—this was something new. This was personal.

I wasn't sure how long we stood there in the silence, both of us lost in the aftermath, but finally, Vance broke it with a soft sigh. "We need to talk to them," he said, the words as raw as the emotion in his voice. "Face to face."

It sounded so simple, yet it felt like a thousand pounds had settled on my chest at the thought. To confront the person who had pulled every string, twisted every emotion, and left us scrambling like fools—it was almost too much to fathom. The fear, the rage, the betrayal. It was a cocktail of emotions that had my head spinning.

"What are we going to say?" I asked, my voice shakier than I liked. It didn't matter how much we'd uncovered, how many times we'd gone over the evidence—this moment was going to change everything. We were about to face the architect of our misery. No one, not even Vance, could predict how that would feel.

"We'll ask them why," he said, his tone firm now, resolved. "And if they don't answer? We'll make them."

I nodded, a faint sense of purpose starting to creep back into my veins. This was no longer about surviving the chaos. This was about ending it. But as I stared at Vance, something gnawed at me. Something I couldn't quite shake. A nagging feeling that this confrontation, this inevitable showdown, would reveal far more than we were ready to face. We had already exposed the puppet master's identity, but the more I thought about it, the more I realized that the truth of this person's motives wasn't just a mystery—it was a mirror reflecting things about us we hadn't yet acknowledged.

The drive to their house was unnervingly quiet. The car's engine hummed in the background, but it felt like the world outside had stilled. No birds singing, no breeze to ruffle the trees. Just the quiet suffocating silence that seemed to settle in every space I entered lately. Every mile that passed seemed to lengthen the distance between the past I thought I knew and the truth that was now crumbling everything in its wake.

We didn't talk during the drive. There wasn't much to say. We both knew what we were walking into. Every mile felt heavier than the last, and by the time we reached the familiar gates of the house—our destination—it felt like a dream. Or a nightmare. I wasn't sure which.

I glanced at Vance, expecting to see the calm determination that usually settled on his face. Instead, his expression was blank, like he was bracing for impact. I had no idea how this would play out, and neither did he. But something in the air had changed, and it wasn't just the proximity to our enemy. It was the way the past, the present, and the future were now tangled together, knots that couldn't be undone.

We pulled up in front of the house, the tall iron gates creaking open as we drove through, the stone driveway stretching ahead like a tunnel. The house loomed in front of us, grand and imposing, a place that had once felt like a sanctuary to me. But now, it felt like the lair of a serpent.

I could feel my pulse hammering in my throat as we parked and got out of the car. The evening sky had darkened, casting long shadows that seemed to stretch out toward us, pulling us deeper into whatever this was going to be. A soft wind ruffled my hair, but it was the chill in the air that made me shiver.

Vance was already moving toward the door, his steps measured and sure. He didn't look back at me, but I could feel the tension in his movements, like he was a coiled spring ready to snap. I hurried to catch up, the heels of my boots clicking against the stone as I matched his pace.

The door opened before we even had a chance to knock, and there they were—standing in the doorway, the person who had masterminded all of this, the one whose face had become both a symbol of trust and treachery in my mind. It was surreal, seeing them like this, so close, so... human.

"Come in," the voice was smooth, too smooth, and I hated how much it sounded like a command. Like they were the one in control of everything, and we were the ones about to fall into their hands.

Vance didn't hesitate. He walked in without a word, his presence filling the space, and I followed behind, the air thick with unspoken words. This was it. The confrontation. There was no going back.

And yet, as I stepped into the room, something inside me froze. The familiar comfort of this place, the elegant decor, the quiet luxury—it all suddenly felt so alien. A stage set for a play I didn't want to participate in. But I was here now. And I had no choice but to play my part.

"So," the voice continued, a sly smile playing at the corner of their lips. "You've finally come. I was wondering how long it would take."

The smile that curled at the edges of their lips was nothing short of maddening. It was a perfect blend of satisfaction and mockery, the kind that only someone who had watched every move, orchestrated every failure, could wear. "So," they repeated, their voice lilting as if nothing in the world could be more delightful than this moment, "you've finally come. I was wondering how long it would take."

It was hard to breathe, harder still to think. Standing there, across the threshold of the very place that had once felt like home, my mind was a battleground—every rational thought was fighting against the growing unease that gripped my chest. This was it. The moment of confrontation, where there would be no more questions, only answers I wasn't sure I was ready to hear.

Vance, still as stone, crossed his arms and gave them a look that could slice through steel. "Enough games," he said, his voice clipped. "You've had your fun. Now it's time to explain yourself."

The air between us seemed to freeze as they leaned casually against the doorframe, a picture of grace under pressure. "Explain myself?" they repeated, an eyebrow arching as though they were amused by the very notion. "My dear Vance, I think you've misunderstood. You weren't meant to understand. None of you were. You're part of something far bigger than your little lives could ever imagine."

A shiver ran down my spine, but I fought to hold my ground. This was no longer about playing catch-up, no longer about trying to keep up with a mystery that was far too big. It was about putting an end to it, once and for all. "So this was never about us," I said, keeping my voice steady, even though my heart raced. "We were just... pawns?"

The word felt heavy, like a stone lodged in my throat. To think, all this time I had believed we were making progress, that we were solving a puzzle. But it had all been a lie. A carefully orchestrated lie, wrapped in the guise of friendship, trust, even love.

"Precisely," they replied, as though discussing the weather. "You were never meant to understand. Just follow the script. But I must admit, I'm impressed. You've lasted longer than I anticipated."

I wanted to scream, to lash out with every bitter word that had built up inside me over the months. But Vance's hand on my arm stilled me, grounding me. His presence next to me was the only thing keeping me tethered to reality, to some semblance of control.

"Enough," Vance said again, his voice taking on a note of finality, one I'd rarely heard before. "Why did you do it? Why drag us through all this madness?"

Their smile softened, turning almost wistful. "Why? Oh, darling," they said, pushing off the doorframe and strolling across the room with an unnerving ease, "because I could. Because I knew that the only way to truly understand people, to control them, is to strip away everything they think they know. And once I had you both in my grip—well, I knew you'd never see it coming."

I blinked, my mind struggling to catch up with their words. It was all a game, a long con, stretching across years of manipulation. But the longer I stood there, the more it became clear: this wasn't just about control. This was personal. It was a vendetta, a sick need to tear apart the very fabric of our lives, to destroy everything we believed in.

"You had no reason to drag us into this," I said, my voice breaking the silence. "We were never part of your plan."

"That's where you're wrong," they said, their voice lowering, and I could hear the steel beneath the silk. "You were always part of it. From the very beginning."

I felt the ground shift beneath me, the weight of their words settling over me like a storm cloud. The pieces that had once seemed separate, incongruent, now began to lock together. I thought of the small, seemingly random moments—those subtle manipulations, the too-perfect coincidences. They had orchestrated it all, woven it into the fabric of our lives, knowing exactly how we would react, knowing exactly where we would go wrong. It had all been carefully planned.

"And the worst part," they continued, their voice a soft, venomous whisper, "was watching you two play right into it. You were so eager to solve the puzzle. But some things, some truths, are better left unsaid. Don't you think?"

I wanted to retort, wanted to scream that they were insane. But the chill in the room, the quiet certainty in their eyes, made me hesitate. What if this was just the beginning? What if there were layers upon layers of manipulation, secrets even darker than this?

Vance took a step forward, his jaw set. "You think you've won?" he asked, his voice low but dangerous. "You think you've got us exactly where you want us?"

"Oh, I don't think," they said, a wicked glint in their eye. "I know."

The atmosphere seemed to crackle with a tension so thick I could almost taste it. I took a slow breath, forcing myself to stay calm, forcing myself to focus. This was the moment—the moment when we either gave in or fought back.

Vance's hand brushed mine, a brief, steadying gesture. "We're not leaving until you tell us everything," he said, his voice hard with resolve. "Everything."

A moment of silence passed, the world holding its breath as they studied us, sizing up what was left of our resolve. Then, with a slow, deliberate motion, they reached for something from the desk—an envelope, thick and sealed. They tossed it onto the table between us with an almost lazy flourish.

"Then you'll want to open this," they said, their voice colder now. "Because once you do, everything you think you know will unravel. And I do mean everything."

I stared at the envelope, its weight more than just paper. It was a promise. A threat. A revelation I wasn't sure I was ready to face.

Chapter 22: The Ties That Bind

The rain hadn't stopped for days. It fell in a steady, relentless downpour, washing away the world outside until it felt as though we were trapped in a glass bubble. The constant drumming on the roof and the fog clinging to the windows only added to the tension that simmered between us.

The fire crackled in the hearth, its warmth fighting the chill that seemed to creep into every corner of the house. But even the flames couldn't melt the icy distance that had settled between Vance and me. Every word, every glance felt charged, like we were both waiting for the storm to break. The space between us, once comfortable and easy, now felt suffocating. I had made my choice. I had walked away from the possibility of a future with him. The truth was too dangerous, too raw, and something told me that neither of us were ready for it.

I had learned to love him in pieces, little by little, until the fragments of my heart that had once been whole were now tangled up in him. But I was a fool if I thought walking away would unmake that love. It had already taken root, deep inside me, its roots twining themselves around my ribs, squeezing whenever he was near. And I had thought I could control it, keep it from spreading. I was wrong.

The door creaked open, and his silhouette appeared in the frame, blocking the light from the hallway. The moment his eyes found mine, something inside me shifted. I wanted to look away, to shield myself from whatever was in his gaze, but I couldn't. His presence was a magnet, pulling me in with an irresistible force.

"You're still awake," he said, his voice rough from what I could only imagine had been a long day of putting out fires—both literal and metaphorical.

I nodded, not trusting myself to speak. It had always been this way between us, hadn't it? A game of silence and half-spoken words.

A battle of wills, both of us too stubborn to be the first to admit that we were falling apart. Or perhaps I had fallen apart already, and he was just waiting for the pieces to settle.

His boots echoed softly on the floorboards as he stepped into the room, his presence as heavy as the storm outside. He stood near the fireplace, his broad shoulders silhouetted against the flickering flames. There was something about the way he filled a room, as though he were larger than life itself, his energy impossible to ignore. I wanted to ask what had happened today, if he was all right, but I couldn't bring myself to care. Not yet.

"You should get some rest," I said, my voice coming out sharper than I intended. It didn't matter. I couldn't let him see how much his proximity rattled me. Not when I still hadn't figured out what I wanted from him, from myself.

His lips quirked into a half-smile, but it didn't reach his eyes. "I'm not tired. And I don't think you are, either."

He was right. I wasn't tired. How could I be? The weight of everything—the decisions, the regrets, the what-ifs—kept me awake long into the night, my mind spinning with questions that had no answers.

"You always know how to read me, don't you?" I said, finally managing a smile of my own, though it felt like a mask. A mask I had perfected over the years.

He studied me for a moment, his eyes narrowing as if he were trying to figure out what I was really saying. But then, just as quickly, his expression softened. "I'm not the only one who knows how to read the other," he murmured, his gaze lingering on my lips.

I could feel the heat between us flare, an undeniable spark that made my heart race in spite of myself. And I knew that if I wasn't careful, this moment, this fragile silence, would shatter everything.

I forced myself to stand, taking a step back, away from the fire, away from him. "We need to talk," I said, even though I was already dreading the words I had yet to say.

He didn't move, but I could feel his presence pressing in on me, steady and unwavering. "I know. But first, let's acknowledge the fact that we're both pretending we're not standing in the same room right now, pretending we're not feeling whatever it is we're feeling."

I didn't respond immediately. He was right, of course. We had danced around this—around us—for too long. But now, with him so close, I could feel the weight of our past, our mistakes, pressing down on me. I had tried to bury them, to convince myself that it was better to walk away than to risk everything for something that could destroy us both.

But there was no escaping it. I couldn't escape it.

"You know," he continued, his voice dropping to a low whisper, "there's only so long I can pretend I'm okay with this. With the distance. With the silence." He took a step closer, his eyes locking onto mine, intense and unyielding. "I'm tired of pretending."

I wanted to tell him I felt the same, that I was tired of fighting this invisible force that had always been there between us. But the words stuck in my throat, heavy with everything I had yet to admit.

Instead, I shook my head. "We can't just—"

But he cut me off with a quiet, "Why not?"

The challenge was there, in his voice. It always had been. His belief in us, in whatever this was, had never wavered, even when I had pulled away. And that belief was both comforting and terrifying in equal measure.

"Because we're too connected," I whispered, barely audible, even to myself. "And that scares me."

The silence stretched between us again, but this time, it wasn't the same. It wasn't heavy with regret or fear. It was different—like the calm before a storm.

And this time, I wasn't sure I was ready to weather it alone.

The storm outside was nothing compared to the tempest raging within me. Each word, each touch from Vance, felt like an electric current zipping through my skin. He was always so close, always within reach, and yet... so far. There was a barrier between us that neither of us had yet dared to break, a distance born of choices and circumstances, of fears we hadn't fully acknowledged, and now—perhaps even more frustrating—the refusal to acknowledge the ache we shared. The ache I could no longer ignore.

The rain drummed on the windows, a steady pulse that matched the rhythm of my thoughts. Every raindrop against the glass felt like a reminder of what we hadn't said. But for the first time, I wasn't afraid to listen to the silence between us. Maybe, just maybe, it was enough for us to exist in this moment of tension—of almost—and let whatever came next unfold naturally.

Vance didn't speak again. He didn't need to. His presence alone was enough to fill the space, to suffocate me with everything unspoken. He knew how to wait. Knew how to push without pushing. It was one of the things I both admired and hated about him. And now, in the quiet after his admission, it was clear he was waiting for me to decide how much further I would go with this. With him.

I could feel him watching me, the weight of his stare heavier than any storm. I crossed my arms, fingers digging into the sleeves of my worn-out sweater, trying to hold on to something tangible.

"You think I don't know what you're doing?" I finally said, my voice steadier than I felt. I hated that we were here again, but more than that, I hated that I was still so willing to fall into the trap he set so effortlessly. "This—this game of yours. The silent dance of who's going to flinch first. I'm not playing, Vance."

He took a step forward, then another. Every movement deliberate, calculated, as if he knew exactly how much it would affect me. When he reached the armchair across from me, he sank into it, folding his long legs beneath him with an ease that made my pulse race. He wasn't close enough for me to touch, but it didn't matter. I could feel him there all the same.

"I'm not playing a game, Jess." His voice was low, but the edges of it held a promise, a challenge. "I'm just... waiting for you to see what's in front of you. What's always been in front of you."

I turned away from him, my gaze falling to the empty glass of wine on the coffee table. I had to focus on something other than the way his words made my heart stumble. He had a way of simplifying everything. A way of stripping me down to nothing but the truth. And the truth was that I couldn't walk away from him anymore. Not when he had already taken up so much space in my life, in my heart.

"I'm not who you think I am," I muttered, my voice tight, almost too soft to hear.

He raised an eyebrow, that familiar glint of challenge creeping back into his eyes. "Who do I think you are?"

"The one who can't possibly fall in love again," I whispered, though I hardly believed it myself. "The one who believes that love only ends in heartbreak. You should've learned that by now."

For a long moment, there was silence, a deep, lingering stillness that stretched between us, both suffocating and sweet. His eyes were fixed on me, studying me in a way I hadn't let anyone do in years.

"You think I haven't learned it?" Vance asked, his voice steady but sharp. "You think I haven't seen that same heartbreak in your eyes every time I get too close?"

I flinched, but he didn't move. "You're afraid of me, Jess. And I get it. But the thing is, we both have scars. We both have pasts that we can't outrun. And I'm not asking you to forget that. I'm asking you to see me. See what we could have if you'd just stop fighting it."

I couldn't hold his gaze any longer. Instead, I turned my face toward the window, my chest tightening with each breath. "I don't know how to stop fighting it."

"You don't have to," he said softly. "You just have to stop fighting me."

My fingers clenched tighter around the sleeve of my sweater. I felt the familiar sting of tears, a wave of emotion threatening to crash over me, but I swallowed it back. There was no room for vulnerability in a world like ours. Not now. Not when the stakes had grown so high.

"I don't know how to do this, Vance," I confessed, finally letting the words slip from my lips, quieter than a whisper. "I don't know how to let you in."

The words hung in the air, heavier than anything I'd ever said before. But it felt different this time. Not like an admission of weakness, but rather of surrender. I was giving in to him. To us.

And Vance—he understood. His eyes softened, and he exhaled a breath he must have been holding in for far longer than I'd realized. He wasn't going to push me. Not tonight.

"I'm not asking you to know how, Jess," he said, his voice gentle, almost tender. "I'm just asking you to try."

A laugh escaped me, though it sounded more like a breathless sigh. "That's rich, coming from you. You always make everything look so easy. I'm not like you, Vance. I can't just... let go."

"You don't have to let go." He leaned forward slightly, his gaze steady, unwavering. "Just take my hand. Let me hold you for once."

His words were a lifeline, and for the first time in ages, I wanted to reach out. To trust.

But it wasn't that simple. It couldn't be. Not with the pieces of my heart scattered across the ground. Not when I wasn't sure I could trust myself with the power of what we could be.

I didn't respond right away. Instead, I just let the silence wrap itself around us, trying to figure out if I was strong enough to make the leap into what I knew would change everything.

Vance was waiting. And for the first time in a long time, so was I.

The tension between us lingered like the fading notes of a symphony, each note pulling at my heart in ways I hadn't anticipated. As I stood there, my hands clammy and my chest tight, I tried to steady my breath. The air in the room had thickened, heavy with unspoken words and unacknowledged truths, but nothing had ever felt more fragile than this moment.

Vance didn't speak again. He simply watched me, his gaze so intense it felt as if he could see straight through me. I wondered if he could, if he knew everything I was too scared to say aloud. I didn't want to admit it, but the truth was undeniable. The wall I had so carefully constructed around myself was crumbling, piece by piece, every time he came near.

His presence was both a comfort and a threat, pulling me in and pushing me away in equal measure. The feelings I had for him were real, undeniable, and terrifying. To love someone with such intensity felt like standing on the edge of a cliff, knowing the only way to find solid ground was to fall.

I took a shaky breath, trying to gather the courage to face him. "I don't know how to let go of the past," I finally said, my voice hoarse. "How can I, when it's all I've ever known?"

Vance didn't flinch. He didn't try to fill the silence with words. He understood. The past we both carried with us was a weight we could never outrun, no matter how fast we ran. But here, in this moment, it didn't matter as much as it had before. The past was a part of us, yes, but it didn't have to define the future.

"You're not supposed to let go, Jess," he said softly, his voice so steady it grounded me. "You don't have to forget the past. Just... make room for something new. For us."

The simplicity of his words hit me harder than I expected. I didn't know what to do with them, what to make of the possibility that maybe, just maybe, I wasn't meant to carry this burden alone anymore. The idea of sharing it, of letting someone else in, was so foreign that it almost seemed laughable. But in the quiet of his presence, it didn't feel so impossible.

I took a small step toward him, my feet moving of their own accord. It wasn't an admission of anything—not yet—but it was the first step toward understanding that maybe we could be something more. Maybe we already were, and I was too afraid to see it.

When I stopped in front of him, we were close enough that I could feel the heat radiating from his body, the energy between us crackling like static electricity. He was so close now that all I could focus on was the steady rhythm of his breathing, the way his chest rose and fell, the way his hands rested at his sides, as if waiting for me to make the next move. It was maddening, knowing that the next decision—the one that could change everything—was mine.

"Why are you doing this?" I asked, my voice barely a whisper. "Why fight for someone who can't even see what you're offering?"

The question hung in the air like an unspoken dare. I wasn't sure what answer I expected. But when he finally spoke, his words were simple, yet profound. "Because I know you, Jess. I know you better than anyone else ever will. And I'm not afraid of what we could be."

The words stung, though not in the way I expected. They didn't feel like a challenge. They felt like a promise. Like something I wasn't ready to face but was going to have to, sooner or later.

The room felt smaller now, the walls pressing in, as if the house itself were holding its breath, waiting for the truth to break free. I could feel the pull of him, his presence, his unwavering belief that we could figure this out together. It was both comforting and suffocating.

"You don't have to do this for me," I said, shaking my head. "You don't owe me anything."

Vance stood then, his height looming over me, and in that moment, I was acutely aware of every inch of space between us, every breath we took in tandem. "I don't owe you anything, no," he said, his voice low and fierce. "But I want to be here. With you."

The words hit me like a wave, crashing over me, drowning any lingering doubt I had. I wanted to fight it. I wanted to walk away and pretend like I could just keep moving forward without acknowledging how much I needed him. But I knew it was too late for that.

I didn't speak, not at first. There was nothing to say, nothing that would make this easier. All I had was the weight of his words, the truth I'd been avoiding for so long. And for once, I didn't want to run.

Before I could stop myself, I stepped closer to him, reaching out without thinking, my fingers brushing against the rough fabric of his shirt. The contact sent a jolt of electricity through me, and I had to fight the urge to pull back. But I didn't. Instead, I let my fingers linger there, tracing the outline of his chest, feeling the steady beat of his heart beneath the surface.

"Don't pull away," Vance whispered, his breath warm against my ear. "Not now. Not when I'm finally here."

I couldn't reply. I didn't need to. The words were unnecessary, because in that moment, all I could hear was the sound of my own heart, racing in time with his.

And then, just as I felt myself sinking into the truth of us—into the possibility of us—there was a sharp knock at the door.

The sound ripped through the moment, shattering the fragile bubble we had created. The sudden intrusion made my heart race for an entirely different reason. The quiet between us was gone, replaced with the sharp edge of tension.

I didn't want to look at Vance. I couldn't. Not when I felt everything shifting so completely. But the knock came again, louder this time, and I knew it wasn't something we could ignore.

Vance's hand was on my wrist before I could even think to pull away. "Do you want me to get that?" he asked, his voice low but laced with an edge of something I couldn't quite read.

I shook my head, unable to form words. This was our moment, and yet it was already slipping away. I wanted to hold onto it, to lock it away somewhere deep inside me, where no one could take it from us. But reality had a way of barging in uninvited.

With a final glance at me, Vance crossed the room, his hand still gripping mine as he reached for the door. And as he turned the handle, I couldn't shake the feeling that the world was about to change again—whether I was ready for it or not.

Chapter 23: Breaking the Cycle

The rain began to fall in a steady stream, relentless and cold, as if the heavens themselves were trying to wash away the sins of the earth. I stood by the window, the chill of the glass biting into my palms as I pressed against it, watching the water cascade down in rhythmic patterns. My thoughts, like the rain, blurred together into a tangled mess that I could no longer control.

Vance's hand on my shoulder was a gentle reminder that I wasn't alone, though the weight of the truth I had uncovered made me feel as though I were drifting, untethered. It had been a day of revelations, and they had left me hollow, a ghost of the person I had been only a few hours ago. The lies had come undone, layer by fragile layer, until the heart of the matter—of my matter—was exposed, raw and trembling in the light. And it was a truth I never expected, one that twisted the very core of what I had believed about myself, about everyone I had trusted.

My mother's name had always been a whispered thing in my family. A name passed through the generations with reverence and fear. She was an enigma, a woman whose absence was more poignant than her presence had ever been. All I knew was that she had vanished when I was just a child, leaving behind an emptiness that had been filled with stories of her beauty, her strength, and the mysterious circumstances of her departure. For years, I had been the product of those stories—fragments of a woman I could never know, an idealized figure I could never live up to.

And then, like a slap in the face, the truth hit me: My mother hadn't vanished. She had chosen to leave. But not out of neglect. Not out of disdain. No, she had walked away for reasons I had never imagined—sacrifices made out of love for me, love for a life I couldn't understand. It had been a choice made in the face of something far darker than I had ever fathomed. A betrayal so deep, so gut-wrenching, that it had torn apart not only her life but mine as well.

"Are you going to tell me what's going on in that head of yours, or do I need to keep guessing?" Vance's voice was warm, the familiar drawl pulling me back to the present.

I turned slowly, the weight of his gaze catching me off guard. His eyes, dark as midnight but full of light, were unwavering. The same eyes that had seen me at my lowest, and somehow still looked at me as though I was worth something.

"It's her," I said, the words coming out in a strangled whisper, as though the very act of saying them out loud would make them more real. "My mother. She wasn't just... lost. She left, Vance. She left because of something I never knew."

He didn't need to ask who. The pain in my voice said it all. And for the first time in weeks, the sharp edges of his usual bravado softened, replaced by a quiet understanding.

"I don't think I'm ready to know everything," I continued, wrapping my arms around myself, as if to hold myself together before I fell apart completely. "But I do know this: whatever she did, however she did it, it changed everything. For me. For her. For us."

Vance stepped closer, his breath warm against the cold air between us. "You don't have to carry it all alone, you know that?"

I closed my eyes, trying to steady the storm inside me. "How could I not? It's my history, my mess to sort through. And now... now I have to decide what to do with it all. What to do with them."

The 'them' was the hardest part to face. The people who had once been allies, the ones I had trusted to protect me, had been complicit in the lies. They had spun the stories that kept me blind to the reality of what had happened in my own home. My father, who had been more of a shadow than a presence in my life, had known everything—everything—and yet he had allowed me to believe I was the victim of some random twist of fate. My aunt, my only remaining family, had done the same, playing the part of the concerned relative while harboring secrets that had never once been mine to carry.

I felt as though I were drowning in a sea of their betrayals, but Vance was the anchor, his presence keeping me grounded. His hand reached out, cupping my cheek, the warmth of his skin a sharp contrast to the cold storm outside.

"You don't have to forgive them," he said quietly, his thumb brushing across my cheek in a slow, soothing motion. "Not yet. Hell, maybe not ever. But you don't have to do this alone. You're not the only one with a past full of shadows."

For a moment, I let myself believe him. I let the heaviness of my burden lift just enough to see the possibility of a future that wasn't defined by pain. But the truth of what had happened couldn't be ignored. It loomed between us, between the words we spoke and the silence we kept. There was something dangerous in the air, something I couldn't name, but I knew it was there, pressing down on both of us.

I took a deep breath, swallowing back the bitterness that rose in my throat. "I don't know what to do. I don't know if I'm strong enough to break the cycle."

His smile was small, but it reached his eyes—eyes that had seen so much, had lived through things I couldn't begin to understand.

"You don't have to be strong enough. Not yet. Just take it one step at a time."

But I wasn't sure if one step would be enough. Because breaking the cycle would mean more than just walking away. It would mean facing the darkness head-on, seeing it for what it truly was, and deciding whether I could ever forgive the people who had set it all in motion.

And deep down, I wasn't sure I could.

The house felt quieter now, as though the walls had absorbed the weight of the revelations and were exhaling a collective breath with me. I wasn't sure how long I had stood in the silence, but when Vance's voice broke through again, it was as soft as a whisper, yet it carried with it the undeniable weight of understanding.

"You're not sure what to do next, are you?" he asked, and I could hear the edge of concern in his tone. It was the way he always spoke when he knew I was trying to hide something, to bury it deep enough to pretend it wasn't there. It wasn't that I didn't trust him; it was just that sometimes, some things felt too heavy to share, even with him.

I shook my head, the movement slow, deliberate. "No. I'm not sure of anything right now."

There was a beat of silence, the kind that stretched long and painful. But when he finally spoke, his words were simple, unadorned, but they landed with the force of something true.

"Then let's figure it out together."

I turned to look at him, really look at him. His face, strong and steady, showed none of the doubt that churned in my stomach. Vance had always been a rock, but this time, it wasn't his usual easy confidence that gave me comfort. It was something deeper, something quieter. It was the trust he had in me to find my own way, without rushing me, without pushing. In that moment, I realized that I hadn't just found someone who was willing to fight alongside me; I'd found someone who understood the importance of letting me fight my own battles.

I opened my mouth to speak, but the words felt wrong, tangled in the sudden overwhelming surge of emotion that had caught me off guard. Instead, I took a step forward, closing the distance between us until the space felt comfortable, familiar. For the first time in what felt like ages, I let myself lean into him, feeling the solid warmth of his body against mine, letting his strength envelope me like a blanket.

"I don't know if I can do this," I whispered into his chest, my voice barely audible over the steady beat of his heart.

His arms tightened around me in response, his fingers brushing the back of my neck in a way that felt like a promise. "You don't have to do it all at once. You don't even have to do it alone. But we'll do it together, okay?"

There was something profoundly reassuring in his words, a balm to the rawness I had been carrying since I learned the truth. Yet, as comforting as Vance's presence was, the reality of what I was about to face loomed large in my mind. It wasn't just about confronting the lies of the past. It was about deciding whether I had the strength to break the cycle—whether I could, in the face of all that had happened, make the choice to forgive.

My thoughts swirled, a cacophony of emotions, but one thing was clear: the choice was mine. It had always been mine. The power to move forward, to let go of the hurt, to break free from the past. Or to keep fighting—to keep feeding the anger that had kept me going this far.

The problem was that anger had become a companion I wasn't sure I was ready to part with. It had been my shield for so long, a sharp and jagged thing that had protected me from the ache of betrayal. But the longer I held onto it, the more I realized it was also becoming a cage. And like any cage, it would eventually start to suffocate me.

Vance must have sensed my thoughts, because he shifted slightly, his fingers tilting my chin upward so I was forced to meet his eyes. There was no judgment there, no expectation. Just steady, unwavering support.

"You've got this, you know," he said, his voice low but filled with conviction. "No one else can tell you how to handle this, but I know you'll find the right path."

I wanted to believe him. I really did. But right now, the only thing I knew for certain was that every step forward felt like a leap into the unknown, and I wasn't sure I had the courage to take it.

A knock at the door broke the moment, sharp and insistent. I tensed, feeling the cold rush of reality settle back in. Whoever it was, they weren't here to offer comfort. My heart lurched as the knot in my stomach tightened.

"Do you want me to get it?" Vance asked, sensing my hesitation.

I hesitated for a fraction of a second before shaking my head. "I'll go."

I turned away from him, the warmth of his presence fading as I crossed the room toward the door. My hand shook as I reached for the handle, but I didn't pull away. I couldn't afford to hide anymore, not from the people who had been a part of this mess.

When I opened the door, the last person I expected to see stood there—my father.

His appearance was a jarring contrast to the vulnerability I had just allowed myself to feel. His suit, crisp and immaculately pressed, was the same as it always had been when he walked into a room to command attention. But it was the tightness around his eyes that caught me off guard. He looked different, older, like someone who had been carrying too much for too long. I couldn't tell if the guilt in his gaze was genuine or just another mask he was wearing, but for once, I didn't care.

"Dad," I said, the word feeling strange on my tongue.

His eyes flicked over my shoulder, searching for Vance, before settling back on me. "We need to talk."

It was the last thing I wanted to hear. But as much as I tried to hold onto the anger that had kept me going for so long, I couldn't ignore the part of me that still needed answers. And so, with a resigned sigh, I stepped aside and let him in.

I stepped back, letting my father into the entryway, my heart thudding in my chest. I hadn't seen him in years, not since he had disappeared from my life the same way my mother had, leaving nothing behind but unanswered questions and the kind of emptiness that gnawed at your soul.

He glanced around, taking in the modest décor of the apartment, his eyes missing nothing. There was a moment's hesitation, just a brief flicker of something I couldn't place, before he met my gaze again. His face, once so familiar, now seemed like a stranger's, his sharp jawline and graying hair betraying the passage of time. He had aged, and yet he looked unchanged in all the ways that mattered.

"Is Vance here?" His voice was low, controlled, but there was a nervous edge to it that I hadn't expected. The man who had once run his life with military precision—without ever breaking a sweat—was suddenly unsure.

I nodded, though I had no intention of letting him see Vance. Not yet. "He's in the other room."

"Good. I'd rather speak to you alone, anyway."

That sent a flicker of disbelief through me. He wanted to talk to me alone? After all these years of silence, now he wanted to keep the conversation between just the two of us? It made no sense. The last time I'd seen him, he had stormed out of the house without so much as a glance back. The man who had left me, my mother, and everything we had built behind was now standing here, asking for my ear?

"What do you want, Dad?" My voice came out colder than I had intended, but there was no warmth left for him, not after everything. His absence had left a hole, but that didn't mean I was eager to fill it with whatever excuse he had this time.

He shifted on his feet, the tailored suit not quite hiding the tightness in his shoulders. "I'm sorry," he began, and the words were so foreign from him that it took a moment for them to sink in. "I should have done this a long time ago. I should have explained."

A bitter laugh bubbled up from my throat before I could stop it. "Explain? After all these years, you think a few words are going to fix it?"

His face hardened, just for a moment, before he seemed to force the expression back into something more controlled. "I wasn't given the chance. And you have every right to be angry. But I never wanted—"

"Never wanted what?" I interjected, my voice rising despite myself. "You never wanted to tear my life apart? You never wanted to leave us in the dark? Don't try to act like you didn't make a choice."

His gaze dropped to the floor for a brief moment, a flicker of guilt passing through his eyes before it was shuttered once more. He took a slow, steadying breath. "What I did, it wasn't just about you and your mother. It was—there were bigger things at play. Things I couldn't control."

"Control," I repeated, the word tasting bitter on my tongue. "Let me guess, Dad. You were always the victim, weren't you?"

I could feel the shift in the air, the tension between us thickening like a storm cloud before a downpour. He raised his hands, as if to calm me, but I wasn't in the mood for his placations. "What I'm trying to say is that the decision I made, leaving, it wasn't about abandoning you. It was... it was about protecting you from something worse."

I blinked, his words striking me like a slap. "Protecting me? From what?"

But I wasn't prepared for the look that passed over his face, the one that spoke of a thousand untold stories. For a moment, I thought I saw a flash of fear, something raw and vulnerable that seemed out of place on the man who had always seemed impervious to anything other than his own will. And then, just as quickly, it was gone.

"I'm not going to get into the details right now," he said, his voice steadying again, though it lacked the confidence it had once held. "But what I'm telling you is the truth. What you learned about your mother, it's not the whole story. There's more. And if you want answers, you'll have to hear it from me."

I could feel my heart pounding in my chest, the blood rushing in my ears as I tried to make sense of what he was saying. My mother? More? The web of lies I had discovered was already complex, but now it was beginning to feel like I was tangled in something much, much deeper.

I swallowed hard, trying to keep my voice steady. "What does this have to do with me, Dad? Why now? Why do you suddenly want to be a part of my life after everything that's happened?"

He stepped forward, closing the gap between us, his eyes now locked onto mine with a kind of intensity I hadn't seen from him in years. "Because, whether you want to accept it or not, you're a part of all this. You always have been. And the choices you make now, they matter more than you think."

Before I could respond, there was a sudden sound from the other room—Vance's voice, low and urgent. It was followed by a sharp knock at the door, then another.

My father's face went white, his eyes darting toward the door. "It's them. They've found us."

The panic in his voice was unmistakable, and for the first time in a long while, I realized my father wasn't the one pulling the strings. The power he had once wielded so easily had been stripped away, leaving him a man backed into a corner, desperate and afraid.

I took a step back, trying to process his words, the sudden rush of fear and confusion swirling in my chest.

"What do you mean 'they've found us'? Who's after you?" My voice was tight, breathless, as the reality of the situation began to settle in.

The knock came again, louder this time, and my father looked at me with something like regret in his eyes, as if he were weighing whether or not to share more.

But before he could speak, the door burst open. And the man standing in the threshold wasn't someone I recognized.

Chapter 24: A Love Forged in Fire

The smoke hung thick in the air, a blanket of gray that threatened to smother the last vestiges of sunlight. It curled around my legs like a living thing, creeping into my lungs with every breath. The ground trembled beneath my feet as the world around me cracked open, a cacophony of chaos and destruction. There was no time to think, only to react. And as I stood there, my sword raised high, Vance's voice rang out in the storm, his words sharp and unwavering.

"Don't stop," he urged, his words a breath in the wind. "We can't afford to let this go any further."

I nodded, barely able to hear him over the pounding of my heart, but the meaning of his words was clear. We were beyond the point of retreat. There was no going back now. The battle we were fighting wasn't just against the forces that sought to tear us apart—it was against everything that ever tried to break us. And for the first time, I knew I wasn't fighting alone.

Vance moved beside me, his back a shield, his presence a constant reassurance. He was like a rock in the tempest, unyielding and steady, even as the world around us threatened to crack under the strain. His dark eyes met mine for a fleeting second, and in that moment, the intensity of our bond flared. The battle raged on, but the connection between us felt more tangible than any enemy in front of us. I was no longer just fighting for survival. I was fighting for him. For us.

The clash of steel echoed in the distance, a constant reminder of the war we were waging. But as the sword in my hand met the shield of a shadowed adversary, I felt something shift within me—a sudden surge of energy, a fire that burned hotter than anything the world could throw at us. It was him, I realized. Vance was the flame, and I was the fuel. Together, we were unstoppable.

"Are you with me?" he asked, his voice low and urgent, the words meant for me alone. The world around us could burn to the ground, but in that moment, it was just the two of us standing at the edge of the world.

"Always," I said, and it wasn't just a promise. It was a declaration, a vow spoken without hesitation.

The clash of our blades was a symphony, the rhythm of our movements seamless. We fought as one, our bodies synchronized in a dance of fury and grace. Every time I struck, I could feel him at my back, guiding me, supporting me. And every time he moved, I was there beside him, a shadow to his light.

There was no room for fear anymore, only the burning determination to keep fighting. The darkness that surrounded us—the enemies that threatened our world, our love—began to lose their power in the face of our unity. It wasn't just skill or strength that drove us; it was the unspoken understanding that we would give everything to protect what we had built together.

The air shifted, heavy with the scent of fire and metal. The final push was upon us, and I could feel it deep in my bones—the moment that would decide everything. We had fought too hard, sacrificed too much, to let it all slip away now. The ground beneath us cracked open once more, the very earth protesting the violence of the battle.

"Get ready," Vance warned, his voice fierce as he stepped closer, positioning himself protectively in front of me. I didn't need to ask what he meant. I could feel it—the pulse of magic, of power gathering in the shadows, ready to strike. And in that moment, I understood what had to be done. It wasn't enough to simply fight. We had to end it. We had to destroy the source of this darkness once and for all.

"I'm with you," I said again, my voice steady as the storm raged around us. There was no hesitation this time. I had made my choice.

Vance turned to face me, his eyes burning with the same resolve. There was no turning back now. The magic crackled around us, a dark force that seemed to bleed from the earth itself. But we were ready.

I stepped forward, my sword raised high, the magic in my veins thrumming to life. We moved as one, our movements synchronized in a single, perfect strike. The world held its breath as the darkness recoiled, a final, desperate gasp before it was consumed by the light we had summoned together.

The explosion of energy sent us both stumbling back, our bodies thrown by the force of the blast. The air was thick with the scent of smoke and ozone, but I didn't feel the burn. I didn't feel the ache of the battle or the weight of our scars. All I felt was him—his hand on my arm, his steadying grip pulling me back to my feet.

"Is it over?" I asked, my voice hoarse, my breath shallow.

Vance didn't answer immediately. Instead, he lifted my chin with his fingers, his gaze searching mine. There was a flicker of something in his eyes, something I couldn't quite place. Then, finally, he spoke, his voice a soft murmur in the midst of the wreckage around us.

"Not yet," he said, his lips curving into a wry smile. "But it will be. As long as we're standing together, it will be."

And in that moment, I knew he was right. The battle might not be over, but we had already won. Because love, real love, was never just about survival. It was about choosing to fight, every single day, for the one person who made it all worth it. And I had chosen him.

The aftermath of the explosion left the world oddly quiet, as though everything had taken a collective breath and was waiting to see what would happen next. My heart still pounded in my chest, the adrenaline pumping through my veins, but there was no time to savor the victory—no time to think. I had to move. Had to stay sharp. The shadows were still out there, swirling in the distance like a storm gathering strength.

Vance didn't give me the luxury of hesitation. He was already on his feet, a few feet away, his back straight and his posture all warrior, even though he was still catching his breath. He was always like that—never one to show weakness, no matter the odds. It was something I admired, though I wished sometimes he'd let himself rest. Just a little.

"Move," he said, his voice gruff but commanding. "We're not done yet."

I nodded, the words barely necessary. We'd always been in sync, even in the chaos of battle. It was as though our souls understood one another, perfectly, completely. I could read his thoughts, anticipate his next move without even trying. And maybe that was what scared me more than anything.

Because as we moved through the smoky haze, I realized that this fight—this war we were in the middle of—wasn't just about saving the world. It was about saving ourselves. The deeper we waded into the storm, the more I understood how much we were entwined. If one of us fell, the other would too. I didn't know how we'd survive that, but I knew I wasn't going to find out. Not if I could help it.

"We need to reach the bridge," Vance said, glancing back over his shoulder. The tension in his voice made it clear that this wasn't a suggestion. "It's the only way we can stop this."

I didn't question him. I didn't need to. The bridge was where the heart of the darkness lay, a twisted thing of shadows and magic that had been threatening to break open ever since we'd set foot in this cursed land. It was a place of ancient power, a place where, if you weren't careful, you could lose more than just your life.

We didn't speak as we moved, but the silence between us was thick with understanding. There were no words for the fear I could see in his eyes, no words for the way his hand tightened around the hilt of his sword. We didn't need words. The weight of our shared resolve was enough.

The ground was uneven beneath our feet, each step a reminder of how fragile this world was. The trees around us, once lush and full of life, were now twisted and gnarled, their branches reaching out like clawed hands trying to pull us back into the depths of darkness. The very air seemed charged with an unnatural energy, as though the land itself was alive, watching, waiting for us to slip up.

"Stay close," Vance warned, his voice low, urgent. "We don't know what's still out here."

I could barely hear him over the rustling of the trees, but I didn't need to be told. My eyes never left him as we moved through the eerie silence, and I knew without asking that he felt the same. There was no room for doubt now. No room for fear.

We reached the bridge just as the last remnants of the storm began to clear. The structure was as ancient as the land itself, its stones slick with moss and covered in an eerie, almost oppressive silence. The air felt colder here, and for the first time, I could feel the weight of what we were about to face. This wasn't just the end of a battle. This was the point of no return.

Vance stepped forward, his hand resting on the railing, his eyes scanning the horizon. He was waiting for something, for someone. And I couldn't help but feel the gnawing sense that this moment, this exact moment, was where everything had been leading. The culmination of every sacrifice, every struggle.

"We have to destroy it," he said, almost to himself. "We can't let it take any more."

His words cut through the air like a blade, sharp and final. I stepped beside him, my hand brushing against his, the contact grounding me. I didn't know what was coming, but I knew that together, we could face whatever it was.

"It's not going to be easy," I said, though I wasn't sure if I was trying to convince him or myself. The darkness in the distance seemed to stir, like it had been waiting for us to make our move. And as I looked out over the bridge, I could feel the weight of what we were about to face.

"I know," he replied, his voice steady but tinged with a bitterness I knew too well. "But we don't have a choice."

The wind picked up, sending a shiver down my spine. The sky was darkening once more, the clouds rolling in like a warning. The bridge began to tremble beneath our feet, and I realized then that it wasn't just a structure we were trying to save. It was a symbol of everything we had fought for—everything we had almost lost. If we couldn't destroy the darkness now, there would be nothing left.

I reached for my sword, my fingers curling around the hilt, and I glanced at Vance. His jaw was clenched, his eyes narrowed, but there was something in them—something fierce, something unyielding. We were ready.

"This ends now," he said, his voice a whisper but one that carried with the force of a thousand storms. "For all of us."

And as we stood on that ancient bridge, ready to face the darkness head-on, I realized something crucial. Love had never been about grand gestures or promises of forever. It had always been about the quiet moments, the shared battles, the unspoken understanding. We had chosen each other, time and time again, and now we had to choose each other one final time. It wasn't just our love on the line—it was everything. And together, we were going to burn it all to the ground.

The air hummed with a tension that seemed to crawl beneath my skin, sending shivers up my spine. I stood at the edge of the bridge, the ground beneath my boots shaky, as though the very earth was holding its breath. The shadows swirled around us like a living thing, a storm of malice that seemed determined to swallow everything whole. But I wasn't afraid—not anymore. Not with Vance beside me.

I caught his eye, and in the depth of his gaze, there was an unspoken promise: we would survive this. We had to. The dark forces that had been gathering for so long were no longer a distant threat—they were here, now, and it was our job to put an end to them.

The bridge trembled once more, the stones shifting beneath us as if the entire structure itself was beginning to come alive, a relic of ancient magic. I could feel it in the very air, a pressure building around us, winding tighter and tighter with each passing second. This wasn't just about fighting; it was about rewriting the future. It was about taking everything we had—our love, our pain, our sacrifice—and turning it into something that could shatter the darkness once and for all.

"This is it," I said, my voice barely above a whisper, though I knew Vance could hear me just fine. "We can't stop now."

He didn't respond at first, but the slight tightening of his jaw was answer enough. There were no words left to say, not with the weight of the world pressing down on us like this. Instead, he stepped closer, his shoulder brushing mine in a small gesture of reassurance. In the face of everything we were about to face, it was everything.

I reached for my sword, fingers trembling ever so slightly as I gripped the hilt. The metal was warm from the fight we'd just waged, and the hum of its magic felt like an extension of my own heartbeat. I didn't know if I had the strength to finish what we'd started. But I had no choice. There was nothing left to do but keep going.

And then it came.

A wave of energy crashed over us, darker than any storm, colder than the deepest winter. The shadows stretched toward us, a writhing mass of smoke and rage, and for a split second, I felt like I might be swallowed whole. But I wasn't alone. Not anymore. Vance was beside me, his presence solid, unwavering, a constant in the face of the storm.

I drew a deep breath and stepped forward, the sword raised high. The power in the air buzzed, almost as if it were waiting for us to strike. And then, with a shout that seemed to come from deep within my soul, I brought the sword down. The force of the strike sent a shockwave through the air, a blinding light that seemed to split the very sky in half. The darkness recoiled, hissing like something that had been burned.

Vance's voice cut through the blinding light, harsh and urgent. "Hold on!"

I had barely enough time to register what was happening before the ground beneath our feet gave way.

The bridge cracked, the stones splitting apart, and before I knew it, I was falling, the wind rushing around me, my heart in my throat. The world spun in a dizzying blur of motion, and I barely managed to catch a glimpse of Vance as he reached out, his hand stretching toward me. His voice—gruff, frantic—reached me just before everything went black.

The sensation of falling was more than physical. It was as though everything around me—everything I had fought for—was slipping through my fingers, leaving me with nothing but empty air and the cold embrace of uncertainty. And as the darkness closed in, the only thing I could think about was him.

And then, nothing.

I awoke to the sound of rushing water, the coldness of it creeping into my bones. My eyes snapped open, but I couldn't make sense of the world around me. Everything was distorted—fuzzy, like I was seeing through a veil of mist. The world felt distant, far away. It took me a moment to understand where I was.

I was lying on the ground, the soft, wet earth beneath me. My body ached, but there was no immediate pain. It was as if I had been tossed around, thrown into the depths of something, and then left to settle. But as I blinked up at the sky, I realized that the sky wasn't right. It was swirling with dark clouds, a storm that seemed to be moving toward me at an unnatural speed.

The weight of everything came crashing down all at once. Vance. The bridge. The darkness.

I tried to sit up, my limbs heavy, and immediately regretted it. My head throbbed with a sharp, pulsing pain that seemed to vibrate through every bone in my body. I reached out, my fingers brushing against the ground for support, and that's when I heard it—the unmistakable sound of footsteps, faint but growing louder.

My pulse quickened.

"Vance?" I called out, my voice shaky. I couldn't tell if the word was an echo of hope or pure desperation. But there was no response. Not right away.

A shadow moved across the dimming light. At first, I thought it was just my mind playing tricks on me—another cruel twist of fate—but when I saw the shape again, I realized it was too solid to be an illusion.

"Vance?" I said again, my voice stronger now, more insistent. But the figure didn't respond. It just... watched.

Fear coursed through me, sharp and sudden, but I couldn't move. I couldn't even breathe. I was paralyzed, the weight of what had just happened, of what might be coming next, heavy on my chest.

The figure took another step forward, and as the last light of the sun dipped below the horizon, the shape came into focus, and my blood ran cold.

It wasn't him.

It was something else entirely. Something dark, something wrong.

And as the figure stepped into the clearing, its hollow, empty eyes fixed on me, I knew that everything had just changed again.

Chapter 25: The Final Stand

The air was thick, humid, like a damp cloth draped over my shoulders, pressing down with every breath. The city—once so full of light and life—now lay still, its streets abandoned and its windows like vacant eyes, staring out into the emptiness. A soft, muffled hum of the old world buzzed in the distance, but it felt hollow, like the sound of a dream fading into nothing. I swallowed, tasting the salt of my own nerves. It had been days, maybe weeks—time was an illusion now. The only thing that remained clear was the singular path ahead.

Vance stood beside me, his jaw set, eyes narrowed, and his hand, warm against my own, clutched mine as if it were a lifeline. I could feel the trembling in his fingers, his fear somehow mirroring mine. His body was the same as ever—muscles taut, brow furrowed—but there was a subtle tension about him now, an uncertainty that hadn't been there before. We had survived countless dangers together, and yet, this felt different. This was the one we couldn't afford to lose.

The villain was waiting for us. I didn't know how or why they had come into being—what twisted fate had shaped them into this thing we now had to face—but I did know one thing: they had to be stopped. The world couldn't afford another day under their reign of terror. I had witnessed their cruelty, their hunger for power, and the suffering it had wrought. But it wasn't just about vengeance anymore. It wasn't about the pain they'd caused, or the people they'd crushed underfoot. It was about us—about Vance and me and what we had found together. The world had tried to break us, to strip us of everything that had made us who we were, but we had survived. And now, we were about to find out if love could be our shield.

The streets had never looked this empty. We walked down them like we were the last two people on earth, or perhaps we were. There were no sounds of life—no children playing, no cars rushing by, no sounds of ordinary people going about their lives. Just silence.

And the wind that whipped through the streets, carrying with it the faintest smell of smoke and decay. The city felt like a ghost, haunted by memories of a time that had passed.

I squeezed Vance's hand, feeling the weight of the moment pressing in on me. "We'll make it through this," I whispered, though even I wasn't entirely sure who I was trying to convince.

Vance didn't answer, but I felt his thumb brush the back of my hand, a silent promise. His eyes were fixed ahead, scanning the horizon as if the villain could leap from the shadows at any moment. His posture was tense, ready for whatever would come next, yet there was something else in him, something softer beneath the steel resolve—a flicker of something I couldn't quite place.

We reached the heart of the city, where the villain's fortress stood like a monolith in the center of everything, looming over us with its jagged edges and dark, brooding presence. I had been here once before, in another life. When the city had still been alive, when hope hadn't been so foreign a concept. But it was nothing like it had been then. The streets were littered with debris, and the once-glorious skyline was now a jagged, broken tooth in the mouth of a beast. The fortress gleamed with an unnatural light, its spires casting long, twisted shadows over the ground below.

"They're waiting for us," I said, my voice strangely calm despite the storm raging inside me. "And they know we're coming."

Vance's gaze hardened. "They can wait all they want," he muttered under his breath. "But we're not going to make it easy for them."

I caught a glimpse of the determined fire in his eyes, that spark of defiance that had always drawn me to him. His strength wasn't just in his body or his ability to fight. It was in his resolve, in the way he carried everything with him—every wound, every loss, every moment that had shaped him into the person he was. He didn't just survive; he made sure everyone around him survived too. That was his gift, his curse.

Together, we walked through the fortress gates, which stood ajar as though welcoming us to the inevitable. I couldn't help but feel a pang of fear at the sight of the darkened hallways that stretched before us. But then I remembered who I was walking with. Vance had never failed to protect me, and I wasn't about to let him down now.

The silence in the fortress was suffocating, broken only by the sound of our footsteps echoing against the cold stone floors. It felt like a funeral procession, each step a reminder of the countless lives lost, of the sacrifices made along the way. My heart pounded in my chest, each beat matching the rhythm of our journey forward. It was hard to believe that in just a few moments, everything could change.

We turned a corner, and there they were—waiting, standing in the center of a vast chamber, their silhouette outlined by the harsh, unnatural light that seemed to emanate from the walls themselves. The villain stood tall, their face obscured by a mask, but the voice that echoed from the shadows was unmistakable.

"So, you've come," the voice purred, smooth and dark, like silk wrapped around broken glass. "How quaint. Do you really think you can stop me?"

Vance stepped forward, his body a shield between me and the threat. "We don't have to think. We know."

The villain's laugh was a cold, calculated thing, cutting through the heavy air like the snap of brittle ice. It echoed off the walls, a sound that reverberated through my bones and into the deepest corners of my mind. I had heard that laugh before, in nightmares, in the moments just before waking when everything seemed too real. But hearing it in the flesh—feeling it wrap around me—was something entirely different. It wasn't just a laugh. It was a warning.

Vance's fingers tightened around mine, his grip steady despite the surge of unease that rattled through us both. The silence that followed was oppressive, broken only by the slow, rhythmic thud of my heart in my ears. I wanted to shout back, to let the words spill from my mouth in a defiant roar. But I didn't. We were past words now.

The figure before us finally moved, stepping forward with a fluid grace that was almost too perfect. A shadow against the blinding light, their every motion deliberate, measured, as though they were savoring the moment. And why wouldn't they? They had us exactly where they wanted us. Trapped in the belly of a beast that had no exit, no escape.

"You really are a hopeless pair," the voice purred, and it made my skin crawl. "Don't you see? You've lost already. It's only a matter of time before everything falls apart. You, all your little friends, this city, everything. It's all gone. Just like that."

Vance stood taller, his face hardening, but I could feel the tension in him, too—the tightrope that was stretched too thin, the impending break. He was ready, but the question was whether either of us could take the first step. This was more than just a battle of strength. It was a battle of wills.

"I think you're forgetting one thing," I said, my voice steady despite the knot that had settled in my stomach. The villain's gaze flicked to me, intrigued, almost amused.

"What's that?" they asked, the words sliding out like silk over jagged rocks.

"Love," I said simply. And before they could scoff, I added, "You don't understand it. You never have."

The villain's eyes narrowed. I could see it now, the cracks in their icy facade. Something was shifting, something was breaking. It wasn't the power that could destroy us—it was the very thing they had tried so hard to extinguish. Hope. It had always been there, buried beneath the rubble, beneath the pain. But it was alive. And it was stronger than they could ever comprehend.

I didn't wait for them to respond. Instead, I pulled Vance forward, my hand in his like it had always been, like it always would be. We moved, not with the grace of warriors but with the determination of two people who had survived far worse. Who had fought through hell and come out on the other side. Who had loved each other enough to make it this far.

The villain raised a hand, fingers outstretched, and the air around us shimmered with the faintest tremor. Electricity crackled in the stillness, a storm just waiting to be unleashed. But I wasn't afraid. I couldn't be—not now. Vance's presence was a grounding force, the steady pulse of his heartbeat syncing with mine. Together, we were unstoppable.

"You still don't get it, do you?" I asked, stepping forward, my voice rising in a defiant challenge. "You've been using fear to control everyone. But what happens when fear is no longer enough?"

The villain's face twisted, their lips curling into something almost... disappointed. "I don't need fear to control you," they said coldly. "I already have you."

Before I could respond, Vance moved. It wasn't a grand gesture, no grand proclamation, but the shift in the air was unmistakable. He was there in front of me, standing between me and the villain, his back straight and strong, a wall of determination. He wasn't just fighting for survival—he was fighting for something much deeper than that. He was fighting for us. For the love we had built, for the future we had yet to see.

"I don't think you understand either," he said, his voice low but filled with authority. "It's not about your power. It's about what we're willing to do to protect what matters." His eyes met mine for the briefest of moments, a silent promise passing between us.

Then, without another word, he surged forward, a blur of motion, reaching for the villain. For the first time, I saw doubt flicker in their eyes.

It was an impossible fight—one we were never supposed to win—but in that moment, as Vance's body moved with a deadly precision, I knew the rules had changed. The villain's power crackled and flared in the air, but it was no match for the force that had been building within us, within our hearts. They had underestimated us. They had underestimated love.

I moved with him, my own steps swift, sure, as I closed the gap between us. The villain was fast—too fast—but for the first time in a long while, we weren't alone. The whispers of everyone who had ever fought for this, the voices of the fallen, filled the air, and I could almost feel their presence with us. They were here, with us, giving us strength. And in that strength, I knew we could defeat this.

Vance's fist collided with the villain's chest with a sickening crunch, and for the briefest moment, everything stopped. Time seemed to stretch out, like the calm before a storm, and then—just like that—it broke. The force of the blow sent the villain stumbling back, their mask cracking, their form wavering. But it wasn't the physical damage that had shattered them. It was the realization that they were no longer in control. They were no longer the one holding the power.

And in that fleeting moment, I saw it. The villain's eyes, wide with something close to panic. The truth they had been running from.

We weren't afraid of them anymore. And that, more than anything, was what had truly broken them.

The villain staggered back, their mask cracked, the eerie glow around them flickering like a dying candle. The shock of it, the vulnerability, was something I'd never expected to see. I had thought we were just pawns in their game, that we would always be outmatched, always a step behind. But now? Now, the balance had shifted. There was power in seeing that crack, that break in the unshakable façade.

For a heartbeat, we stood there in the silence, the world holding its breath. My pulse raced, my legs trembling beneath me, but it wasn't fear that rattled me now—it was something else. Something that felt like the beginning of an end, but not the one we'd been led to expect. The villain, standing so tall and confident just moments ago, seemed smaller now, a mere shadow of the figure that had haunted our every step.

Vance, always the one with the steady resolve, was the first to move again. His fists clenched, ready to finish what had been started. But I caught his arm, just for a moment, grounding him. His eyes flicked to me, confusion flashing briefly before the recognition settled in.

"What is it?" he asked, his voice a low growl.

I couldn't answer right away, not because I didn't know what to say, but because there was a sinking feeling in my stomach that refused to go away. Something was off. The villain had crumpled in a way I hadn't anticipated, but that didn't mean we were out of danger. The world had a way of playing tricks, of making us think we were winning when, in reality, we were only one false move from disaster.

I nodded slowly, releasing his arm. "Watch your back," I whispered, even as the words left my lips, I knew how futile they sounded. They were the words of someone who had seen too many endings, who understood that everything—every hope, every victory—could be snatched away in an instant.

Vance didn't respond, but the look he gave me spoke volumes. He knew. The villain, who had stumbled back, was rising again, their form growing taller as the shadows began to curl around them, feeding from the very air. The crack in their mask was no longer the sign of defeat—it was a signal. A warning.

For the first time, I saw what lay behind the mask. The person—or what was left of them—stood there, their face not twisted in rage, but contorted by something more primal: fear. It was a raw, desperate fear, not of us, but of something much darker. I didn't know what it was, but I could feel it in the air, a storm building in the distance, something that was much bigger than the two of us standing here.

"You think you've won?" the villain's voice trembled. "You think you've shattered my control? You have no idea what you've unleashed. You're nothing. This...this is bigger than all of you."

I stepped forward, ignoring the chill that crept up my spine. "What are you talking about?" I demanded, my voice stronger than I felt. "What's bigger than us?"

The villain's lips curled into a bitter smile. "A power you can't even comprehend. It's already started. Your world is already crumbling, and you're too blind to see it."

A crackling sound filled the room, like thunder rolling in the distance, but it wasn't coming from the skies. It was from beneath our feet.

Vance's hand shot out, grabbing my arm, and yanked me back just as the floor beneath us began to shake. A low rumble, like a growl from the bowels of the earth itself, vibrated through the stone beneath our feet. The lights flickered, casting long, jagged shadows that danced like specters across the walls. The villain's laughter rose once more, this time high-pitched, manic, like the sound of someone who had finally snapped.

And then, as if they had known this moment was coming, they lifted their hands, and the world around us seemed to hold its breath. The ground cracked wide open, splitting in jagged lines, and the very air felt as though it were being sucked away. I gasped, the world tilting, as everything around us seemed to pulse with a violent energy, a force I couldn't see but could feel in my bones.

"What is this?" I managed, my voice barely audible over the noise that filled the room. "What are you doing?"

The villain's smile widened, but it was no longer the smile of someone in control. It was the smile of someone who had lost everything but still held the power to take down those who dared to challenge them.

"You never understood, did you?" they said softly, the words cutting through the chaos around us. "You thought you could stop me. But this was never about me. This is about what happens after."

Before I could respond, the ground trembled again, and the lights died completely, plunging us into an abyss of darkness. I felt Vance's hand tighten around mine, but even his strength, his unwavering certainty, couldn't erase the creeping dread settling over me. There was something else happening, something beyond our comprehension.

The silence that followed was deafening. And then, a low hum began, vibrating through the very air we breathed. It wasn't like the electricity from before—it was deeper, more resonant, like a pulse that belonged to something older than the city, something ancient and untamable.

And then, I saw it.

A glowing, crackling shape, coalescing in the darkness—a force too massive to be seen in its entirety, yet too close to ignore. It was not just power. It was a presence. A being. Something older than time itself, and it was rising, moving toward us like a tidal wave.

I opened my mouth to shout, to tell Vance to run, but no sound came out. The weight of it pressed in on me from all sides, suffocating, paralyzing.

And just as the figure came into full view, its presence dominating everything else, I saw the true horror in the villain's eyes: the realization that they had no control over what was coming.

We had never been fighting for survival. We had been fighting to keep the darkness at bay.

And now, the darkness was here.

Chapter 26: The Dawn of New Beginnings

The morning light was soft at first, a delicate haze that kissed the edges of the rubble, turning the shattered cityscape into something almost beautiful. The ground beneath my boots was still warm from the night's fires, and the air held the tang of smoke that hadn't quite been banished yet, as if the city itself was taking slow, deep breaths. Crescent City had always been a place of contradictions, where the dazzling lights of high-rise buildings sat next to the shadows of alleyways no one cared to visit. But today—today, the sun broke over the skyline like it was trying to make sense of everything too, hesitant yet determined to rise.

Vance stood beside me, and I couldn't help but glance at him out of the corner of my eye. His broad shoulders were a silhouette against the light, his jaw set in that way that meant he was still trying to figure it all out. I didn't know if it was the city he was trying to understand or himself. Maybe both.

The truth was, we were walking a thin line between what had been and what could be. The echoes of our past—of the people we'd been before the battle, before the secrets and betrayals and the things we'd done to survive—still clung to us. But somewhere between the smoke and the devastation, something had shifted. I could feel it in the way the air tasted now, fresh and alive with the promise of something new. It was like waking from a long nightmare and finding yourself standing in the sunlight again, blinking, trying to adjust.

I wondered, briefly, if Vance felt the same. If he looked at me the way I looked at him—an amalgamation of everything we'd been and everything we could still be. There had been too many moments between us, too many things said in whispers and glances, in the heat of battle and the dark corners of quiet rooms, to let it all slip away.

I didn't know if it was love—too much had happened for me to be sure of what love even looked like anymore—but it was something. Something worth holding onto.

We didn't speak right away. Sometimes, silence was the only language that made sense. I let the weight of it settle between us, comfortable and real. There was no rush for words. We had plenty of time now.

"Where do we go from here?" Vance asked after a moment, his voice low, rough. The question hung in the air, unspoken, a challenge we both knew we had to face.

I turned to face him fully, letting the sun stretch its golden fingers across his face. He looked... different. Not just the way the light fell on him, but the way his eyes held mine—clearer now, without the shadows of anger and distrust that used to darken them. There was a vulnerability there, too, one I hadn't expected, but maybe it was one I had been hoping for. It made him human, in a way. Imperfect. Real. And I couldn't look away.

"I don't know," I replied honestly, my voice steady despite the turmoil inside me. "But we'll figure it out. Together."

His lips curved in the faintest of smiles, the kind that didn't quite reach his eyes, but it was enough. It was more than enough.

"I like that," he said, his tone playful despite the gravity of the moment.

For a fleeting second, I forgot about the city, the damage, the debris that littered the streets like forgotten dreams. I forgot about everything except Vance and the way he made me feel like we could rebuild everything, not just around us but inside us too. Maybe that was the thing about surviving—about seeing what remained after everything else had crumbled—it made the possibility of rebuilding something new seem a little less impossible.

But then a sound broke through the quiet, a sharp crack, like a twig snapping underfoot. My heart stuttered, and instinctively, I reached for the knife at my belt. Vance tensed beside me, his muscles coiling as if the world was still on the verge of breaking in two.

"I don't think we're done yet," I muttered, my voice low, barely above a whisper.

Vance didn't answer right away. Instead, he took a slow, deliberate step forward, his eyes scanning the horizon like a predator on the hunt. I followed his lead, my senses sharpening. The calm, peaceful morning that had felt so right just seconds ago seemed to slip away, replaced by an edge of tension I hadn't expected. We hadn't just fought the war—hadn't just won the battle—because the game had changed. No, we'd become part of something much bigger. And no matter how much we tried to deny it, there would always be shadows creeping in the corners, ready to pounce when we least expected it.

A figure appeared in the distance, moving through the ruins with a quiet grace, a stark contrast to the chaos surrounding us. The figure was tall, their silhouette slender but unmistakable. My breath caught in my throat.

"No," I murmured, almost too softly for anyone to hear. "Not now."

Vance turned sharply at the sound of my voice, his eyes narrowing as he followed my gaze. The figure approached, and as they drew nearer, the details became clear: it was a woman. Her face was hidden beneath the shadow of a hood, but I knew that profile. Knew it all too well.

"Is it... her?" Vance asked, his voice barely a whisper, the tension palpable.

I nodded, my stomach twisting into knots. "It's her. And she's not here for a friendly chat."

I had half a mind to turn and walk the other way. It wasn't a coward's escape, though I wasn't sure how much courage I had left. It was more of an instinct—one honed by years of surviving on the edge of a city that had no regard for boundaries or mercy. This woman, whoever she was, hadn't come this far just for a chat. And if I was being honest, I didn't think we were in the mood for another fight.

Vance's hand brushed against mine, the touch barely there, but it was enough to steady me. I glanced at him, and his expression, still hard and unreadable, gave nothing away. His eyes flickered to the stranger and then back to me. A silent question passed between us, one that had no easy answer.

"We can't just stand here," he said, his voice edged with something I couldn't quite place. Maybe caution. Maybe curiosity. Maybe just the simple fact that we were both bracing for the worst.

I took a slow, deliberate breath, letting the sharp edge of panic fade into something more manageable. "You're right," I said, but my voice felt thinner than I wanted it to. It didn't matter, though. She was too close now, the rhythm of her footsteps betraying a sense of purpose that made my gut twist. I tried not to think about the last time I had seen her—darkened skies, blood on the streets, and the way she had looked at me as if I were nothing more than a pawn in a game that was far above my pay grade.

"Do we fight, or do we talk?" I asked, glancing sideways at Vance.

He didn't answer right away, his eyes still locked on the approaching figure. But I saw the flicker of something behind them, something complicated, tangled up in old histories. He knew this woman. I could tell. They had shared a battlefield once, and I wasn't sure what secrets lay in the space between them.

"We talk," he said finally, his voice tight but firm. "For now."

For now. That phrase echoed in my mind, and I couldn't help but wonder just how much of a concession that really was. Because something told me that this wasn't going to be a peaceful exchange of pleasantries. Not with her.

As she came closer, I caught more details—her stance, measured and sure, the way the sunlight danced on the edge of her hood, like a halo of danger. I tried to tell myself it was nothing. Just another survivor, just another face in a broken city. But the truth was, she wasn't just anyone. She was someone who had come too close to the heart of everything I had feared, and every step she took toward us felt like an unspoken threat.

She stopped a few paces away, her gaze flickering briefly to Vance before settling on me. Her lips twitched, just slightly, in what could have been a smile or a sneer. Hard to tell with her.

"Well, well," she said, her voice smooth, but laced with an edge that felt like steel wrapped in velvet. "Look at this. The two of you, still breathing."

I swallowed, willing myself not to flinch at the sound of her voice. I had spent too long avoiding her, hoping the past would remain buried in its own shadow. But here she was, pulling everything I had buried back into the light.

"You didn't think it was going to be that easy, did you?" she continued, her eyes scanning the wreckage behind us, the distant smoke curling into the sky like a reminder of all the things we hadn't yet finished.

I didn't answer at first. What could I say to that? The idea that any of this was ever easy seemed laughable. Surviving had always been about endurance, about outlasting whatever storm decided to hit next. But I wasn't sure how much longer that would work if people like her kept coming.

Vance stepped forward, his stance protective but measured. He didn't look at me when he spoke, his attention focused entirely on the woman in front of us.

"I thought we were past this," he said, his voice low but with an undeniable bite. "I thought we'd settled things."

She chuckled, the sound like the click of a knife blade being sharpened. "Oh, we've settled nothing. You've just forgotten how much of the game you've lost." Her eyes flicked toward me again, and for a split second, I swore I saw something like recognition in them. But it was gone as quickly as it came, replaced by that same cold smirk.

"You've always been a pawn, Vance," she said, her voice carrying the weight of a hundred old wounds. "And so have you," she added, turning her gaze on me. "I don't know why I'm surprised you've managed to survive. You were always too stubborn for your own good."

I bristled at the insult, but I didn't let it show. Not now. Not when there was still so much left unsaid.

"So, what now?" I asked, my voice sharp despite the uncertainty gnawing at the back of my mind. "You come here to lecture us, or is there something else?"

For a moment, she didn't answer, as though weighing the worth of my words. And then, just as I thought she was going to turn away, she took a step closer, her eyes narrowing in on me.

"You've survived," she said, her voice softer now, but with an undercurrent of something dangerous. "But not everything has been dealt with. And you're not as free as you think you are."

I could feel my pulse quicken, the weight of her words settling heavily in the air between us. There was a truth to what she was saying, one that I hadn't wanted to acknowledge. The world had shifted around us, but some things—some people—just wouldn't let go.

Vance's expression hardened, and he took another step forward, his shoulders squared. "Then tell us what you want, and be done with it. You're wasting our time."

The woman didn't flinch, didn't even blink. Instead, she smiled, a slow, knowing curve of her lips. "Oh, I'm not here to waste anyone's time. I'm here to remind you of the choices you made and the consequences that are still to come." She took another step forward, closing the distance between us, her eyes glinting with something darker than amusement.

"You think you've won," she said quietly, almost like a promise. "But the real battle is just beginning."

The words hung in the air like smoke, heavy and suffocating. "The real battle is just beginning." Her voice had a way of slicing through the quiet aftermath of our fight, leaving a jagged edge in its wake. I had braced myself for any number of things, but somehow, I hadn't expected that.

I glanced at Vance, searching his face for any sign of recognition, any hint that this wasn't just another cryptic warning from someone who liked to toy with us. But his eyes were fixed on the woman with a kind of sharp, wary focus that made the hairs on the back of my neck prickle. There was history there—history that I hadn't yet cracked open, like a book with pages I wasn't sure I wanted to read.

For a long moment, no one spoke. It was one of those silences that makes your skin crawl, that quiet before everything unravels. I felt my pulse hammering, the thud of it drowning out the sounds of the city beyond us—the distant calls of birds, the faint hum of the city coming to life again after the storm. But here, with her standing in front of us, the air felt thick and unbreathable, as if the city had held its breath too.

I knew I had to speak. If only to break the tension.

"You keep saying things like that," I said, keeping my tone cool, but a flicker of frustration crept into my voice despite myself. "You keep dropping these ominous little tidbits like they mean something. But we're done playing games. If you want something, just say it."

Her smile was slow, deliberate, as though she were savoring every word I'd just said. "Oh, I'll say it," she said, her voice turning soft with the kind of honeyed menace that makes you question whether you're walking into a trap or being offered a deal. "But first, I need you to understand something. You may have won this round, but there are always others." Her eyes flickered to Vance, and then to the shattered remains of Crescent City behind us. "You're in over your heads."

I clenched my fists at my sides. "If you're trying to scare us, it's not working."

Her laughter echoed, a sharp, unsettling sound that made the hairs on my neck rise again. "I'm not here to scare you, darling. I'm here to remind you how much you've yet to lose."

I shook my head, trying to dismiss the chill creeping up my spine. The city had been through enough. We had been through enough. And yet, here we were, standing on the edge of whatever this was, with her serving as the reminder of how fragile everything really was.

"Enough with the riddles," I snapped. "If you've got a point, get to it. What do you want from us?"

She tilted her head, studying me as if I were a puzzle she'd been working on for too long. Finally, she spoke, her words soft and deliberate. "I want you to understand that there are consequences for every choice you've made. For every person you've crossed. For every line you've crossed. You might think you've won, but someone always pays the price."

There was something almost gleeful in her tone, a kind of satisfaction that made my stomach turn. I knew she wasn't talking about Vance. She was talking about me. About us. About the things we'd done—things I hadn't been able to shake, no matter how far we ran from them.

I met her gaze, refusing to look away, even as a thousand thoughts raced through my mind. I couldn't let her see that she had gotten under my skin. That would be admitting defeat.

"So, what now?" Vance's voice cut through the tension, steady and low, though I could see the tension in the set of his jaw. "You're going to make us pay for something we've already paid for? Because if that's the case, I think you'll find we're done with that."

The woman's smile widened, but there was something far colder in it now, something sharper. "Oh, Vance. You really don't get it, do you? This isn't about what you've paid. This is about what you owe. And I'm here to collect."

Before either of us could react, there was a sudden, sharp noise—a crack, like something breaking through the air itself. I spun, instinctively reaching for the knife at my belt, my heart pounding in my chest.

A figure emerged from the shadows, silhouetted against the brightening sky. The figure was tall, cloaked in a dark, weathered coat, the edges fluttering as if caught in the wind. My breath caught in my throat. I didn't know who they were, but I could feel the shift in the atmosphere as soon as they appeared. The woman—my shadowy visitor—turned, her eyes narrowing, lips parting in disbelief.

"What is this?" I muttered, unable to keep the edge from creeping into my voice.

The new figure didn't speak at first. They simply moved closer, each step slow and deliberate. The woman's posture had stiffened, and I could feel the tension building in the air around us, thick and tight. Something was about to happen. I could feel it in the way the city seemed to hold its breath again.

Vance's hand tightened around the hilt of his sword, his eyes flicking between me and the approaching figure. His voice was low, steady, but I could hear the flicker of concern beneath it. "Who is this?"

The figure stopped just a few feet away from us, and for a long, silent moment, nothing else moved. Not the wind, not the world around us. Just the crackle of tension, the weight of a thousand questions hanging between us. And then, without a word, the figure reached up and pulled back the hood, revealing the face beneath.

I froze, my blood running cold.

It was someone I thought I'd never see again. Someone who was supposed to be long gone.

"You..." I whispered, my voice shaking despite myself.

And in that moment, everything shifted. The city, the world—it all felt like it was unraveling beneath my feet.

Chapter 27: Rebuilding from Ashes

The air in Crescent City was thick with the scent of smoke and rain, a mixture of destruction and renewal. I stood on the balcony of our temporary home, watching as the last of the flames from the battle flickered out in the distance, giving way to a darkened sky filled with ominous clouds. The rain had started, soft at first, then heavier, washing the streets below in cleansing torrents. The city, once vibrant and full of life, was now a tapestry of broken glass and twisted metal, its heartbeat stilled for the moment. But in the midst of it all, there was an undeniable hum—a sense that the land itself was holding its breath, waiting for us to breathe life back into it.

Vance's footsteps behind me drew my attention, his presence a quiet comfort. I didn't need to turn around to know he was there. I could feel him, the warmth of his energy mixing with the chill of the air. His arms slid around me, pulling me back into him, his chin resting on the top of my head. The weight of everything, the destruction and the loss, seemed to momentarily lift when he was near. "We'll rebuild," he said, his voice low and steady, a promise wrapped in raw truth. "Not just the city. Us, too."

I exhaled, leaning into him, the rhythm of our breaths syncing as if we had always been like this—entangled in a way that felt inevitable. "I don't know where to start," I confessed, the weight of his words settling over me. "It feels like too much."

"One step at a time," he murmured. His hands were gentle as they ran down my arms, steadying me, grounding me. "Start with us. We've got all the time in the world to figure the rest out."

There was a vulnerability in his voice that I hadn't heard before—an openness that both scared and comforted me. It was a rare gift, this willingness to expose the raw, tender parts of ourselves. But in that moment, I understood something fundamental about us.

We weren't just rebuilding Crescent City. We were rebuilding each other.

It hadn't been easy, this dance we'd been doing since the battle. We'd fought not only the forces that had threatened our world but also the fears that had held us back from fully surrendering to what had always been between us. Trust. Hope. Love. It was hard to imagine, in the immediate aftermath of chaos, that anything could be whole again. Yet, here we were—together, surrounded by ruins, somehow still standing. Still breathing.

The rain began to fall harder, a steady thrum against the windows, and I could hear the city waking up around us. The first of the rebuilding teams had already arrived, gathering in groups to assess the damage, to make plans. We hadn't spoken much about the logistics, mostly because we didn't need to. The people of Crescent City knew how to survive. They always had. They just needed a spark—a leader. A reason to hope again.

Vance's grip tightened around me, and I turned in his arms, meeting his gaze. His eyes were darker now, not from the storm, but from the weight of the world we both carried. "How do we do it?" I asked, my voice barely above a whisper, unsure if I was asking about the city or something far more personal.

"We do it by trusting in what we have," he said, his fingers gently brushing the hair away from my face. "By trusting in each other."

The words were simple, yet I felt their truth ripple through me, pulling me closer to him. There had been a time when I couldn't have imagined letting someone in this far. The walls I'd built around myself were thick, layered with years of pain and disappointment. But Vance had torn them down, piece by piece, with his quiet patience and his unyielding faith. Not just in the city, but in me.

I reached up, tracing the line of his jaw, the familiar texture of his stubble grounding me. "And what if it's not enough?" The question escaped before I could stop it, a thread of doubt that I hadn't realized was still clinging to me.

He smiled then, a slow, deliberate curve of his lips that held none of the bravado he often wore but all the softness I was coming to adore. "Then we build something better. Together."

I didn't know what the future held. The city was broken, and so were we, in ways that neither of us could articulate. But I did know one thing for certain. We would rebuild. Not just the city we loved, but the parts of ourselves that had been lost along the way. It wouldn't be easy. We would stumble, perhaps even fall. But in the end, the city would rise, and so would we.

I stepped back from him, the rain soaking through my clothes now, but I didn't mind. The coolness of it was grounding, a stark contrast to the heat between us. "We should join the others," I said, my voice steadying, a spark of resolve flickering in my chest. "It's time to get to work."

Vance didn't hesitate. He took my hand, his fingers wrapping around mine with a quiet certainty that made the world outside feel a little less heavy. We walked together into the storm, both of us knowing that the road ahead would be long, but that we would walk it side by side, one step at a time.

The days following the battle were an odd mixture of quiet and chaos. Crescent City was at once a place of devastation and renewal, a city with a heartbeat that hadn't quite given up, even though it was bruised. Every corner seemed to offer a new reminder of the destruction we'd faced: a crumpled tower that once housed the finest restaurant in the district, a shattered fountain where children once played. But there was also something else, something almost imperceptible at first, like a whisper threading through the debris. It was hope.

Vance and I found ourselves more often than not on the streets, surveying the damage, talking to the citizens who were already picking up the pieces. There were so many of them—brave faces smeared with dirt, hands rough with work, but their eyes, oh their eyes—they were tired, but they burned with something undeniable. Resolve. And that was something Vance and I were learning to cultivate in ourselves.

We'd fallen into an unspoken rhythm, a dance of sorts, as we navigated our own fragile relationship amidst the wreckage. Sometimes I'd catch him staring at me when he thought I wasn't looking, his eyes soft yet full of intent, as if he was trying to read me like a map he hadn't quite figured out. Other times, I'd look up and find him waiting for me to speak, his mouth a thin line, as if he too was searching for the right words. It wasn't easy—finding that delicate balance between what we had been and what we were trying to become.

The city felt like a metaphor for us. I could almost hear the cracks forming beneath our feet, the fractures threatening to split wide open. But there was something in Vance's steady presence that kept me from falling. Or maybe it was the way we both understood the cost of silence, how it had a way of hardening the spaces between two people until the cracks turned into chasms. So, I spoke when it was hard. And he listened. And sometimes, when words failed, he would reach out, his hand a quiet promise that we were in this together.

It was a Saturday when it happened—just another gray day, rain threatening but not yet delivered. We were at the square, gathering with the rebuilding teams to plan what came next. I could feel the weight of it all settling into my chest, the enormity of the task, the questions that swirled in my mind like the storm clouds above us. How do you rebuild something so broken? How do you even begin to fix what feels irreparably lost?

Vance caught my eye across the crowd, his lips twitching into that rare, crooked smile of his. It was a look that never failed to turn my heart over, like I was the only person in the world who mattered. He beckoned me over with a nod, and I walked to him, the ground slick underfoot, the scent of wet earth thick in the air. I stepped into his arms without hesitation, his familiar warmth an anchor in the storm of thoughts I'd been swirling through all day.

"Something on your mind?" he asked, his fingers brushing a lock of wet hair behind my ear.

I met his gaze, hesitated, then nodded. "Everything feels... heavy. I don't know where to start."

His smile softened, and for a moment, he said nothing. He didn't need to. His presence alone was enough. "Start with today. You can't fix everything at once. Neither of us can."

"I know." The words were a release. I hadn't realized how tightly I had been holding myself together until that moment.

There was a long pause, filled only with the sound of rain tapping against the cobblestones. Then, Vance turned slightly, pulling me with him toward a gathering of locals near the fountain—the fountain that used to be the centerpiece of the district. It was a sad, collapsed version of its former self now, the stone rim cracked and water pooling in shallow depressions. But the people were working, laughing, rebuilding it as if it were a symbol of something they couldn't afford to lose.

"You see this?" Vance gestured to the workers, all of them moving in harmony, like the city's pulse was beating just beneath their feet. "This is how we start."

I took a deep breath and looked closer, at the laughter that bubbled through the rain-soaked air, at the way hands that were still raw from the battle now touched the stones with tenderness. There was a rhythm to it, an unspoken understanding that the small, deliberate acts—those everyday gestures—were what would carry them forward. It wasn't grand. It wasn't perfect. But it was progress.

"It's all we can do," I said softly, stepping closer, my shoulder brushing his as we watched the group work together. "One stone at a time."

Vance nodded, his gaze never leaving the workers. "One stone at a time."

For the rest of the afternoon, we worked with them. Not because we had any particular skills to offer—though, I did have a decent knack for organizing people—but because it felt right. We weren't standing apart anymore. We weren't just observing; we were part of it, the pulse of the city slowly coming back to life beneath our hands.

As the sun dipped low, casting a golden hue over the city's wreckage, I found myself beside Vance again, our hands brushing occasionally as we moved to different sections of the square. The tiredness was there, pulling at me, but it wasn't the heavy kind of exhaustion that made you want to shut down. It was the kind that made you feel alive. The kind that came from doing something that mattered.

"I don't think I've ever done something that felt this real," I said, my voice a little breathless from the work. "Something that... really mattered."

He shot me a sideways glance, the corners of his mouth turning upward. "I've got a few things that really matter, if you're interested."

I glanced at him, laughing despite the seriousness of everything. "I'm listening."

He stopped walking, catching my arm with a gentle tug, pulling me toward him. "You matter. The city matters. And, despite all the craziness around us, you know what else matters?"

"What?"

He grinned. "The fact that I'm starting to think you might actually be the only person I'd do this with."

My heart stuttered in my chest. It wasn't what I'd expected, and yet, in a way, it was exactly what I needed to hear. The walls that

I hadn't even realized were still up started to crumble then, and I knew—I just knew—that no matter what came next, we would face it together. One stone at a time.

We'd worked through the night, long past the point where the rain had stopped and the streets began to glisten with the damp, empty silence of a city still in shock. The only sounds now were the occasional creak of a support beam shifting in one of the old buildings, or the low hum of the wind weaving through the cracked windows. But beneath that stillness, there was a growing pulse, like the city was slowly, tentatively waking from a long, painful slumber.

I hadn't realized how much I needed this—how much I needed to be doing—until we'd thrown ourselves into the work. It wasn't the grand, sweeping gestures of leadership that I had imagined at first. No speeches, no promises to the masses. It was the quiet, unglamorous work of lifting bricks, mending foundations, wiping away the dust of the past to reveal the bones of the future. And somehow, it felt right.

It had been days now, and while Vance and I had learned how to balance the weight of our shared quiet moments, there was still something between us that hadn't quite been resolved. A silent understanding, maybe. The tension of unspoken words, or rather, a collection of words we weren't ready to speak. There were mornings when I would catch him staring at me over coffee, as if he was waiting for me to make the first move. But it wasn't just about the words. It was the other things—the subtle gestures, the way he'd reach for my hand when he thought no one was watching, or the way he lingered a fraction too long after a kiss, his lips soft and searching.

But just as the city was healing, so too were we. The cracks that once defined us were starting to soften, to fill in with something new, something deeper.

The morning was clear and fresh, the air cool enough to make me shiver as I stepped out onto the balcony. The sun had begun to burn away the fog that had settled on the city overnight, revealing what seemed like a world reborn. The golden light spilling over the rooftops made everything feel possible, even if just for today.

Vance was already at the makeshift command post, his head bent over a stack of papers, his jaw set in that familiar, determined line. He was always the first one up. Always working. Always planning. Sometimes I wondered if he ever stopped, ever let himself breathe.

I found myself drifting towards him, almost instinctively, my steps quieter than usual. I wanted to ask him how he was really doing, but something told me he wouldn't answer. Not yet. So instead, I leaned against the wooden doorframe and simply watched him.

After a moment, he looked up, and for the briefest second, I saw something shift in his eyes—like he'd just realized I was there, not in a distant, "I'm just passing through" kind of way, but in the way that meant he'd been thinking about me even before I stepped into his line of sight. His gaze softened, and without a word, he motioned for me to sit across from him.

I moved without hesitation, sliding into the chair, my hands resting on the edge of the table, the weight of the conversation I'd been avoiding pressing heavily between us.

"So," I said, the word a little breathless, "I think we've got the city on its feet." It was a weak attempt at lightness, but I needed to break the tension. We both did.

Vance's lips twitched, but it wasn't the smile I'd been hoping for. It was something more guarded. "We're getting there," he agreed. "But the real work is just beginning. The political alliances, the trade routes, the rebuilding of infrastructure—Crescent City won't fix itself."

"I know." I nodded, trying to ignore the weight of the truth in his words. It wasn't just about the physical labor anymore. It was about rebuilding the trust that had been lost, about reconciling the factions that had been torn apart during the battle. It was about hope. But that was something neither of us could promise, not without making ourselves vulnerable in ways we hadn't quite figured out how to navigate yet.

The silence stretched on, and I could feel the distance between us, not in the way we had been before, but in something more intricate. A tension in the air, a quiet humming that pulled at me, made my pulse quicken.

"Vance," I started, the name feeling like it carried more weight than it ever had before. "Do you think we'll be enough? To rebuild all of this?" I gestured vaguely to the city, the streets below now filled with workers, each one a small part of the larger whole. But despite the movement, despite the progress, I could still hear the question echoing in my mind, unanswered and pressing.

He leaned back in his chair, his eyes never leaving mine, as though weighing my question against the world that hung heavy around us. "I don't know," he said quietly. "But I think we're better together than apart."

I let out a breath I hadn't realized I'd been holding, the weight of his words settling into me like a heavy truth. The air between us felt thick, but this time, it wasn't uncomfortable. It was just real.

"Sometimes, I wonder if I'm even capable of this," I said softly, gesturing between us, between the work, the city, everything. "I wasn't built for this—any of it."

Vance reached across the table, his fingers brushing against mine, the warmth of his hand grounding me. "You are," he said, his voice so sure that I almost believed him. "You just don't know it yet."

I squeezed his hand, trying to find something solid in the unspoken promise between us. But just as I opened my mouth to say something, a shout came from outside. We both stood instantly, the tension in the room snapping into action.

"What's happening?" I asked, moving quickly toward the door.

Vance was already ahead of me, his steps swift and purposeful. "I don't know, but we'll find out."

As we stepped out onto the balcony, I saw the commotion below. People were scattering, shouting, running toward the edge of the district, toward the crumbling gates. There was something in the air now, something different—something that wasn't right.

I turned to Vance, my pulse racing. "What's going on?"

His face had gone pale, and for the first time since I'd met him, there was fear in his eyes.

"I don't know," he said, his voice tight. "But I think we're about to find out."

Before I could respond, a figure emerged from the crowd, their silhouette framed by the setting sun. They were coming straight for us. And I knew, with a sinking feeling in my chest, that nothing—nothing—would be the same again.

Chapter 28: Threads of the Future

The café was quiet, the kind of quiet that felt heavy in the air, as if the world outside had just taken a deep breath and paused. I could hear the clinking of porcelain cups, the soft rustling of a newspaper, and the distant murmur of the barista behind the counter, pulling espresso shots with an efficiency that bordered on surgical precision. But it was the heat that had settled in the room that caught my attention, thick and comforting, wrapping itself around my skin like a familiar embrace.

I sat at the far corner, my fingers absentmindedly tracing the rim of my coffee cup, feeling the warmth seep into my palm, grounding me in the present. I liked this moment—these stolen few minutes when everything seemed just right. When the chaos of the outside world was muffled by the soft murmur of conversations and the gentle hum of the espresso machine. I had a lot on my mind, too much, maybe. But for the first time in weeks, I wasn't rushing to figure it out.

Across the table, Alex was scribbling something in a notebook, his brow furrowed in concentration. His pen moved with a kind of fluidity, as if the words were already in his head, just waiting to escape onto the paper. I couldn't help but admire the way his mind worked, how he could get lost in a thought and yet remain so entirely present at the same time. It was a rare gift.

"Penny for your thoughts?" I asked, breaking the silence, my voice teasing but genuine.

Alex glanced up, a flicker of amusement crossing his face before he set the pen down. "That's an inflationary rate for something so trivial," he said with a wry grin, but his eyes softened as they met mine. "But sure, if you insist."

I chuckled, shaking my head. It was impossible not to love him when he made me laugh like that. His charm was subtle, the kind that didn't demand attention but earned it all the same. There was something effortlessly magnetic about him. "Okay, fine. I'll take that as a yes."

He leaned back in his chair, tapping his fingers on the edge of the table, eyes drifting to the window where the light was beginning to shift, casting long shadows over the street. "I'm thinking about the future," he admitted, his voice quieter now, as if he'd let the words slip out before he could stop them. "About what comes next. After this... after everything."

The shift in his tone wasn't lost on me. I could feel the weight of the conversation hanging between us like a fragile thread, one that could snap at any moment if pulled too hard. My stomach tightened, and I swallowed, the reality of our situation creeping back in. There were no easy answers. The world had a way of complicating things, and the more I thought about the future, the less certain I became of what I wanted or what was even possible.

"I know," I said softly, trying to sound more confident than I felt. "Me too."

Alex tilted his head, his expression unreadable for a moment before his lips curled into that teasing smile. "You know, it's kind of strange," he mused, "how two people can sit in the same room, be caught in the same storm, and yet feel like they're on entirely different paths."

I met his gaze, searching for the meaning behind his words. "What do you mean?" I asked, my voice barely above a whisper.

He exhaled slowly, rubbing the back of his neck. "I mean... you're all about the bigger picture, right? The grand design. But me? I get lost in the details. The little moments. Sometimes I feel like I'm drifting, but then I find something, some little piece of the puzzle, and it makes sense again. For a while, at least."

My heart clenched. His words rang so true, but it was the way he said them—so matter-of-fact, as if he was trying to convince himself— that made something shift inside me. We had always been two sides of the same coin. He was the dreamer, the one who could see the endless possibilities and the beauty in the chaos, while I was the planner, the one who wanted to put everything in its place. It worked, most of the time. But lately, I wasn't sure if our worlds were still aligning.

"I don't know where the road goes from here," I admitted, my voice barely audible as I watched his face. "But I don't want to lose what we have. I don't want it to just fade away because we didn't figure it out in time."

He leaned forward, his gaze intense and unwavering. "Then we won't let it fade. We don't have to figure everything out right now, but we can figure it out together."

His words were a balm, soothing the unease I hadn't even realized had been gnawing at the edges of my thoughts. It wasn't a solution, but it was something. And something was enough.

We sat in silence for a moment, each of us lost in our own thoughts, the quiet hum of the café providing a backdrop for the tension that hung between us. Outside, the sky had darkened, and the city had begun to come alive in the way it did at twilight, bathed in the soft glow of streetlights. The air had taken on a slight chill, and I could hear the distant honk of car horns and the shuffle of feet on the sidewalk.

For the first time in what felt like forever, I wasn't thinking about the future. I wasn't thinking about what might go wrong or what might never come to be. I was here, in this moment, with him. And that was enough to keep me grounded.

The streets outside had begun to pulse with life as the evening set in, and yet, here we were, still wrapped in the cocoon of this little corner, holding on to the calm before the storm. I could almost hear the city breathing, a deep, steady hum that seemed to reverberate beneath the quiet chatter of those around us. It was one of those nights where the world felt both infinite and impossibly small at the same time, where everything felt heavy with promise but also just a little fragile—like an old book teetering on the edge of a shelf, waiting to be opened.

Alex stretched his arms, a little too dramatically, but it made me smile despite myself. He was always a bit theatrical, like the kind of person who would make a grand entrance even if it was just to grab a coffee. "I think I've had enough introspection for one day," he muttered, tapping his pen against the table. "Time to focus on the important stuff."

I raised an eyebrow. "The important stuff?" I echoed, my tone teasing, as I watched him shift in his chair, clearly preparing for whatever quirky tangent he was about to go off on.

"Yep. The really important stuff," he said, his eyes narrowing playfully. "Like where we're going for dinner."

I couldn't help but laugh, shaking my head. He had a knack for deflecting heavy moments with his humor, and I was starting to realize just how much I appreciated that. Sometimes, when things felt too raw or too real, it was easier to lean into the absurdities of life rather than let yourself get lost in the gravity of it all.

"You're impossible," I said, but there was no malice behind it. I liked that about him—that ability to lighten the mood when I needed it most.

"I try," he replied with a smirk. "So, how about Italian? I'm thinking something cheesy, saucy, and completely unnecessary."

I considered it for a moment, letting the absurdity of his suggestion settle in. "That sounds... dangerously tempting," I admitted, my fingers still tracing the edge of my cup, "but I'm not sure I'm prepared to deal with the carb coma that comes with it."

His eyes glinted with mischief. "Oh, please. You and I both know you've already surrendered to the carb coma. It's just a matter of when."

I let out a mock gasp, feigning outrage. "I resent that. I'm a woman of self-discipline."

"Uh-huh. Sure you are," he said, grinning. "So... Italian? Or do we want to make a wrong turn down the path of shame and go for sushi instead?"

"Sushi?" I scoffed, putting my hands on my hips. "I thought you were better than that."

His eyes widened in mock horror. "Sushi? Better? Pardon me for daring to mention something fresh and healthy. You wound me." He clutched his chest dramatically, causing the couple sitting a few tables away to glance over in mild confusion.

"I'm not going for sushi. You're getting pizza. And no, you can't add pineapple," I said, leaning back in my chair, satisfied in my decision.

"You can't just ban me from pineapple. That's a human rights violation."

I raised my eyebrows, giving him my most serious look. "You'll thank me when you wake up tomorrow, staring longingly at the gym's elliptical machine."

He opened his mouth as though to argue, but then stopped, his expression softening slightly. He ran a hand through his hair, eyes distant for a moment as he shifted in his seat. "Yeah. You're probably right."

The weight of the change in his demeanor didn't escape me. It wasn't like him to fall quiet—he usually filled the air with jokes or lighthearted commentary, always the first to make some snarky remark. But this, this was different. There was something pulling at him, something I couldn't name, but I felt it, a kind of tug at the edges of my thoughts, like the beginning of a storm just on the horizon.

"You good?" I asked, my voice softer now, no longer teasing. It wasn't like me to press, but it had been a long while since I'd seen him so... still.

He blinked, as though pulled out of his thoughts. "Yeah. Just... thinking. It's nothing, really. Just... future stuff."

I tilted my head, studying him more closely. "The future again?"

He gave a little shrug, his lips curving into a half-smile. But it didn't reach his eyes, and that made the air feel heavier somehow. "Yeah. You know. The usual. What's next. How things work out."

"Are we still talking about dinner?" I asked, trying to draw him back into the lightness, to crack the mask he'd slipped on.

He laughed, the sound a little strained. "Maybe not."

"Okay," I said, setting my coffee cup down, locking eyes with him. "Let's skip the future for a second. Just tell me about your perfect day. No rules. No 'what comes next.' Just... you. What does a perfect day look like for Alex?"

It took him a moment to answer, his fingers tapping idly on the table. When he did speak, his voice was quieter than I expected. "Perfect day? Hmm. It's funny, I think about it more than I should. Maybe I'm just trying to picture a life that makes sense." He paused, and I saw a flicker of something pass across his face—something raw and unspoken. "But I guess it'd be one where I wake up, not stressed about the next thing. A day where I get to just... be."

I nodded slowly, absorbing the weight of his words. "And me? Where do I fit into your perfect day?"

A slow smile spread across his face, genuine this time. "You'd be there, of course. You're the part that makes it real."

I swallowed hard, a lump forming in my throat. "And the rest of it?"

"The rest of it?" He leaned back in his chair, the playful spark in his eyes returning. "That's the easy part. I'd get to spend the whole day teasing you about your food choices."

I laughed, the tension breaking, and the lightness returned. But somewhere deep inside, the future—the one we didn't dare speak of directly—still lingered. And despite the laughter, it wasn't going anywhere. Not yet.

The evening had taken on a soft, golden hue as the last of the daylight lingered, casting long shadows across the tables and stretching across the worn, wooden floors of the café. The air smelled faintly of cinnamon and roasted coffee beans, and for a moment, everything outside those thick glass windows seemed like an afterthought, a place I couldn't quite grasp. I wanted to stay here, in this cocoon of warmth and fleeting moments, where the world felt manageable and the future didn't loom so large. But of course, life had other plans.

"So," I said, breaking the comfortable silence that had settled between us. "Do you think we're crazy for thinking this could work? You know, all of this... whatever this is."

Alex didn't look up right away, his gaze still fixed on the street outside, his fingers playing with the edges of his notebook. I could tell he was avoiding the question, letting it hover between us like a balloon someone was afraid to pop.

"Do you?" he finally asked, voice light, but his eyes flickering with something more serious beneath.

I took a deep breath, the cool air feeling almost foreign in my lungs. "I don't know. Some days, I feel like we're making sense of a mess. And other days... it's like we're pretending we have it figured out."

"You mean today?" he asked, glancing at me now, his lips curling into a teasing smile.

I shot him a look. "Exactly."

He grinned, the tension in his eyes melting for a moment. "Yeah, well, it's not like we're alone in that. Everyone's pretending they've got it figured out. Even people who really, really don't."

"I know," I said, shifting in my chair, suddenly uncomfortable with how true that felt. "But you know what I mean. It's like we're supposed to have a plan, like we're supposed to know where we're going. And we don't. And maybe we never will."

Alex leaned forward, his expression serious now, a sharp contrast to the casual tone he usually wore. "Maybe that's the point, though. Maybe we're not supposed to know exactly what comes next."

I frowned. "You're starting to sound like a self-help book. Are you going to tell me to 'embrace the journey' next?"

He chuckled, but there was a flicker of something else in his eyes. Something deeper. "Maybe. Or maybe I'm just realizing that all the planning in the world doesn't stop things from... happening."

I felt a chill crawl up my spine. "What do you mean?"

"Nothing," he said quickly, but the way his jaw tightened gave him away. He was holding something back, something that felt heavier than the easy jokes he usually used to deflect things.

"Alex," I said softly, pushing my coffee cup aside, "what's going on?"

He hesitated, his fingers tapping against the table, the rhythm unsteady. "I don't know, Penny," he muttered under his breath, the words barely audible over the rising hum of the café. "I just... I feel like we're at a crossroads. Like we've reached the point where we either figure it out, or we just stop pretending we can."

I swallowed, the weight of his words sinking in. "And you think it's that simple? You think we just... stop?"

He exhaled sharply, his gaze shifting to the street again. His voice was low, almost to himself. "I don't know if it's simple. But I think it might be the only way forward."

The finality in his tone caught me off guard. I could feel the distance between us growing, not in any physical sense, but in a way that made everything feel more fragile. Like the bond we had built was held together by nothing more than the thinnest thread, one that could snap if either of us moved too quickly.

For a moment, I didn't know what to say. The silence between us stretched long, heavy with the weight of unspoken things. The world outside was still turning, the hum of life continuing unabated, but inside this small bubble of space, everything felt suspended, hanging in limbo.

"I don't want to stop," I whispered, almost afraid to say it aloud. "I don't want us to stop."

Alex's eyes met mine, searching, as though weighing the truth of my words. "Neither do I," he said softly. "But sometimes, the harder we try to hold on, the more we hurt each other."

I felt my chest tighten at his words. It wasn't that I didn't understand what he was saying—it was that, in this moment, it felt like the only thing that was certain was that nothing was certain anymore.

"I don't know if I'm strong enough to let go," I admitted, my voice barely a whisper.

Alex's expression softened, his lips pressing together in a line of quiet sympathy. "Maybe you don't have to. Maybe the letting go isn't about giving up. Maybe it's just about letting things... unfold."

I wanted to believe him. I wanted to believe that whatever was happening between us could be fixed by time or patience or the sheer force of our will. But I wasn't sure anymore. The future felt like a distant shore, just beyond reach, and I didn't know if we had the strength to swim toward it.

We sat there for what felt like an eternity, the moments stretching out until they became threads in themselves, weaving a story that neither of us knew how to finish.

The air in the café had grown thick, the fading light casting soft shadows over the table, but there was an undercurrent of tension now. The kind that made it impossible to focus on anything but the conversation at hand.

Then, just as I was about to speak, I saw something—someone—through the window. A figure crossing the street, moving with the kind of urgency that instantly drew my attention. Something about their posture seemed... familiar.

My heart skipped a beat. And just like that, the fragile thread between us snapped.

Chapter 29: A Love Eternal

The wind whipped through my hair, tugging it free from its careful knot, and I laughed, shaking my head. It felt absurdly perfect. The last rays of the setting sun clung to the edges of the horizon, a fiery orange glow bleeding into the midnight blue of the sky. But it was the breeze—wild, untamed—that made the whole scene feel like something pulled from a dream, not reality. And yet here we were, on the edge of something real and terrifyingly fragile.

Vance's hand tightened around mine, and I glanced at him. His expression was one of quiet resolve, the soft curves of his face still carrying traces of the boy I had once thought I knew. It was the strangest thing—how much of him felt familiar, even after everything that had happened. As if, somewhere deep inside, we had always been this version of ourselves, destined to meet here, where love and chaos collided.

"Are you sure you're ready for this?" he asked, his voice a low murmur that barely rose above the wind's song.

I smiled, but it wasn't one of those easy, carefree grins. It was the kind of smile that comes with a knowing, the kind that comes with the weight of everything we'd gone through. The fight, the loss, the pain that sometimes threatened to swallow us whole. And yet, here we stood, together.

"I'm as ready as I'll ever be," I said, squeezing his hand back. It was the truth, more than he knew.

The streets of Crescent City stretched out before us, lit by the gentle glow of the street lamps that lined every corner. It was quieter tonight, a Sunday evening that most people had chosen to spend indoors, curled up with their families or escaping into the arms of books and films. But not us. We had bigger plans, ones that didn't involve comfort or easy resolutions. Our story had never been about ease. It had been about surviving, about finding each other through the rubble we had once thought would bury us.

"You know," I said after a pause, "I think we might be the only ones still here. I haven't seen anyone for blocks."

Vance chuckled, the sound warm and rich, but there was an edge to it, a quiet unease beneath the humor. He had always been good at hiding his feelings—something I admired about him, and at times, resented. But I had learned to read the small signs, the subtle shifts in his demeanor. I saw it now—the flicker of uncertainty that passed over his features, and it made me wonder what he was really thinking.

"Well, maybe that's because we're not like everyone else," he said, his voice carrying a faint but discernible trace of bitterness. "Not in this city, not in this world."

I let the silence stretch between us for a moment. There was so much weight in those words, so much history that neither of us had truly faced. He wasn't wrong. We had always been different. There was a part of us, buried deep down, that wasn't bound by the same rules as the rest of Crescent City. And that had made us targets—first of our own fears, then of people who sought to tear us apart.

I ran my fingers along the smooth leather of his jacket, grounding myself in the present. There was something comforting about the feel of his warmth, the steady pulse of his heartbeat beneath the fabric. It reminded me that we had made it through everything and still found our way back to each other.

"Maybe," I said, my voice soft, but filled with resolve, "but that doesn't mean we don't deserve to be here."

I saw him glance at me, a surprised expression flickering across his face. He opened his mouth, as though to say something, then closed it, seemingly unsure. His gaze dropped to where our hands were still entwined, and I couldn't help but wonder what he was thinking. It was rare for him to be quiet like this, as if he were weighing words that could change everything between us.

The sudden sound of footsteps echoed down the cobblestone street, breaking the fragile moment we shared. We both turned toward the sound, the hairs on the back of my neck prickling. It was late, too late for anyone to be wandering this far out, and I had a feeling we were about to find out why. A shadow appeared at the end of the street, tall and unmoving, just beyond the light.

I sucked in a breath, ready for whatever would come next. With everything we had faced, there was no room left for fear, only readiness. Vance stepped closer to me, his protective instinct kicking in.

"Stay behind me," he murmured, but I didn't need to be told. I had learned long ago how to stand on my own two feet, even when it felt like the earth was giving way beneath me. We both knew that whatever was approaching wasn't going to be something we could outrun.

The figure stepped into the light, and I froze. It was too familiar. The way the silhouette leaned forward slightly, the way the moonlight caught in the glint of dark, unsettling eyes. I didn't need to see more than that to recognize him—Lucas.

"What the hell is he doing here?" Vance muttered, stepping closer, his body tense, ready to strike if need be.

I swallowed, the weight of his presence making my throat tight. Lucas. Of course it was him. And of course, he would find us here, in this fragile moment where everything felt like it could finally come together. But nothing with him ever did.

Lucas didn't step forward, not at first. He just stood there, like some wraith in the fading light, his hands casually shoved in the pockets of his black leather coat. The wind pulled at his dark hair, and for a moment, I almost thought the scene would play out like some old noir film—him standing there, impossibly cool, ready to deliver a cryptic monologue that could either make everything make sense or drive me mad.

But Lucas wasn't that kind of guy. No, he was the type to leave everyone on edge with just his presence. A presence that had never once been for my benefit.

"Didn't think I'd find you here," he said finally, his voice flat, almost too calm. He didn't seem surprised to see us together. If anything, he sounded... bored.

I had no idea how to respond to that. How do you respond to someone who's the personification of bad decisions, especially when the bad decision that is you, standing here, still feels like the worst one you've ever made?

"Lucas," I said, making the word come out sharper than I intended. "Should've known you'd show up when things started looking up."

Vance shifted beside me, his posture stiffening, and I felt his muscles coil like a predator preparing to strike. It was all too familiar, the way he always seemed to anticipate conflict. But it wasn't just that. He had the same kind of eyes as me, a mirrored reflection of the rawness I'd learned to hide.

"Vance, relax," I muttered, sensing the tension tightening around us like a trap.

"I don't like the look of this, Lena. You know what he's capable of."

I nodded, though the truth was that I wasn't sure I did anymore. Lucas had always been the kind of person you could never quite get a read on—too charming one minute, too cold the next. He had the kind of look that could break a person's heart in one word and then rebuild it with another. And that was what made him dangerous: the uncertainty.

"Don't flatter yourself," Lucas said, his eyes narrowing as if he could see the gears in Vance's head turning. "I'm not here to fight."

The words hung in the air, heavy with unspoken meaning. Not here to fight, but still standing right in front of us, like a bad penny that refused to stay away.

"I didn't ask for your company, Lucas," I said, my voice firmer than I felt. "Why don't you take your charming self elsewhere?"

For a long moment, he didn't respond. His gaze flickered between me and Vance, calculating. Then his lips curled into something that could've been mistaken for a smile if it weren't so… off.

"You're still the same, aren't you, Lena?" he said quietly, almost to himself. "So damn predictable."

"Predictable?" I couldn't help the laugh that escaped me. It was bitter, sharp. "You can't be serious. If there's one thing I'm not, Lucas, it's predictable."

Vance's eyes shot to me, but I held my ground. Lucas always had a way of prying things open, exposing wounds I thought had long since closed. The way he knew exactly where to poke, where to twist. It was exhausting. And infuriating.

"Maybe not," Lucas conceded with a smirk, "but you're still here, aren't you? Still tangled up in this mess. You know, I can't help but wonder… What is it about him? What makes him so special?"

Vance's grip tightened around my hand, and I could feel the muscles in his arm flex under the pressure. But I didn't flinch. Not this time.

"Why don't you ask him?" I said, stepping just slightly forward, putting myself between Lucas and Vance. The last thing I needed was for Vance to start playing Lucas's game.

Lucas raised an eyebrow. "Oh, believe me, I'm more than aware. I've seen the way he looks at you."

His words hit me like a slap. There it was again— that old thing between Lucas and me, that unspoken claim he always tried to put on me. And yet, I knew, even as I stood there feeling my pulse quicken with unease, that what had been between us had died long ago, even before everything had gone to hell.

The thing about Lucas was that he had a way of making everything feel... unfinished. Even the air felt incomplete around him, like an open sentence with no period. It wasn't just the past, but the way he could crawl into your present, uninvited, and suddenly make you question everything.

"I never should've gotten involved with you," I muttered under my breath, more to myself than to him.

His lips twisted, the smirk fading just a fraction. "Yeah, well, neither of us had a say in that, did we? Or does that escape you now?"

I bristled, the heat rising in my chest. No, it didn't escape me. Nothing about that time escaped me, not even the darkest, ugliest moments. Those moments shaped everything that had come after, and I knew better than to pretend I could wipe them from my memory.

"You're still here, Lucas," I said, my voice colder than I wanted it to be. "Still acting like you own the place. It's pathetic."

Lucas's eyes glinted, and for a moment, I thought he might say something to cut me to the quick, like he always had. But instead, he held my gaze and shrugged, the last hint of his smirk returning.

"Maybe I do," he said, taking a slow step back. "But I don't need to stick around for this. Consider this a warning, Lena. You may think you've won, but the game's not over yet."

And just like that, he turned and disappeared into the shadows. It was over as quickly as it had begun, leaving nothing but the unsettled air between us.

I stood there for a beat, my breath still a little shallow. The adrenaline still buzzed in my veins, but I didn't let it show. I couldn't. Not now. Not with Vance so close, his presence still warm against the cool night air.

I felt his hand on my shoulder, the pressure light but firm.

"Are you okay?" he asked, the concern clear in his voice.

I nodded, though I wasn't entirely sure I was. "Yeah. But I have a feeling it's far from over."

The night seemed to deepen around us as Lucas's shadow disappeared into the shadows, but the weight of his presence lingered, like smoke you couldn't quite shake. The cool breeze that had once felt refreshing now seemed to chill straight through my bones, leaving me uneasy. I turned to Vance, but he wasn't looking at me. His eyes were narrowed, scanning the street, tracking every movement that might suggest Lucas was still somewhere close. He wasn't wrong to be suspicious. Lucas had a way of creeping back into your life when you least expected it.

"You don't think he's really gone, do you?" I asked, though I wasn't sure I was asking him or myself.

Vance finally looked at me, and his expression was unreadable. The quiet strength he exuded always made me feel safe, but there was something in the way his jaw tightened, something more guarded than I was used to seeing.

"I hope so," he said, his voice low, "but I wouldn't count on it. We've dealt with him before, Lena. He doesn't just... disappear."

I let out a breath, running my fingers through my hair, trying to shake the feeling of being tangled up in something I couldn't quite control. I had thought, maybe foolishly, that the worst was behind us—that we had survived the storm, and all that was left was to find our way back to the calm. But I knew better. It wasn't that simple. Nothing ever was.

"I'll take the bet that he's gone for good," I said, my voice a little more confident than I felt. "But if he isn't, we'll handle it. Together."

The words hung between us, heavier than they had any right to be. Vance didn't say anything right away. Instead, he reached over, brushing his thumb along my wrist in that quiet way he had, grounding me in the moment.

"Together," he repeated softly, almost like a promise. And for some reason, that promise felt like something I could cling to.

We stood there in silence for a moment, letting the world spin around us. I could hear the distant hum of city traffic, the occasional rattle of a car driving by on the old cobblestone streets. Crescent City had always been a place that felt stuck in time—old-world charm mixed with modern chaos. It wasn't a city that ever seemed to sleep. But tonight, everything felt different. Like something was just beyond the horizon, waiting to push its way into our lives.

"I don't trust him," Vance said suddenly, breaking the silence. "There's something more going on with him. I can feel it."

I nodded. I didn't trust Lucas either. But what worried me more was that he had always seemed to know how to get under my skin, to worm his way back into my life just when I thought I had closed that chapter for good.

"Maybe he's just... causing trouble because that's what he does," I said, trying to shake the dark thoughts that clung to the edges of my mind. "He's a mess, Vance. Let him be."

But Vance didn't look reassured. His eyes were sharp, focused on something only he could see in the distance. A glint of something dangerous flickered in his gaze, and it made me uneasy.

"We can't let our guard down," he said firmly. "Not with him. Not yet."

I opened my mouth to argue, but before I could get a word out, the sound of something—someone—approaching caught my attention. The soft, quick footsteps echoed off the walls, and I turned just in time to see a figure emerge from the alleyway. The light from the streetlamps barely touched the stranger's face, but I could see the sharpness in the outline of their silhouette.

Vance stepped forward instinctively, his posture suddenly rigid, like a coiled spring ready to snap. I felt the change in him, a shift I was too familiar with. It was the kind of tension that always preceded something bad.

The figure took a step closer, and I recognized the gait. Not the face, but the walk. I could hear the quiet breath of recognition from Vance beside me as well. His hand shot out, grabbing mine in a tight grip as I took an instinctual step back.

"Stay close," he murmured under his breath, his tone even more serious than before. I didn't question it. There was no time for that.

The figure came into the light, revealing a woman—her face half-obscured by the shadow of her hood. She looked nothing like Lucas, but I couldn't shake the feeling that this encounter was just as dangerous. Her eyes, though, were unmistakable. They were cold, unblinking, and filled with a knowing that didn't belong in this place.

"Can I help you?" I asked, my voice barely above a whisper, but firm enough to let her know I wasn't afraid.

She didn't immediately respond. Instead, she stepped closer, her presence seeming to expand, filling the space between us. It was like she was a force of nature, something I couldn't quite understand but could sense was far too important to ignore.

"I think you can," she finally said, her voice smooth but layered with something like tension. "And you will. Whether you want to or not."

Vance tensed beside me, but I could see his eyes darting between the woman and the darkened street behind her. His instincts were alive, sharp, and I knew he was already calculating every possible outcome. Me? I was still trying to figure out who she was, and why the hell she seemed so familiar.

"What's this about?" I asked, trying to sound braver than I felt. "Who are you?"

The woman didn't respond right away. Instead, she took another step closer, and her gaze shifted to Vance.

"It's him, isn't it?" she asked, her voice now tinged with something darker. "You're the one who's been interfering."

Vance stiffened, his jaw setting in that hard line I recognized so well.

"If you're here because of him," he began, his voice low and measured, "you'll leave just like he did. Understand?"

But the woman just smiled, a sharp, unsettling grin that didn't reach her eyes.

"I think you'll be the one leaving soon, Vance," she said softly. "The game has just begun."

And in that moment, with the words hanging in the air between us, I knew that nothing would ever be the same.